Guardian Bride

The Quinter Brides, Book Four

by

Lauri Robinson

Guardian Bride: The Quinter Brides, Book Four

COPYRIGHT © 2010 by Lauri Robinson

Cover Art by *Nicola Martinez*

The Wild Rose Press
PO Box 708
Adams Basin, NY 14410-0706
Visit us at www.thewildrosepress.com

Publishing History
First Cactus Rose Edition, 2010
Print ISBN 1-60154-857-5

Published in the United States of America

**The jingle of harnesses and the creak and
clatter of wagon wheels interrupted
the casual tweets of the prairie songbirds.**

Frowning, Snake moved beyond the end of the long
rows of wheat. The small plume of dust had grown
closer. He squinted. With the force of a lightning
bolt, his heart plummeted into a dark, spooky place.

An old mule, wearing a hat that someone had
cut long slits in the brim so the animal's ears could
stick out and full of purple and pink flowers, trotted
along the trail. Dust rose into the air in the animal's
wake. Two women sat on the seat of an odd shaped,
little wagon. He began to shake. They didn't need to
come closer for him to know who they were. The
driver wore a hat to match the mules, minus the ear
slots, and the woman beside her toted a well-used
shotgun.

Fear like he'd never known raced over his body,
and he scanned the vast ground, erratically trying to
figure out which way to run.

Just as he hefted a leg, which felt like it weighed
three hundred pounds, a rough voice sliced the air.
"Don't move! I got you in my sights!"

"Aw, shit!" The two women—together—could
only mean one thing. Turning back to the wagon, he
shouted, "Put the gun away, Ma, you ain't gonna
shoot me."

"You don't know that!" she reiterated.

On second thought, a good round of buckshot
wouldn't be as bad as the alternative—marrying the
woman who sat beside his mother, glowering at him
like he'd just killed her mule, hat and all.

Summer Austin flinched as the gun in the
woman's hands clicked. Out of the corner of her eye,
she checked if the woman sitting beside her had
cocked the trigger.

Praise for the Author

Dedication

To Virginia Robinson, my mother-in-law.
Rest in Peace.

Chapter One

Southwestern Kansas
1885

"What the hell?" Snake, otherwise known as Scott Andrew Quinter, jerked against the eerie sensation rippling his spine. He lifted his head, scanning the area with a good once over. The rich, fertile soil of the plains making up western Kansas lay out in all directions. It was like a mine, a gold mine, and he was a miner claim-staking the mother lode.

A spectacular sky, profound blue and adorned with clouds that looked like pillows of bleached cotton, housed the bright sun that made sweat pour down his back. He let his gaze make another circle, convinced it took more than a trickle of perspiration to make his entire body quake.

Other than a small puff of dust far off on the horizon, there was nothing to blame for the uneasiness that seared his bones. He shrugged, but it was to no avail. Besides the eeriness, a heavy gloom shrouded him lately. Forcing his mind to ignore it all, he bent to examine the roots of the winter wheat he'd sowed last fall. The hearty plant had thrived in the rich soil and was well on its way to proving this hybrid of wheat he'd created was the one—the seed that would turn Kansas into the breadbasket of the nation.

The quiver came again, eating at his bones like a bug devouring a leaf. He snapped upright and stomped toward the end of the field, kicking clods of dirt out of the way as he went. What the hell was wrong with him? Ever since that stupid poker game in Dodge, he'd had a dark cloud hanging over his head and an irritating, nagging voice in the back of his mind. It wasn't as if he'd cheated anyone, in all reality, he'd folded—threw away a full house, Queens over Aces. In his mind, it had been the only honorable thing to do. July Austin—the man he'd played against—had thrown his daughter into the pot.

Austin had said she was of age and more than willing to comply with the deal, but Snake didn't think it was appropriate. No, siree, gambling a daughter away wasn't right, no matter how willing she was. Another shiver raced over his shoulders, and sweat not caused from the sun, dripped off his forehead.

In all actuality, the whole situation had been too close to home for comfort. His mother had married off three of his brothers—against their will for the most part. Not that it hadn't worked out for Kid, Skeeter, and most recently, Hog, but he, Snake, wasn't about to let it happen to him. His brothers were all happier than peas in pods, but marriage wasn't in his future. He had farming to do, between this hybrid, and the new irrigation system he was structuring—he flat out didn't have time for anything else—but more than that, women made him nervous.

He was all male, and had visited the upper floors of saloons before. What flesh and bone man didn't? Those visits were needed, and those girls didn't make him uneasy—there were a few he grew damn right excited to see again. It was women like his sisters-in-law that made his throat swell up like he'd rolled in a patch of poison ivy. They were sweet, kind, and could make a man run in circles faster than a cat with two tails.

The jingle of harnesses and the creak and clatter of wagon wheels interrupted the casual tweets of the prairie songbirds. Frowning, Snake moved beyond the end of the long rows of wheat. The small plume of dust had grown closer. He squinted. With the force of a lightning bolt, his heart plummeted into a dark, spooky place.

An old mule, wearing a hat that someone had cut long slits in the brim so the animal's ears could stick out and full of purple and pink flowers, trotted along the trail. Dust rose into the air in the animal's wake. Two women sat on the seat of an odd shaped, little wagon. He began to shake. They didn't need to come closer for him to know who they were. The driver wore a hat to match the mules, minus the ear slots, and the woman beside her toted a well-used shotgun.

Fear like he'd never known raced over his body, and he scanned the vast ground, erratically trying to figure out which way to run.

Just as he hefted a leg, which felt like it weighed three hundred pounds, a rough voice sliced the air. "Don't move! I got you in my sights!"

"Aw, shit!" The two women—together—could only mean one thing. Turning back to the wagon, he shouted, "Put the gun away, Ma, you ain't gonna shoot me."

"You don't know that!" she reiterated.

On second thought, a good round of buckshot wouldn't be as bad as the alternative—marrying the woman who sat beside his mother, glowering at him like he'd just killed her mule, hat and all.

Summer Austin flinched as the gun in the woman's hands clicked. Out of the corner of her eye, she checked if the woman sitting beside her had cocked the trigger.

Stephanie Quinter had. Moreover, one gnarled finger was set to pull the lever back the rest of the way.

Summer swallowed, stirring up the bile that already churned in her stomach. Marrying Snake Quinter wasn't necessarily what she wanted, but he was her ticket out of Dodge, and she had to take it. Another option wasn't likely to come along, and time had run out.

He, the man she was about to marry, stood at the edge of a fading-green field. Soon the stalks of wheat would turn gold—that is if locusts or hail didn't wipe the crop out before it ripened and diminish the entire lot. Summer had seen it before, the way Mother Nature could destroy a crop in the blink of an eye, and a piece of her hoped it wouldn't happen to Snake.

For the most part, from what she knew anyway, he was a good man, kind to strangers and children alike. Nor was he a drinking or gambling man, the game he'd played with her father had been the only time she'd seen him at the Long Branch. He'd been in Dodge helping his brother build a new hotel for several months, but had only stopped at the saloon that once.

Summer pulled on the reins, and while Maisy, her faithful old mule, brought their slow, steady pace to a halt, Summer closed her eyes and offered up a quick, silent apology. *I'm sorry. Sorry to do this to this man, but he's my only hope.* Her thoughts juggled to include, *You better be right about this.*

A comforting and warm aura floated over her, as common to her as the sound of the wind. She drew her eyes open, glancing around, expecting to see the image of her Guardian Angel. Jonas was nowhere in sight. A touch of disappointment rippled her spine. He'd been with her off and on for the past decade, guiding her through many dark and dismal nights, but, in all honesty, she really shouldn't expect him to offer comfort now—after all she was about to force his son into marriage.

Maisy, tired as all-git-out, plopped her hind end on the ground like an old hound. The wagon jolted and creaked, and the gun Stephanie Quinter held juggled about. As the wagon gave a final groan, the woman let out a sigh. She'd managed to keep the gun from either dropping or firing and kept herself from toppling. Summer scrunched her face with regret she hadn't pre-warned Stephanie about Maisy's habits.

"What's going on?" Snake asked, resting one arm on the top of his hoe handle.

He wore brown pants, held up by thick, black suspenders that stretched over his wide shoulders. The shirt beneath the straps was a speckled gray undershirt, with all five buttons undone, and dotted with blots of sweat. The garment was tight, and Summer felt a hint of apprehension at what was about to happen. He must be as strong as an ox. Mounds of muscles covered his arms, shoulders, and chest.

Squaring her shoulders, she met his stare—and quivered again. His eyes were the same soft, faded green as his field of wheat, but their gaze was stone cold. If it was just she who needed to get out of Dodge, she would have bolted, but this—no, he—was August and September's only hope, and she couldn't let them down.

"Good afternoon, Mr. Quinter," she said, surprised at how calm she sounded.

His eyes glowed like an animal's at night, and then with a somewhat disgusted squint, he pulled his gaze off her and settled it on his mother. "What's going on?"

Stephanie Quinter rested the butt of her gun against her shoulder. "I didn't raise any cheaters," she all but spit.

"Cheaters?" His furrowed brows looked like one

long, dark, caterpillar crawling across his forehead.

"Yes. Cheaters," Stephanie repeated. "This here gal says you cheated in a game of cards with her father."

Regret for her father's behaviors wasn't new. Summer bowed her head, peering out through her eyelashes.

Snake took the floppy brimmed hat off his head, wiped the crook of his arm over his forehead, and then replaced the hat. Anger seemed to float off his tall form as he lifted the flat-end hoe and thrust the spade deep into the ground. The handle wobbled, and he took a step closer to Maisy.

"I didn't cheat," he snarled.

Summer pinched her lips together and sucked in a bit of air for fortitude through her nose before she lifted her face. "You won the pot, and you didn't claim it."

He reached out a hand. To Summer's surprise he merely patted Maisy on the snout. The mule, who undoubtedly thought she was a dog instead of a mule, turned her head and ran her cheek up and down his arm. He let the mule nuzzle him, patting her a bit more as he glanced up.

His cold stare once again settled on Summer. "I folded."

"But the other players didn't accept the fold. You won. Your Queens over Aces, won."

He let out a short huff of air and closed his eyes for a moment. When he opened them again, his face looked like it was carved out of granite, hard and cold. "Miss Austin..." he started.

A chill told Summer he fought hard to hold his anger in check.

"There is nothing to accept in a fold," he stated.

She opened her mouth, but he held up one hand and stopped her from speaking. "I folded, your father won, end of game."

Her chin quivered and try as she might it wouldn't cease. Scratching her nose, which had started to burn, she explained, "My father didn't win. Sam Wainwright was still in the game."

A look of confusion overtook his features. "Wainwright?"

She nodded.

His face twisted into a scowl. "That Mexican trader?"

She nodded again, blinking at the pressure building behind her eyes.

He shook his head. "No, he didn't. He'd already passed out. Was snoring up a storm in his chair."

"He has witnesses who say he'd already thrown his money in, and his cards were still in his hand. Three Jacks and two Kings."

"So? He was passed out," he argued.

"He woke up after you left and claimed the win. But he—" She took a breath to block the sob rising up her throat. "He didn't want me. He wanted my little sister September, instead. She's only eleven, and I can't—" She stopped, needing a moment to quell the fear overtaking her system. Gasping for air, she quickly added, "George Hinkle stepped in and said your fold wasn't accepted. The next day he came by our place and said you'd left town right after the game, and that he'd send you a telegram that said you had two weeks to claim the win."

At some point Stephanie Quinter had lowered her gun, now she held out a folded, yellow sheet of paper. "I got the telegram right here. She's not lying, Snake."

Summer wished he'd take his eyes off her so she could wipe her stinging ones, but he didn't, just kept staring at her as he reached out and took the note from his mother. He read it quickly, glancing between the telegram and her.

The paper crinkled as he balled it into his fist.

He hung his head and rubbed at one temple as if it hurt. Summer took advantage of the moment to wipe her nose on the sleeve of her dress, and then brush away the water welling in her eyes with both hands.

When he lifted his head, his hat was pushed back. A mass of wavy, gold hair fell over his forehead. He brushed it aside, pulled the hat back down, and pointed one finger at his mother. "I'm not marrying her," he declared.

"Snake—" Stephanie Quinter started.

"No," he interrupted, sternly. His eyes settled on Summer. "I'll go to Dodge and claim the win. And then—" He blew out a long, heavy sigh. "I'll figure what the hell to do about it."

Relief came as welcomed as spring after a long, cold winter. Summer's shoulders relaxed as if she'd just shed a heavy, woolen cloak. "Thank you, Mr. Quinter."

He looked at her, and then he closed his eyes, giving his head a slow shake, like he had a hard time believing what had just taken place. She couldn't blame him. It was a bit out of the ordinary—winning a person in a poker game. It was even more unordinary to be the person who was won. Then again, there wasn't a whole lot about her life that was run of the mill.

"Where's your little sister?" he asked, jolting her attention.

Summer pointed at Stephanie Quinter. "At your mother's house. So is my little brother, August. He's eight," she added, for no real reason.

Snake took a deep breath, but the air was hot and stifling. His body was as well, steam threatened to ooze out of every pore. He should have left Dodge when the rest of his family had, but instead he'd decided to spend a day talking with the local miller. While waiting for his appointment with Mr. Everest, he'd decided to stop in at the Long Branch and joined the game just to pass the time, not really caring if he won or lost.

The thought of Wainwright, a filthy man who'd stunk to high heaven, made his stomach churn. The man boasted about being a Mexican trader, boldly laughing about transporting wagons full of young girls down to the border. Snake had no doubt the man wanted the little sister. He looked up and met the watery gaze of Summer Austin.

A straw hat, decorated with a splattering of flowers, shielded her head and face from the midday sun. Beneath the rim, glossy, raven-black hair looked like it had streaks of deep blue shimmering in it as is flowed over her shoulders and down her back. Her eyes were so dark he wondered if they were black too, and her skin had a bronze tint to it, like she spent many hours out of doors. She was attractive, in a dark and elusive sort of way, and Snake wondered if her little sister looked like her. Not that it mattered. Wainwright most likely didn't care how beautiful the girls were.

He closed his eyes for a moment, tossing the thought of the evil man aside. A new subject instantly took its place. It didn't matter how nice looking Summer Austin was either, he wouldn't have any part of keeping her around. The last thing he needed was a young woman and her siblings underfoot. He'd already been away from the farm too long while helping Hog get the Majestic up and running. Besides, Ma was too quick with that shotgun of hers—marrying her sons off as if they were a litter of pups looking for homes.

He'd go claim the bet, make sure Wainwright was long gone from Dodge, and then give the whole kit and caboodle—Summer and her brother and sister—back to her father. Hopefully, Snake glanced back to his field, he'd get it all accomplished before it was time to harvest his wheat.

"Snake," his mother said.

Before she could start in on one of her rants, or tell him what she thought he needed to do, he interrupted, "You two head back to the house. I'll be along shortly and saddle up to ride to Dodge."

"I think—"

"Ma," he warned sternly, holding up a hand.

For once in her life, his mother didn't argue. His brows lifted in surprise, but he quickly tugged them down.

"All right," she said, and then gesturing toward the mule added, "Summer, can you get that animal to stand up?"

"No."

Summer's reply made him snap his head towards her. "No?" he asked.

She shook her head. "Once Maisy sits down, you just have to wait until she stands up. No prodding or coaxing in the world will get her going until she feels up to it." Summer glanced toward his mother. "She's old," she said, as if that explained everything.

A sigh of disgust fluttered from his chest. He wrapped his fingers inside the mule's halter and clicked his tongue. "Come on, girl, up and at'em."

The mule looked at him with big brown eyes, and then rubbed the side of her face against his shirt. He tugged harder. "Come on. Up."

The hide covering the animal's back quivered from rump to neck, but the mule didn't make any attempt to rise.

"Up! Up, now!" he demanded, a bit fiercely.

The mule snorted and turned her head, defiantly staring straight ahead.

"It's really no use. She'll get up when she's ready. It's usually no more than half an hour or so," Summer assured.

"You're joshing, right?"

"No," she answered solemnly.

Snake walked to the front of the animal and bent down to stare in the big eyes. They were clear and bright, and the rest of her looked good, too, no sign of illness or mistreatment. The mule met his stare and yawned.

More than a bit frazzled, he glanced up at the driver. "How often does she"—he pointed to the mule with his thumb—"take a little rest?"

Summer shrugged. "It was only about four or five times a day. But the trip from Dodge was long. Most likely the longest one she's ever taken."

"Oh." Unable to think of anything else to say, he shook his head with disbelief and walked over to gather up his tools. It was a good three miles back to Ma's house, too far for the women to walk in this heat. His mother would most likely blister him if he left them out here alone, so after loading up his pack, and unable to think up a solution, he sat down in the shade of the wagon to wait until Maisy, the mule, decided to stand up.

Chapter Two

The ride to Dodge City was hot, dusty, and long. Snake knew all this before leaving home, but somehow, today—his second day on the trail—seemed to have no end. It wasn't even noon yet. Buster, the dapple gray gelding he'd bought from his brother, Kid, two years ago, knew the way, so there wasn't a whole lot for Snake to do—but think. Ponder about that dim-witted mule, Maisy, and her outrageous behavior.

An uncontrollable grin formed on his face, as if someone tickled his chest with a rooster tail-feather. Dang if that mule wasn't ornery. Stupid critter had sat down again as soon as they got to Ma's place, wouldn't even budge an inch for him to get the harness off her.

The animal's antics didn't faze Summer. She'd just gone about other tasks until the animal stood up, and then moseyed over to unhitch her. He'd also learned Maisy didn't like to have her hat taken off. When he'd attempted, the blasted mule tried to bite him. It had been Summer again, who rushed over to inform him Maisy's hats stay on until they fall off. She proceeded to explain that a new one must be put on before the animal will stand up again.

He left shortly after that lesson, having already learned enough about Maisy to last a lifetime. With one hand, he patted Buster, "Good thing you ain't that stubborn. I'd have had to put you out to pasture. No man has that kind of patience."

Buster tossed his head, as if agreeing with the statement, and they continued to amble along.

The wire from Hinkle said he needed to talk with Pat Sughrue, the Sheriff in Dodge. George Hinkle was the previous sheriff, and a family friend. Snake had met Sughrue while in Dodge, found him to be a good sort, but didn't really know what the sheriff could do about a poker game.

It had started out fine enough, just five men passing a lazy afternoon with a deck of cards. July Austin was the fifth one to join, had thrown in a single gold coin, and ended up winning the first pot. The next couple hands had lessened the man's stack of coins and bills, and by the last hand, he'd been once again down to his gold coin.

It was amazing how someone as attractive as Summer, with her dark hair and eyes, could be July's offspring. But then again, most of July's unsightly image had to do with the smallpox outbreak a few years back. The man's face was scared with deep craters, and from what Snake knew, the disease had also taken his wife.

He'd seen Summer back there, at the Long Branch, washing out spittoons and other tasks. She'd stuck her head and arm out of the back room, handing the clean dishes to the bar keep, and July had made a point of singling her out, telling everyone at the table she was his daughter.

"Come here, girlie, see what your pa won," the man had shouted. That of course had been while the coins were stacked up in front of him. She'd bowed her head shamefully and slid back into the backroom. July had spouted on then about his other daughter.

A frown tugged at Snake's brows. If he remembered correctly, July had gone on to say his other daughter was the pretty one.

A sense of foreboding hit him like a gust of wind. Snake turned to investigate. He'd had the sense someone followed him—he'd half expected his little brother, Bug, to walk into camp last night.

This feeling was different.

Behind a patch of brush there was a quick flash of light. Before he had a chance to decipher what it might be, fire shot up his leg, a split second later, a hard force hit his shoulder, and the ricochets of gunfire rolled across the plains.

Pain exploded across his chest as he caught the saddle horn, keeping his seat. Buster bounded sideways and then took off in a full, wild run.

Snake could do little more than hold on and feel the blood flowing out of the holes in both his leg and shoulder. The gun shots continued, but his one arm was useless, and he needed the other just to stay in the saddle.

The ground flowed beneath them, and the bouncing gave teeth-clenching pain the opportunity to eat away at his body. His vision became blurred, and his hearing muffled.

Through the thick fog encompassing him, hoof beats behind grew closer as Buster, winded from his wild race, slowed. With his good leg, Snake tried to nudge the horse, make him continue to run, but it was futile. Beyond dizzy, Snake slumped lower over the saddle horn. The pace really didn't matter, he couldn't hold on much longer.

"Don't let go," a faintly familiar voice shouted. "Don't let go!"

He attempted to lift his head, to glance behind him, but the movement was too much and the fog too thick. Snake laid his head against Buster's bouncing neck, and the world as he knew it, ceased to exist.

Later, or maybe not, he couldn't really decipher when, a man stood several yards away. He was familiar. When the man raised his hand, holding it out, Snake lifted an arm. Oddly enough, the movement didn't hurt. "Dad?"

Jonas Quinter nodded but then held his hand all

the way up, silently telling Snake to stay where he was.

His mother's voice filtered in his fuzzy mind and pain like he'd never experienced ripped him in two. There was more pain, more voices he half recognized, but couldn't muster up the strength to respond to them. Jonas appeared again while those voices called to him, his father, calmly, assuredly told him to nod his head. Nod in acknowledgement to the far away voices. Snake nodded because he hadn't seen his father in ten years. He had so much to ask him. So much to say. Then they all—his father and the voices—faded away.

****

It was the warmth on his face and a light so bright it filtered through his eyelids that he responded to next. It took effort, and he was worn out by the time his eyes open.

Sun shone through the open window. He blinked at it, wincing at how his head, swollen and thick, pounded. Dull aching throbs filled his arm and leg. Over all discomfort consumed his body from head to toe. The groan in his throat caused more pain.

"Here," someone said, "drink this."

He turned toward the sound, but stopped, cringing and closing his eyes against the pain. Something bumped his bottom lip. A glass. He sipped from it. A nasty, bitter taste filled his mouth. He shuddered as it flowed down his throat, burning.

"It'll help. Drink some more."

He shook his head.

Something refreshingly cool settled on his forehead, and he sighed at the relief it brought.

"Try to sleep some more." The voice was feminine, and slightly familiar. However it didn't belong to his mother or sisters-in-law.

Flames of fire ate at his vocal cords by the time he managed to mutter, "N-not t-tired."

Lauri Robinson

"Just try to sleep," she said.

"C-can't," he forced out. Something twisted deep in his guts, told him he had to wake up, there was danger or something he needed to remember, respond to.

"Just try."

The cool cloth left his forehead to run down the sides of his face and over the skin of his neck. It was heavenly. The knot in his stomach dissolved, and he sighed with reprieve.

"That's it, just sleep," the voice faded into oblivion.

Summer continued to dip the cotton in the basin of water by the bed, wring it out, and pat his clammy skin. It had been almost a week since he'd been shot, and though the doctor had shown her two bullets, assured there weren't any more in either Snake's leg or shoulder, she wondered if he'd truly survive.

What would she do if he died? Where would she and September and August go? They couldn't return to Dodge. Yet, even if they were married, she and Snake, she and the children couldn't remain here. Wainwright would find them. She couldn't put the rest of the Quinters in danger.

A cool, calm feeling overcame her body, and she closed her eyes, accepting the sensation like one welcomes a visit from a long lost friend. There were no words, not even the faintest hint of a whisper, yet he spoke to her. Jonas assured her all would be well. The heaviness in her chest lifted, floated away like a feather on a warm breeze. When she opened her eyes, Summer knew Snake would survive.

Voices, those of August and September blew in through the open window, and she let the air out of her chest. There'll be bumps in the road, she intuitively understood, but in the end, the children would be taken care of, and that was all that mattered—besides Snake's recovery.

He'd fallen back to sleep. The wide span of his chest rose and fell with each breath. Summer placed her hand in the center of his torso, and ignoring the heat of his skin and the softness of the splattering of curls, concentrated until she could feel the steady rhythm of his heart beating.

The doctor had said he was lucky, another inch and the bullet would have torn through his heart, killing him in the saddle. She lifted her face upwards, and whispered, "Thank you."

There was no answer, but she hadn't expected one. Jonas never acknowledged her gratefulness. His silent assurance Snake would survive was more than she anticipated.

She rose from the chair beside the bed. After repositioning the sheet over his sleeping form, she gathered the rag and water bowl and carried them from the room.

"How's he doing?" Stephanie, who'd been a beacon of kindness, wanted to know.

"He woke up for a minute, but is sleeping again now." Summer dumped the bowl in the sink and hung the cotton cloth on a hook above the cupboard. "He's going to be fine." Even though she knew the words to be true, a lump formed in her throat.

"I know he is, sweetie," Stephanie patted her shoulder. "My boys are tough. Practically made of nails."

Summer nodded a response.

"Did I tell you about Bug? When he was hit in the head, and we didn't know if'n he was gonna make it?" Stephanie asked while she carried a basket of beans to the table. "We were out at the Badlands, building Skeeter's house. You ain't met him yet. Most likely we won't see them now 'til the holidays." The woman plopped into a chair and began to snap the ends off the beans. "He and Lila got two kids. I've mentioned that."

Summer nodded and took a chair to assist with the green beans. She replied when appropriate but for the most part didn't hear a lot of what Stephanie said. The woman had five sons and talked non-stop about them. Summer didn't think there could be much about the brothers she didn't already know.

Kid, married to Jessie, lived on a cattle ranch a few miles away. Skeeter, married to Lila, lived near the Kansas Badlands. Snake was next, he owned the land next to this farm, but hadn't built a house there yet so still lived here. Hog, married to Randi, owned the Majestic in Dodge. Bug was the youngest. He lived at home with Stephanie and Snake. As they snapped beans, Bug and Kid were towing the big thrashing machine out to the wheat field. Tomorrow, with the help of Kid's ranch hands, they'd start to harvest Snake's wheat.

In the past few days, the wheat had turned golden brown, and the big heads had opened up to let the sun and wind dry out the seeds. Summer would help with the harvest as well, so would August and September. The field was massive, the largest one she'd ever seen. Not that work scared her, but the possibility they'd be able to thrash the entire field while the wheat was in its prime seemed almost impossible. Of course there was also the fact she wanted to stay behind and nurse Snake.

Stephanie would watch over him, she'd been doing so right along with Summer, but Summer liked to know for herself how Snake was doing. Even before she met him, before he won her in the card game, Summer felt as if she'd known Snake, knew he would be a part of her life. He'd been the one Jonas told her the most about.

Jonas never really said anything. He didn't actually talk to her. Not with words anyway. But over the years, he'd let her know things about all the brothers, but mainly Snake, and he'd led her to believe she was destined to be connected with the Quinter family. Then again, she'd known that ever since Jonas had died in her arms—the day July Austin had killed him.

"You coming?"

Summer, brought back to earth by Stephanie's question, glanced up.

"Someone just rode in. You coming to see who it is?" Stephanie moved to the door.

Summer snapped the bean in her hand, throwing the ends in the scrap pile and the center in the bowl as she stood. Wiping both hands on the long apron covering her green striped dress, both gifts from Stephanie, she followed the other woman out the door and onto the small porch.

August and September ran around the corner of the house and bounded onto the porch to stand behind her. The children were wary of strangers, rightfully so given the life they'd lived the past few years. She stretched her hands behind her and drew them to her sides like a mother hen does her chicks in a rain storm. Arms draped around their thin shoulders, she held them as three men dismounted near the water trough.

The children, who looked healthier than she'd ever seen them before—due to the fact they now had plenty of food and were able to sleep, feeling safe and sound—glanced up. She offered them each a smile.

Their gazes, cautious and questioning, settled on her face. "It's all right," she assured, though her insides swelled with heavy doom. The metal badges pinned on two of the men's vests were impossible to overlook.

"Mrs. Quinter," one said as all three walked toward the porch.

"Malcolm," Stephanie nodded. "What brings you out here?"

He tilted his head toward the men on either side of him. Summer knew both of them. One was Pat Sughrue, the sheriff of Dodge City, and the other was George Hinkle, the past sheriff who acted as a deputy every now and again. The one who'd spoken was the sheriff of the small town a few miles from the Quinter place, Scott City, formerly known as Nixon. The town had recently renamed itself after an army man of some sorts.

"We're on official business," Malcolm Turley said. His gaze then settled on Summer. "Miss Austin, we need to speak to you."

"What for?" Stephanie asked, none to friendly.

"Perhaps we could speak to you," Malcolm said, his gaze briefly touching on August and September, "alone for a moment."

Summer trembled so hard she had to plant her heels on the floor to keep her knees from knocking.

Stephanie Quinter huffed and folded her arms across her amble bosoms. "Her name ain't Miss Austin. It's Mrs. Quinter. Mrs. Scott Quinter."

Malcolm looked surprised. "Snake's all right? He's recovered? I thought Doc said he was still unconscious."

"Of course he's still unconscious." Stephanie threw her arms in the air. "He was shot up worse than a rabid coyote. Bullet holes all over him."

Malcolm frowned. "If he's still unconscious how are he and Miss Austin married?"

Stephanie propped her hands on her hips. "The usual way, by a preacher."

The sheriff took off his hat and ran a hand over his thinning hair. "Stephanie," he said, shaking his head. "You can't marry off an unconscious man."

"I didn't," she said. "He agreed to it. Ask Reverend Kirkpatrick if'n you don't believe me."

"How—" the lawman shook his head, stopping his own question. "Stephanie," he said a moment later. "You can't keep marrying your sons off in the middle of the night. One day one of those boys is gonna shoot you with that old cannon you got. And there isn't a thing anyone's gonna do about it."

"Malcolm Turley!" Stephanie screeched. "You little whipper-snap! I oughta—" she took a step toward the man, "I'm gonna smack—"

George Hinkle stepped between Sheriff Turley and Stephanie Quinter. "Break it up." His sad eyes looked at her. "Summer," he said, "maybe August and September could go in the house for a few minutes?"

Summer let out the breath she'd been holding. "Children," she tried to sound calm, and assuring, "there's a basket of beans on the table that need to be snapped. Please see to it."

August and September, used to minding when strangers came around, scampered into the house without a hint of disappointment. George Hinkle lifted a hand. Summer took it, letting him lead her down the steps and across the dirt.

Stephanie, as well as the other two men followed. When George stopped in the shade of a large cottonwood, the rest gathered around.

"What you need to talk to her about?" Stephanie asked, placing an arm around Summer's shoulders.

"I'm afraid we have some news," George said, removing his hat.

"What is it, Mr. Hinkle?" Summer asked. A thousand thoughts raced through her mind. Snake had never made it to Dodge. Had never been able to claim the win. Were they here to take her and the children back, give September to Wainwright? Her throat burned. She wouldn't let it happen. Couldn't let it happen.

"I'm afraid Miss A—" George paused when Stephanie cleared her throat and then continued, "Mrs. Quinter, that your father, July Austin, was found dead earlier this week."

Her legs went weak, would have collapsed beneath her if Sheriff Sughrue hadn't stepped forward and took her elbow. It was news she'd known would someday be delivered, but still, like a wagon wheel one knew would eventually let loose, it shocked her beyond belief now that it had happened.

A thump sounded behind her. "Here set her down."

She glanced over her shoulder. Malcolm Turley had set a bucket upside down and gestured to Sheriff Sughrue to let her rest on it. The sheriff on one side and Stephanie on the other eased her until she sat on the bucket. It wobbled as her weight settled.

Summer lowered her head, squeezing her temples with one hand. "What happened?" she asked.

George crouched down in front of her. The man had always been nice to her, especially over the last couple of years when she took to cleaning at the Long Branch. He'd watched out for her, kept an eye out as she made her way home after work. His wife was the school teacher, and Summer had no doubt the couple knew the hard life August and September had. It was bad enough to have the town drunk as your father, but a half-breed for an older sister caused many more problems for the children.

"He was shot," George said sympathetically. "Most likely by the same men that shot Snake. The card game was never settled. Snake never made it to Dodge."

"I know," she said, nodding. "It was Wainwright, wasn't it?"

"We think so," Pat Sughrue said.

"I told them you didn't see who shot Snake," Malcolm Turley offered.

Sheriff Turley had questioned her after she

brought Snake home. Summer covered her face with both hands, attempting to rid the images of Snake's blood encrusted body. She'd been afraid he was dead by the time she'd led his big horse into the yard. Terrified the men would catch up to them, she'd barely covered his wounds before she'd forced their mounts to the limits racing back toward Stephanie's house. When Jonas had assured no one followed, she'd slowed their pace, but never once had she allowed the animals to completely stop until they'd arrived at the barn late that night.

"You didn't see anything?" George asked.

She took a breath and wiped at her eyes and nose before lifting her face. "They were too far away. All I saw were two men on horseback. I couldn't even make out the color of their animals."

"No one's seen hide or hair of Wainwright. We're assuming he headed back down to Texas, but we can't be sure," Sheriff Sughrue said.

"What's going to happen now? Do I need to go back to Dodge to bury—" Choking on her words, she couldn't continue.

"No, that's already been taken care of," George said.

Thankful she didn't have to attend to the task, she realized something else. "The undertaker will want money."

"July had some, enough to bury him." Sheriff Sughrue then asked, "Is there anything at the house you need, want? The landlord wants to rent it to someone else."

"No. No, I took everything the children need when we left."

George patted her shoulder. "You're safe here. The children are safe here, and we'll put out some posters for Wainwright. We just had to come and tell you the news. I know it doesn't sound like much, but I'm sorry Summer. So very sorry."

"Thank you," she said. "All of you, for riding out, for telling me." She squared her shoulders, and her gaze went to the house. "I best go talk to the children now."

"Do you want me to come with you?" Stephanie asked.

Summer stood and let out a shaky breath. "No, thank you. This is something I have to do myself."

Chapter Three

This time when he woke up his mind wasn't quite as fuzzy, at least that's what Snake thought when he first opened his eyes. Moments later, the nagging suspicion of being watched made him twist his neck. Two bright blue eyes gazed at him. The child—a boy—knelt beside the bed with his chin on the edge of the mattress.

"Hi," the kid said with a grin that showed his front two teeth were surprisingly large.

"Hi," Snake responded, somewhat cautiously. He glanced around the room, taking a double check that it was in fact his bedroom. The curtains, the dresser, the bed, all were familiar. It was his room, but who was the kid?

"You awake?" the kid asked.

Snake took a moment to contemplate, making sure he was indeed a wake. "Yes." His voice crackled like a bullfrog's.

"'Cause I'm supposed to holler for Sissy if'n you wake up." A thick blanket of blond hair hung around the kid's round face. It was somewhat disheveled and reminded Snake of his own hair when he was growing up. Ma had forever been greasing it down. He could still remember the stench of the oil she used.

The kid spoke again, and Snake turned to him. "What?"

"Should I holler for Sissy, or are you gonna go back to sleep?"

"Sissy?" Snake asked. "Who's that?"

"My sister. September."

Memories hit Snake like a spring flood. The card game. Summer Austin and her little sister and brother. The ride to Dodge. He glanced down. A thick, white bandage held his left arm across his chest. With his other hand, he lifted the sheet. His left leg had a bandage wrapped around it. The glance also let him know he was as naked as a newly hatched bird.

He laid the sheet back down and scowled at the boy who'd been peering underneath the covering as well.

The boy grinned. "So, you awake?"

"Yes, I'm awake." He tried to swallow, but his mouth was drier than straw. He pointed to the glass sitting on the table. The boy handed it to him. Snake downed the water in one swallow. "Thanks." He handed the glass back.

The boy set it down. "I'll go holler."

Snake snatched his arm. "Not so quick there fella. Where's my mother?"

"She and Summer are out in your garden."

He stretched to see out the window on the far side of the room. The movement hurt, but he strained harder. Little more than the tops of far off trees could be seen through the glass. "The vegetable garden out back?"

The boy shook his head.

He plopped back down, flinching with pain. "The flower garden out front?"

"No, your big garden. The one that's got all the wheat growing in it."

"What are they doing out there?"

"Thrashing."

"Thrashing?" He breathed past the pain his new movements caused. "How long have I been asleep?"

The kid shrugged.

He pointed across the room. "Get me some britches out of that dresser over there."

The boy frowned. "I don't think I'm supposed to do that. Summer said if'n you woke up I was supposed to holler at September, and she'd take Maisy and go get Summer."

Snake used his good arm to scoot into a sitting position. Pain poured down his arm and leg, and though he imagined, it had lessened some since the shooting, it hurt like hell. He clenched his teeth until the knife-stabbing throbs eased a mite.

"August?" he asked, "You're name's August, isn't it?"

"Yup."

"I remember Maisy," Snake said. "It's going to take your sister half the day to get to the wheat field. Just get me a pair of britches, would you?"

The boy bit his lip, glancing from Snake to the dresser. "I don't think Summer w—"

"August," Snake interrupted. He really didn't give a damn what Summer Austin thought. He had to get out of this bed. "Now that's an interesting name," he offered, noticing how the boy looked at him questionably.

August grinned. "It's cause I was born in August." He nodded proudly. "September was born in September. My pa was born in July and my Ma in June. That's how we all got our names." He gave a slight shrug. "Summer was just born in the summer I guess, 'cause that's her name."

Snake nodded. His family had some unconventional names, but they were just nicknames, their given names were normal enough. "Good thing you weren't born in May," he said. "To be a man named May would be tough."

The kid giggled.

The light carefree sound brought a smile to Snake's face. He winked. "How about you get me those britches?"

August shuffled his feet and scratched at the

back of his neck.

Snake didn't say a word, just waited for August to make up his mind.

With a shrug, August agreed, "All right." He walked to the dresser and tugged out a pair.

"Thanks." Snake, keeping the sheet over his waist, swung his legs to the side of the bed. The movement sent flames ripping up his thigh, and the room spun. He clenched onto the sheet until his knuckles grew numb.

"You all right?" August asked.

"Yes," Snake groaned between clenched teeth.

"Your face looks like you're mad or something. You want a different pair of britches?"

The room no longer spun. Snake let out a breath and tried to sound friendly as he took the clothes. "No, these pants will do just fine. Thanks."

August hung near the side of the bed. Watched.

Snake tried several ways to get one foot into a pant leg—a difficult task with only one hand holding the waistband open. Huffing through the pain every movement caused, he flipped them out and tried again.

"You need some help?" August asked.

"Yeah." He tucked the sheet tight across his midsection. "If you could just set them on the floor by my feet, I'll step into them."

August did so, and by the time Snake had them pulled up to his waist, he was breathing heavily and sweating profusely. Unable to put any weight on his left leg, he plopped onto the bed. The mattress bounced. Another surge of pain took his breath away completely.

"I better go yell for September. You don't look so good."

Snake couldn't muster up a response. He laid back and wished the room would stop spinning again. The motion was enough to make him throw up. He closed his eyes, willing his stomach and the room to settle.

When he came to, August sat near the edge of the bed—again, with big blue eyes staring at him—again.

"Hi," August said.

Something about the kid made him grin. A rough chuckle bubbled up his chest. "Hi," Snake replied.

"You gonna be my pa?" August asked.

"No." Snake ignored the stitch in his chest. "You already have a pa."

August shook his head. "Not anymore."

A chill raced over his shoulders, and Snake eased himself up to sit on the edge of the bed. He took it slow this time, and then positioned his feet on the floor, careful not to put any pressure on his left leg. "What do you mean?"

"My pa died. The sheriff was here and told Summer."

"When?"

"Day 'afore yesterday."

A million subjects darted around in Snake's head. Who'd killed July Austin? Who'd shot him? How'd he get home? Had he really seen his father? Had that been some kind of mystical vision?

August's sad voice filtered in amongst Snake's thoughts. "It's all right," the boy said. "If'n you don't want to be my pa. I was just thinking having a ma and a pa would be kinda nice. Jeffrey Mohler has both a ma and a pa and bragged about it all the time."

"Who?" Snake asked, trying to follow the child's words.

"Jeffrey Mohler. Summer worked for his pa back in Dodge, at the Long Branch. Jeffrey went to school with me. Mrs. Hinkle had to tell him to leave me alone." August's eyes were cast down and a frown pulled on his lips. "He's lots bigger than me."

Snake's heart tugged on the wall of his chest. It had to be hard, growing up without parents. Poor August was so young, and he was a good kid, for all Snake had seen so far anyway.

"Summer said even though she's my sister, I could pretend she was my ma."

A smile tickled Snake's lips. He could see her saying that. It was evident how much she loved her siblings. He'd noticed that right off. "That was nice of her," he said, unable to think of a better answer.

"I was hoping now that the two of you are married, I could pretend you were my pa."

For a moment he thought he'd been shot again. "What?" Snake pressed a hand so hard on his stomach he could almost feel his backbone. "What did you say?"

August jumped back. "Sorry!" He glanced about the room nervously. "I won't pretend you're my pa, I promise."

Snake took a deep breath and told himself not to shout this time. "No, not that part. What did you say about Summer and I?"

"That you two are married?" August mumbled questionably.

"No, we aren't."

"Ah, ha," August said nodding his head.

"Uh, uh," Snake said, shaking his.

Still nodding, August supplied, "The preacher man was here."

Snake went ice cold, inside and out. "When?"

"While you were sleeping. When the doctor was digging out the bullets."

The air in his chest, hotter than Hades, burst from his lungs as Snake bellowed, "Mmmaaa!"

Just then the door flew open. Summer Austin, sweat running down her face and chest heaving with gulps of air, blasted into the room. Following closely on her heels was his mother.

Snake glared. His mother's eyes grew wide, and quicker than a horsefly, she buzzed in, grabbed August, and soared back out the door.

"Ma!" he yelled, thrusting himself onto his feet. Blinding pain made him grab for the table beside the bed. It collapsed. He went down with it, growling and cursing a blue streak at the hell tearing across his body.

Hands tried to assist him, and he pushed them aside. "Get away from me!"

When a little more than a constant ache filled his system, he eased himself off the floor, grunting, and silently cursing, until he finally sat on the edge of the bed again.

Summer Austin stood before him, tears streaked her cheeks. As if she hadn't noticed them until just now, she wiped her face with the backs of her hands, and then met his stare. Her eyes weren't cold, but there was hardness in them, a strength he'd never seen in a woman before.

The sight took him aback, made him stare longer, harder.

She didn't flinch, just met him eyeball for eyeball.

"Are you through trying to kill yourself?" she asked.

His lips grew tight.

She lifted her eyebrows.

He raised a hand, pointed to the door. "Get my mother."

She didn't even blink. "No."

"No?"

"No," she stated, pointedly.

"Fine, I'll get her." He put his hand on the edge of the bed but knew full well he couldn't put any weight on his left leg. If he could get up, he might be able to hop to the door. Fear of the pain he'd felt

31

moments earlier kept him from attempting to stand.

"I didn't think so." Her voice was soft, and she stepped closer. "Tell me what you need, and I'll get it."

"My mother. I need to speak to her."

She lifted the table and checked the legs for breakage. "Why? I can tell you what happened." After settling the table beside the bed, she looked at him. "What do you want to know?"

Snake couldn't make his eyes move. It was as if they were glued to her. Had she been that pretty the last time he saw her? Her long black hair hung past her elbows, and her eyes weren't black, but the deepest, darkest blue he'd ever seen. They were the color the sky turns just before night falls. Her face was long and finely shaped so that each feature stood out, clearly, proudly, yet blended with the others to make the entire image flawless and overly appealing.

His heartbeat increased again, and this time it wasn't caused by pain from his wounds. He wet his lips and tried to come up with something to say. But for the life of him, he couldn't remember why he'd wanted to hop across the floor.

She blinked and the tiniest grin flickered upon her lips as he relaxed. "What was it you wanted to ask your mother? We aren't sure who shot you, but believe it was Wainwright."

His mind cleared with a rush. He pushed one palm deep into the mattress. "August said the preacher was here."

Her eyes grew round, and she twisted, glancing at the door.

"Was he?" Snake asked. "Are we married?"

She spun back around.

Her face had grown beet red. "Uh—" Her hair flew about her shoulders as she twirled again, pointing toward the door. "Umm—" Once again, she spun back toward him. "Oh..." she let out a long sigh that carried a moan.

"Ma!" he bellowed loud enough to be heard in Dodge.

Chapter Four

Summer had never wished to be dead before, but at this moment, being planted six feet under sounded pretty good. Snake Quinter was a large man. She'd bathed him while he slept, washed the bulging muscles more than once. But alive, sitting on the edge of the bed, those muscles seemed much larger, and he, overall appeared much fiercer than his sleeping formed had demonstrated.

Her knees knocked together like spindly tree limbs. She took a restorative breath, told herself there was no need to panic, and flipped around to race for the door.

He bellowed again as she slapped the door shut. Leaning her head against the wood, she gulped as if she'd just floated up from the muddy bottom of the Arkansas River. When her heart no longer tried to beat out of her chest, she glanced around the room. The kitchen area, holding a big table, stove, cupboards, and all the other household necessities, stood empty before her. Empty of people anyway.

There was no sign of Stephanie Quinter anywhere.

The door stood open. Had Stephanie taken the children and headed back out to the wheat field? The thrashing was coming along well, the field more than three quarters done, but it would take every available hand to complete it before night fall.

Maybe Stephanie had gone to get Bug, or even Snake's oldest brother Kid. Summer's shoulders drooped. There wasn't anything they could do. She stepped away from the door, and spun around, gazing at it. To keep Snake from being extremely angry at his mother, she surmised. Who wouldn't be?

Shaking her head, she lifted her hair off her shoulders with both hands and held it up for a moment to let a touch of coolness lick at the sweat that had accumulated as she rode for the house. September had arrived at the field, shouting that Snake had woken up and then fallen back on the bed.

Fearful he'd hurt himself or opened his wounds, Summer had leaped on the closest horse and raced for the house. Frowning, she let her hair fall down her back and walked to the front door. The yard was empty. The horse she'd ridden on was gone. So was Maisy. As were her little brother and sister.

She turned around, looking across the long room to the doorway at the far end. Balling her hands into fists, she tossed her head and squared her shoulders.

"I'll do whatever it takes to keep September and August safe, and that, Mr. Scott Quinter, includes facing you," she said.

Her feet were heavier than cast iron skillets full of rocks, but Summer kept them moving, barely let them stall as they came to his bedroom door. Thrusting it open, she marched into the room and didn't stop until she stood beside his bed. "Yes, Mr. Quinter, we're married."

"Where's my mother?" he asked so calmly she squinted to make sure it was him who'd spoken.

He lifted one brow in question.

"She must have gone back out to the wheat field. The harvest is almost complete, but they need every hand they can get out there to make sure they finish up before the storm that's threatening bursts."

His gaze went to the window.

Summer walked across the room and held the curtain fringed with eyelet away from the glass so he could see through the panes. "It's in the air," she insisted. "You can feel it."

"Who's thrashing the wheat?"

"Your mother, your brothers, Kid and Bug, and several of Kid's ranch hands." She let the material fall back into place and turned to face the bed. "How are you doing? The doctor left laudanum. I've been giving you a little every time you stirred. Would you like some now?"

"No," he said, and as if it were an afterthought added, "thank you." He glanced toward the window again. "Who's running my thrashing machine?"

"Bug. He said he helped you build it, and that he's used it before."

"He did and he has. How's the yield?"

"Kid says it's the highest you've ever had," she answered. Kid had been over to see Snake several times since the shooting, almost daily, and so had his wife Jessie. It was Kid who'd said it was time to get the field harvested, and Jessie brought a noon meal out to the workers every day. "He also says there's not another field around that needs to be harvested yet. You must have early seed."

Snake's face made a tiny frown and then he nodded. "It's a winter wheat hybrid I've been working on."

"It looks good," she admitted. "It's sure to bring a good price at the mill."

His gaze roamed up and down her frame before it settled on her face. "How do you know so much about wheat?"

She shrugged and moved back toward the door. "July did some farming. We lived out by Cimarron. In the river valley, had good water out there."

He nodded. "When was that?"

"Over ten years ago. The grasshopper plague wiped us out."

"You...you had to have been just a little girl then."

"Eleven. But you don't forget something like that. Those little bugs didn't leave a strip of green anywhere." She bit her lip, not wanting to say more, not wanting to remember that was also where and when Jonas died.

"Did you move to Dodge then?"

"No, not right away. We went to the eastern part of the state for a few years, and then came back to Dodge. Had only been there a month when the smallpox outbreak hit. August was just a baby, September only three. September got it first, then July and Ma caught it. Ma didn't survive."

"So you've been raising August and September since you were fourteen?" he asked.

She took a moment to ponder at how quickly he'd done the math to figure out her age. "Of course I have. They're my brother and sister."

"In Dodge?"

"For the most part. July moved us a couple of times, but we always ended up back in Dodge somehow or another." She moved to the doorway, not wanting to answer any more questions. "I'm going to get you something to eat and drink. You have to be starving."

"No, don—" he stopped and shook his head. "I'm really not hungry."

"You will be once you start eating." Summer left the room, wondering why she'd told him so much about herself. She wasn't one to talk, let alone share her life story with others. Perhaps it was because they were married and she felt she should. Her feet stumbled. Luckily a chair was close enough to grab.

He hadn't said anything more about their marriage. Quickly, as if her feet had grown wings she flew to the ice box and pulled out the soup she'd made last night. The house had one of the finest kitchens Summer had ever seen, a root cellar full of provisions and cupboard full of other supplies, but after tasting two meals Stephanie Quinter had prepared, Summer had started to do the cooking. The morning Stephanie had fed them oatmeal with lumps the size of biscuits, Summer determined if Snake had been destined to die at an early age, it would have been due to his mother's cooking.

Summer frowned, and silently chided herself for thinking so rudely about someone who'd been so kind and considerate. Stephanie had welcomed September and August into her home as if they were her long last grandchildren, and Summer would forever be grateful to the woman for that.

While the soup heated, she pumped water into a pitcher from the spigot at the sink, filled a glass, and set it along with bread and other necessities onto a tray. She also took a moment to wash her face and smooth her flyaway hair. When everything was ready, she carried the laden tray into his room. He still sat in the same position, legs dangling over the edge. She set the tray on the small table he'd knocked over earlier and moved it in front of him.

"Try to eat something. I haven't got much down you the last week."

He lifted the spoon, watching the soup flow off it. "Where'd this come from?"

"I made it," she said.

"Ma help you?"

"No." She almost smiled, understanding his apprehension.

He nodded and lifted the spoon to his mouth. After several spoonfuls he laid the spoon down to take a bite of the bread. "This is good," he said after swallowing. "Ma's not much of a cook. We knew it before, but since Hog moved to Dodge, Bug and I have been wondering if we'd starve to death." He took another bite. "We were afraid Kid was going to chase us off his porch with a stick if we kept begging the way we were."

She couldn't help but laugh. He looked at her in such a way that Summer wished she could read his mind. He didn't smile—not really anyway, but she kind of felt it.

His gaze went back to the food and after a few more bites, he sat back. "That was good, thanks."

"You should finish it," she said.

"No." He shook his head.

Maybe her food was as bad as his mother's. Summer had never cooked for anyone outside her family, who never complained about having something to eat.

"Really," he said. "It was good. I just can't eat any more. I'm full."

She lifted the tray and turned to carry it back to the kitchen.

"Will you come back, after you've put that away? So we can talk."

Summer didn't turn around. "Yes," she said, walking out of the room. He wanted to know if they were really married. Her stomach pitched. She'd told Stephanie he didn't know what he was doing. Couldn't possibly know he was agreeing with the ceremony by simply nodding his head.

After cleaning the kitchen and putting everything back in its rightful place, she closed her eyes to prepare herself for what was about to come. Now that July was dead and Sam Wainwright was a wanted man, there really wasn't any reason to stay married. Yet, for some reason the thought tugged at her heart. She'd only been at the Quinter farm a week, but from the moment she'd seen it, she'd felt as if she'd finally come home.

Summer walked back into the bedroom and wiping her hands, which had begun to perspire, on her apron, she sat down on the chair in the corner.

He stared at her for several silent moments, until she wondered if she had something on her face, or maybe stuck in her hair. She brushed the long strands aside, wishing she'd taken a moment to brush it, or at least peer in the mirror.

"How'd the marriage happen?" he asked.

She glanced up. "What?"

He waved a hand. "Our marriage. How'd it happen?" A scowl formed. "Did Bug go get the preacher?"

"Bug? No."

"Kid did?" He looked shocked.

"No," she answered.

"Then who did?"

"Your mother."

"Ma?" Again he sounded as if she hadn't told the truth.

"Yes," she assured. "There wasn't anyone else here, except August and September."

"How'd I get here?"

"I brought you."

"Really?" he sounded skeptical. "For some reason I thought it was Kid or Bug. Where'd you find me?"

Summer bit her lip, wondering how much to say. She most certainly couldn't tell him his father, Jonas Quinter, was her guardian angel. At least that's what she called him. For the past ten years, he'd came to her when she needed him, told her where to find things, how to make ends meet when they were miles apart, as well as many other things.

She swallowed and met the gaze coming across the room. Snake no longer looked furious. He behaved quite amicable, friendly even, considering the position he was in. Injured and married, all because of her.

A cool breeze blew in the window and flowed over her. It was as soft and gentle as being cloaked in pure silk must be. A calming sensation grew from the pit of her stomach, swelling to encompass her.

She sighed. Jonas was here, and would help her through the conversation.

"Not long after you left, I-um-I had a feeling something was wrong. I borrowed one of your horses and followed you." She held back the part where she camped close enough to hear him breathe that night, or how she stayed back the next morning, fearing he'd sense her. "Before I caught up with you, I heard shots. Two men on horses were chasing you. I fired at them, but they were too far away to hit. They took off in the other direction, and I chased your horse down. After I pressed some bandages to your wounds," she didn't bother to tell him the bandages were actually her petticoat, "I tied you in your saddle, and we rode all day to get back home."

He didn't comment so she continued, "Stephanie was the only one here, besides the children. She rode to town to get the doctor. He said the bullet was close to your heart, and he didn't know if you'd survive the surgery to take it out." She paused, biting her lip until the pain made her stop. "Stephanie said we had to get married before he started working on you."

"Why?"

"She said since you hadn't made it to Dodge, the win hadn't been claimed."

"So?"

Summer swallowed. Stephanie must have explained it better, because that night it made more sense. It had seemed like it was their only option— then. Now, she didn't feel quite as confident. "Well," she said, checking the back of her mind for more details. "If you'd never claimed the win, Sam Wainwright would be able to come and take September. But if you and I were married, it would be the same as if you'd claimed the win, and Wainwright's win would be void."

"And this had to happen before I had surgery?"

She nodded. "In case you died."

"Jesus," he swore under his breath.

Summer flexed her toes, giving herself something to do. The story did sound a bit callous—even to her ears. At the time she'd have agreed to just about anything, fearing he'd soon expire. And it hadn't been because she was worried about herself or September. It had been him. She couldn't let Snake die, not because of her. Her family had already killed one Quinter. Jonas didn't hold it against her, but the rest of the family surely would.

"The preacher wouldn't perform the ceremony until you agreed to it," she offered with condolence.

A frown pulled on his face, and his eyes moved about, as if he tried to remember. Glancing back her way, he asked, "Was I awake?"

"N-not really. But you're mother, the preacher, and the doctor kept asking if you agreed and you finally nodded." She looked at her shoes. Dust from the field covered them. She flounced the hem of her skirt over her toes. "The preacher performed the ceremony while the doctor dug the bullet out of your leg."

He cursed again, quietly, and shook his head.

They sat in silence for some time. Summer couldn't think of anything to say. He looked about as sad as anyone she'd ever seen. She almost wished he was angry again, shouting and glaring at her with fire in his green eyes.

The room—though large enough to hold the big bed, tall wooden dresser complete with an oblong mirror, a wash stand, the table beside the bed, the chair which she sat on, and still leave plenty of walking around space—began to close in on her. A weight pressed on her chest. The air in her lungs grew as heavy as clay.

"I think I'm going to lie down for a bit," he said soberly.

"Oh," she jumped to her feet. "Let me help you."

He didn't refuse and though he didn't give verbal approval, she took his silence as acceptance. Lifting his bad leg as he swung the good one onto the bed, she carefully set it down and then pulled the sheet up. She stopped before laying the material across his chest.

"Do you want to take your britches off?" Her cheeks warmed.

"No."

She let the cover fall over his chest and carefully tucked it around his legs. "Would you like some laudanum?"

"No," he said, eyes closed.

An incredible urge to lean down and kiss his forehead like she did August when she tucked him in overcame her. Jolting upright, she stepped away from the bed. "I'll be in the kitchen. Let me know if you need anything."

He didn't make a move, not even an eyelash flickered. All of a sudden exhaustion settled on her like a winter snowfall. She rubbed her arms, moving toward the door.

"Summer," he said before she pulled the door shut.

"Yes?"

"Thank you for rescuing me. I most likely would have died if you hadn't caught up with me when you did."

"You're welcome, Snake."

He turned his head and opened one eye to look at her. A tiny smile graced his face before he closed the lid and rolled his head back onto the pillow.

Regret. Shame. Disgrace. Something of that sort swelled her throat. She swallowed the huge lump. It hit her stomach so hard she barely made it outside before losing her lunch.

Chapter Five

The merriment in the other room was enough to wake the dead. Snake rolled onto his side and using his good arm worked his body around until he sat on the edge of the bed again. The nap had helped, he felt stronger and more alive than earlier today, but a rock of hurt or anger, he wasn't sure which, still sat in the pit of his stomach.

His mother had always been a bit unseemly to some, but he'd never doubted she loved him and his brothers, that is until he'd been told she'd been more worried about a poker game than his life. More worried about getting him married off than about him living to see tomorrow.

He slapped the mattress. *Damn, if that don't beat all.*

The door opened just then, and Summer Austin poked her head around the edge.

His heart skipped a beat or two. Why the hell did Ma have to marry him off to the prettiest woman around? Couldn't she have found an ugly toothless creature so he could be really pissed off?

"Hi," she said, slipping in the room as graceful and precious as a butterfly. The door clicked shut behind her. "I wondered if the noise woke you."

"Hi," he greeted, unable to keep a smile from forming. Her grin was so adorable his stomach did cartwheels. Ignoring the commotion in his guts, he asked, "What's going on out there?"

"The harvest is over for one." She moved closer. "For two, your brothers just learned that when you woke up today"—she avoided looking his way as she straightened out the bedding he'd managed to twist into a tangled mass—"you weren't very happy with your mother."

The flipping in his insides had worked its way into a laugh that bubbled out before he had a chance to stop it. "Really?"

She moved to his other side, straightening out the pillows. A tiny giggle escaped before she answered, "Yes, really."

Her long, black hair hung over her shoulder, blocked him from seeing her face. He reached up to brush it aside. When their gazes met, it was as if he'd been shot again, dead center.

The door opened, and Kid stuck his head in. "You are up." Pushing the door wide his oldest brother strolled into the room. "How you feeling?"

"Not so bad," he admitted.

The room filled up quickly. His sister-in-law, Jessie, wrapped him in a soft hug and kissed his cheek. Bug slapped him hard enough on the shoulder he almost tumbled off the bed. His nephew, Joel, ran across the room on chubby little legs, and Snake caught the child moments before he jumped up on his bad leg. Placing the child on his good one, he hugged Joel and realized just how lucky he was that he didn't die. Overall he had a good family. A damn good family.

Ma hung back, a nervousness he'd never seen before flittered about her. He stared at her until she couldn't help but meet his gaze. No matter how mad he was, she was his mother, and damn-it-to-hell, but he loved her. He grinned and winked at her.

Ma let out a little squeal and hopped across the room. She wrapped both he and Joel in a hug. "Don't scare me like that," she said. "My heart's getting too old for such shenanigans."

"It wasn't all my fault." He kissed her wrinkled cheek. "But, I'll try to not let it happen again."

"You do that." She pinched his chin. "I need my boys, all of them."

Kid lifted Joel from his knee when Ma stepped aside. "Come on, little brother. We'll help you out to the table." He handed the child to Jessie. "Supper's almost ready. Bug, get his other side."

Summer had disappeared. Snake searched the room for her as his brothers half-carried him to the door.

"She's cooking," Kid whispered in his ear.

"Yeah, thank God," Bug said in the other.

Both of his brothers hooted like jackals. When they lowered him into a chair, Snake would have laughed, too, if their rough movements hadn't made his chest and leg hurt like hell. No one else restrained themselves, and soon merriment filled his mother's house.

The meal had been delicious, certainly not prepared by Ma, Snake conceded. Her foods were either raw or burnt. She'd never mastered that in-between stage. They'd never noticed it growing up, not until Hog started cooking anyway, and they all got a flavor for what food should taste like. Ma said it was because she didn't like cooking. Which was no surprise given she was always in her bedroom, kicking away on her stitching machine. The thought made his gaze wander to Summer.

A silver colored skirt flanked her hips and fell to the floor, streamlining her trim form, and a pristine white blouse was tucked into the waist line. The ties of an apron, long and white, dangled from the big bow tied in the small of her back. She and Jessie stood at the sink, doing dishes, talking as they washed. A single white ribbon held Summer's long black hair together at the nap of her neck. The glistening strands flowed down her back like a long rope, swaying now and again as she moved.

An odd, not unpleasant sensation filled his

chest, and he frowned, wondering what it was. Another consciousness, that of being watched, tickled his spine, and he turned slightly.

September Austin, as light as her sister was dark, glared at him across the table. Snake raised a brow, staring back at the young girl with her faded blue eyes and wheat colored hair. The girl had yet to speak to him, even when he'd greeted her earlier; she'd merely sent him a quick and somewhat disgusted glance.

He smiled and gave her a slight nod. Her eyes narrowed, and she grabbed the plate in front of her holding a piece of peach pie they'd had for desert. The legs of her chair scraped the floor loudly as she pushed away from the table.

Snake continued to watch as the younger sister carried her dish to the sink. As soon as she set it on the counter, September turned back to the table.

"August," she snapped haughtily.

"Uh?" The brother, who'd all but plastered himself against Snake as soon as he sat down, looked up, chewing the food in his mouth with all his might.

"We have chores to do," September said, moving to the door.

"What chores?" Snake asked.

She ignored him. "August!"

"I ain't done eating yet."

September, her blond curls bouncing, stormed across the room and reached for the boy's plate. "You can finish it later."

August clutched the plate with one hand, shoveling the pie in his mouth with the other. His mumbled answer couldn't be understood, but his actions proved he didn't want to go.

"What's so important it can't wait until he's done?" Snake asked, placing a hand on the boy's shoulder.

September's glare became downright hateful. Her little nose wrinkled up, and her eyes all but fired buckshot. "We don't take charity from anyone. We work for our keep."

Snake, taken aback, couldn't come up with a response quick enough. Or maybe Summer, used to the girl's behavior, was just that much quicker.

"September," she said with warning. When the girl looked at her older sister, Summer continued, "You can wait until he's done with his pie."

"He is done." September grabbed the now empty plate off the table. She stomped across the room and plopped the dish on the counter. Her gaze snapped to her brother, and she tipped her head to the door.

"Come on, partner, I'll help you," Bug said, lifting August from his chair.

The glare September sent Bug wasn't any too friendly either. "We don't need help. We know what needs to be done."

Kid stood. "Jessie and I should head home. Bug, would you mind harnessing the horses while I help Snake back into bed?"

"Sure. You want me to help get him back to bed first?" Bug asked.

"I'll help," Summer said from her stance near the sink.

The slam of the door, behind September as she bolted outside, rattled the windows.

Summer, drying her hands on her apron, glanced toward the door. Jessie laid a hand on her arm. "I'll go see if I can help her. You help Kid with Snake."

Snake had never been around children much, his nieces and nephew were little more than babies, but he'd been around plenty of pissed off people before, and something had September Austin madder than a hornet. And the fire blazing in her young eyes had told him her sting would be much worse than an insect's.

"I don't need any help. I can get back to bed on my own," he said.

Shouts of, "No!" filled the room. Summer at least had the decency to sound nervous. While Ma, Kid, Jessie, and Bug sounded downright rude. Annoyance vibrated his spine, he'd been shot, but he wasn't some kind of an invalid. With his good hand, he pushed away from the table and planted both feet on the floor. Agony raced up his leg, he tried to ignore it, grasping the edge of the table. Everyone stepped forward. Snake leveled a steely gaze at the crowd.

Kid hooked an arm around his good elbow. "Come on."

Snake wanted to protest, but his injuries said whether he liked it or not, he needed help getting back to bed. To make matters worse, he needed to use the water closet.

Sometime later, after he'd grudgingly asked Kid to help him restore his britches before his older brother helped him back into his bedroom, Snake laid his head on the pillow and closed both eyes. His shoulder and leg throbbed as if a good sized mule kicked him every other second. He gritted his teeth, breathing through the pain as Kid slid his pants off.

"You need some medicine?" Kid asked, covering Snake's legs with the sheet.

Snake shook his head.

"It'll help. I have it right here."

His eyelids flew open. Had Summer been in there the whole time? While Kid undressed him? The undeniable heat of a blush racing over his face made Snake swallow and close his eyes again. He didn't have any drawers on beneath his britches. What was Kid thinking, letting her be in the room like that?

"No," he snapped. "I don't need any medicine. I just need to be left the hell alone. That's what I

49

need."

He didn't bother to open his eyes to make sure she left the room, but at the sound of the door clicking shut the sting of shame hit his guts. He hadn't meant to sound so rude, Ma didn't abide bad manners no matter what the situation and would probably come storming into the room at any moment.

When the door remained closed and the hushed voices in the other rooms faded, he let the muscles bunched up around his neck relax and begged the constant ache surrounding his wounds to ease. Ma must have put his boorish behavior off to his injuries, which was true. He'd never known getting shot was so painful. He'd be more sympathetic to those inflicted with a bullet next time the need arose.

In the distance, the clop of horse hooves and the creaking and rattling of wagon wheels mingled with the chirping crickets. Even though the barn was on the other side of the house from his room, Snake opened his eyes and gazed at the window. It would be Kid and Jessie along with their children Joel and baby Winifred leaving. He blew the heavy air out of his lungs. Had he even thanked them for thrashing the wheat? His fuzzy mind couldn't remember. It seemed visions of the dark haired Summer were the only things filling the space between his ears.

More sounds filtered into the room, the ones of a household preparing for bed. The creak of the floorboard overhead as someone thudded across the upstairs loft. A swoosh of water—the hightail sign someone had used the tank toilet he and Kid had installed a few years ago in the water closet.

The twinge of a smile tugged at his lips. Dang if Ma didn't like that thing. She'd walked around prouder than a French hen for months after they'd installed it, as if indoor plumbing had somehow elevated her status in life. He and Bug had promised her they'd install hot and cold water, just like Hog had in his Dodge City hotel as soon as thrashing season was over. That would have to wait for a bit longer now, at least until he could put weight on his injured leg. How long did it take for bullet wounds to heal? He couldn't fathom lying around for days on end. He'd become as loco as a cross-eyed bull—and most assuredly as ornery.

The water sounded again, and this time he wondered if it was Summer using the water closet. Did she like indoor plumbing as much as Ma? Most likely all women did. His sisters-in-law sure gaggled about it while everyone was in Dodge. They went on about those porcelain bathtubs as eagerly as they did about a new born babe. Which was something else he never quite fathomed—a baby was a baby. Not a whole lot new about anyone of them. Yet, now that he thought about it, his brothers had all carried on like their babies had been the first kids ever born. Raved about their hair, the tiny fingers, their bright eyes...

His gaze went to the door. Summer would have some pretty babies—especially if they had her striking midnight eyes and hair. A frown tugged at his brows. Now, why the hell was he thinking about her babies and getting kind of giddy about it?

Because she's your wife, a little voice inside his head proclaimed.

"No, she's not," he argued out loud.

Yes, she is.

"No, she's not. Not really anyway." Snake squeezed his eyes shut, as if that could stop the little voice. "Aw, hell," he muttered. "What's the matter with me? I'm arguing with myself."

A soft knock rapped on the door seconds before it opened. "Are you doing all right in here? Need some medicine?"

The space behind her was dark, lit by nothing more than the same moon beams filling his room. Unfathomably, Snake's heart rattled his chest. The faded light caught in the long tresses of her hair, making each strand sparkle.

Breathless, he grunted, "No."

She took a step into the room. "I thought I heard you talking, asking for something."

Only the God-given good sense I was born with, he thought, but said, "No, I don't need anything."

She didn't move right away, and his wandering mind took yet another direction. "Where are you sleeping?" he asked.

Her head twisted as she glanced over her shoulder. "On the divan." She pivoted back his way. "Why? Are you uncomfortable? Need another pillow or something?"

That would make sense—her sleeping on the divan. There were two beds upstairs. Ever since Skeeter moved out, Snake had claimed this room downstairs with a flip of a coin, which had left Hog and Bug up in the loft. They all had slept up there at one time—when Kid—and Pa—had lived at home.

A slight pressure settled his shoulder. Assuming it was from his injury, he rubbed the area.

"Are you sure you're all right?" Summer asked from her doorway stance.

The other downstairs room was Ma's. Most likely September and August were sharing Hog's old bed while Bug slept in the other, which ultimately left only the divan for her.

"It's not very big," he said.

"What?" She stepped closer, pointing to his shoulder. "Your wound? It's actually a good sized hole."

He shook his head. "No, the divan. It's not very big. It can't be too comfortable."

"Oh, it's fine." Walking across the room,

stopping near the bed, she said, "Here, let me check it. Hopefully you didn't disrupt the healing moving around tonight."

"No, it's fine. Kid checked it. B-but...thanks."

She paused beside the bed, as if she was unsure what to do next. He didn't know what to do either, but he didn't want her to leave, not yet anyway. Inching over, into the middle of the bed, he patted the open space with his good hand. "Want to sit down for a minute?"

Her head twisted as she glanced over her shoulder toward the door.

"Just for a minute," he encouraged. "I've slept so much the past few days, I'm not very tired."

Moonlight basked upon her, making her look almost dreamlike. With a slight shrug, she lowered onto the edge of the bed. "You have slept a lot. But that's what the doctor wanted. He didn't want you waking up and ripping out your stitches."

"Ma didn't use her stitching machine, did she?"

Her hair flipped and flopped as her face whirled around to gap at him. "Of course not!"

He winked. "Just kidding. She loves that machine so much I wouldn't put it past her."

The giggle that escaped her mouth tinkled like a sleigh bell. A swell of happiness expanded his chest. It felt good. He'd always considered life was a whole lot easier when you carried a good disposition. Therefore, he usually did. He was a likeable sort of guy, he knew that, and didn't have any real enemies, not that he could think of anyway.

A buckling of doubt made him ask, "Did I do something while I was sleeping that made September hate me?"

"No," she said quickly—almost too quickly. "And September doesn't hate you."

"Yes, she does," he responded. "A person can tell when someone doesn't like them, and your little sister likes me about as much as a dog likes a flea."

"September's just scared. We left Dodge in a hurry, and she feels it's her fault. She probably blames herself for you being hurt as well."

Snake didn't think so, but he didn't want to dispute Summer's belief—not yet anyway. "Tell me about it."

"About what?"

"Leaving Dodge."

She took a deep breath and exhaled it out long and slow. The soft hiss floated on the air until it almost echoed off the walls. He reached over and wrapped his hand around the one she had resting on the mattress beside her hip. The soft, warm skin of the back of her hand filled his palm perfectly, and he gave it a little squeeze.

"I didn't know what else to do," she said despondently.

"Tell me what happened."

"I was at the saloon during the card game. In the backroom. I heard the bet"—she paused, staring at the doorway—"and how angry you were when you folded. Right after you stormed out, Wainwright woke up and claimed the win. July said he could come get September the next day—after he had a chance to tell her. I left then, out the back door, and ran into George Hinkle. He asked what was wrong, and I told him. He told me to go home and not worry about it. The next day he came by to say you'd left town. He wanted the kids and me to go stay with him and his wife for a few days, but I couldn't do that. But after two nights of...." She paused and then said, "We packed up and traveled out here—to your place."

"Why?"

"Why? So Wainwright wouldn't take September. Why else?"

"That was dangerous. Wainwright could have

followed."

She shook her head. "George had him arrested. When he claimed the win, a fight broke out. George broke it up. July was taken to Doc Jones and Wainwright to jail."

Her hand trembled beneath his. Snake gave it a gentle squeeze. She glanced down at the mattress, looking at their hands for a moment before her gaze rose to meet his. There was strength and honesty in those dark eyes, but Snake saw more. He saw a scared little girl. On the outside, Summer Austin may have grown up, but on the inside there was a frightened little girl who was lost in a big, scary world, with two siblings to take care of. Something inside him snapped then. Whether it was a piece of his heart breaking for what she'd been through, or a part of his soul disengaging to merge with hers, he wasn't sure.

As if she felt what went on inside him, her fingers folded around his, and her grasp tightened. A silent, inner thought said as sure as the sun would rise and set tomorrow, they were bound together. Not because Ma had called in some preacher, but because he had to. There was no way he'd let someone as low and downright bad as Wainwright hurt her or her siblings.

"August said your Pa died."

A tiny gasp emitted, and she gave a slight nod.

"What happened?"

She shrugged. "He was shot. The Sheriff thinks it was Wainwright. Thinks that's who shot you, too."

Snake had no doubt that was who shot him. Though he hadn't seen anything, it had happened too quickly, but a gut feeling said it had been Wainwright. That same gut feeling said the man would be back. A simple marriage wasn't going to stop the Mexican trader.

"You should try to get some sleep."

She hadn't moved, but Snake squeezed her hand anyway, as if he could hold her to the spot where she sat. "No, I'm really not tired." He wasn't, not in the least. Lying here, holding her hand, did a better job of healing his wounds than all the doctors and medicine in the world. "Tell me," he said. "What I can do to help September? She has to know it's not her fault."

Chapter Six

Summer had to squeeze her eyes closed to keep the tears at bay. He sounded so sincere, like he really wanted to help September—and Lord knows her little sister needed all the help she could get. July had blamed the girl for their mother's death for as long as September could remember. He claimed if she hadn't came down with the pox, June wouldn't have died. Summer tried over the years to convince September it hadn't been her fault, but every time July found a bottle—which was every day—he'd start blaming the child all over again.

"It'll just take some time is all," she said, knowing she'd been quiet too long. "September just needs time."

"Time is a good healer, but sometimes it's not enough. Sometimes a person needs more. The truth or reason."

Summer stared into his eyes. They were clear, didn't seem to be hiding anything, but was he suspicious? Did he know her father was the cause of Jonas' death? Did he want the truth?

He squinted at her, which caused a slight frown to pull his brows together.

She swallowed the lump in her throat.

"All right. We'll just give her time," he said. "But I'll need your help. She really doesn't like me."

Summer's fingers had tingled to the point they'd had all but gone numb. Holding his hand caused a sensation not unlike the invisible comforting blanket that surrounded her when Jonas paid a visit, but stronger, more real in some way. It was strange, for she'd truly never felt a connection like this before. It was a tiny bit scary to know another person could silently affect her so. Her thoughts paused, and she waited, searching to see if it was Jonas making her feel this way and not Snake.

"You will help me, won't you?"

The sound of Snake's voice was enough to pull her mind back. Jonas wasn't around. "Yes, I'll help you." It was an honest, simple answer. She'd known for years there'd be a time when they'd need each other, and this was it—no doubt.

"Where do we start?" he asked.

Her expression undoubtedly said she had no idea.

"What does she like?"

"What?" she asked.

"What does September like to do? Like to eat? What are her favorite things? That could be a place to start."

Summer had to smile. He really was an intuitively nice man. "Well," she started, "she does like to read. She was always borrowing books from Mrs. Hinkle."

"Kid has a room full of books. We'll take her over there and let her pick out a bunch."

Her heart tick-tocked faster than a mantel clock wound too tight. She chanced a peek, making sure he was serious. September would be ecstatic to spend a day in a room full of books. A golden beam from the moon bounced off his face, displaying a soft, sincere smile. "She'd like that."

"What else," he asked softly, "does she like?"

Summer searched her mind, but nothing formed. Wasn't there anything else September really liked? She tried harder, forced herself to recall times she'd seen September happy or content. Nothing appeared. Did she really not know, or was sitting this close to Snake turning her fuddle-headed?

"I'll have to think about it," she admitted after several silent minutes.

"All right," he said, "then tell me about August. What does he like?"

"You," she blurted out before she had time to bite her tongue.

He let out a deep chuckle, which caused her to glance to the open doorway, hoping his mother hadn't heard. She didn't want to disturb Stephanie's sleep, but more than that, she didn't want to leave his room yet.

"Don't worry, she sleeps like a rock."

She twisted, gaping at him.

He laughed again, but muffled it this time. "I like August, too. He's a good kid."

Happiness made her smile. "Yes, he is," she admitted. "Always has been."

"What does he like?"

"Everything." She scrunched her face as August was known for doing. "Except reading."

Snake chuckled. "A true boy."

"Hmm, yes he is." A giggle slipped out as she added, "Full of snip and snails, and puppy-dog tails."

"Puppy dogs tails," he said thoughtfully.

"Oh, it's just a saying—"

"I know. Kid also has puppies. His old dog, Sammy, is getting up in years so he bought his kids a new dog last Christmas." His smile grew. "About a month ago, she had pups. Maybe August would like one."

Excitement made her skin quiver, and she squeezed the fingers wrapped around her hand. "Oh, he'd love one."

His intent gaze wandered over her face for a long, silent moment before he asked, "What about you, Summer? What do you like?"

This time she did stop herself from saying *you*. But just barely, for it surely was the only thought zipping around in her head. All of a sudden, she knew it was time to leave—while she still could. "I like patients who follow doctor's orders. And it's time you get some sleep."

"There's not a doctor here."

Had his voice always sounded so husky and persuasive? She squirmed, preparing to stand, but his hold on her hand tightened.

"The doctor left orders with me for you to follow." Was that her voice sounding so shaky? She swallowed. "And one of those orders was lots of sleep."

He closed his eyes. "I guess I am a little sleepy. But will you stay a little longer? Just talk as I drift off."

"About what?" she asked, more than willing to stay.

He yawned. "Whatever you want." He rolled his hand, lacing his fingers with hers. "Just don't leave."

"I won't," she promised.

"Neither will I," he said, clearly drifting off into slumber land.

Summer sat there, on the edge of the bed, holding his hand for a very long time. She didn't talk, and even after his fingers went lax, telling her he was fast asleep, she sat, simply absorbing a deep, satisfying security she'd never experienced.

Closing her eyes, she once again searched for Jonas. It had to be his presence easing her fears, quelling her doubts. But try as she might, she couldn't feel the spirit who'd been with her the past few years. She'd almost told Snake, a few minutes ago, that it had been Jonas who told her to leave Dodge. For two nights he'd hung in her mind, and when she finally conceded, he led her directly to the Quinter house.

"Summer?"

She jumped off the mattress, lids ripping open

as she turned toward the door.

"What's wrong? Did Snake tear open his stitches this evening?" Stephanie asked quietly, moving into the room.

"N-no, I don't think so. A-at least he said he didn't. H-he just-just wanted—" Summer stammered, searching for an answer.

"Has he had you in here talking to him?" Stephanie's voice held a hint of humor, and love.

A warm sensation rippled her insides, and Summer paused to consider what it meant. The Quinters, strong and resourceful, loved one another unconditionally, something she'd never thought much about before.

"He's always been a talker. Why, he even talks to his plants. Almost as if they were humans and could hear him." Stephanie stopped beside the bed and stroked Snake's wavy hair away from his forehead.

A wave of loneliness or loss rolled across Summer's shoulders hard enough to make her quiver. She'd missed her mother often over the years, to the point at times it turned into anger. Pinching her lips, she held her breath, looking inward for Jonas. He always came when thoughts of her mother attempted to overwhelm her common sense.

Low and behold, there was no sign of him, even when her lungs began to burn and she had to let the air release. Where was he? She needed him, and he was no where around.

"Come on," Stephanie urged, placing a gentle hand on her shoulder.

The weight was enough for her to abide. Summer let her fingers slip away from Snake's and allowed the other woman to lead her from the room.

As she closed the door, Stephanie asked, "Are you sure you don't want to share my bed? It's big enough for two. And I don't snore." She let out a silly snort. "Not much anyway."

Summer had to smile. In the pale light, with the older woman grinning like a school girl, Summer could see a youthfulness that years and wrinkles distorted in the light of day. In her younger years, Stephanie Quinter had been a beautiful woman. Catching the remnants of that beauty in every tiny, well-sculptured feature, Summer believed she saw the woman Jonas knew. The woman he fell in love with, and though he no longer walked the earth, she knew the man still loved his wife with a deep passion.

"No. I'll sleep out here." Summer glanced to Snake's bedroom door. "In case he needs something in the middle of the night. But, thank you for the offer." She reached out a hand and squeezed Stephanie's. "And thank you for being so kind to us. To me and September and August."

"You're family, girl. All of you. Of course we'd be kind to you. Take care of you." Stephanie patted Summer's cheek. "One's gotta take care of family. It's all that really matters on this earth."

A surprising lump formed in Summer's throat, and she swallowed. It refused to be dislodged. She bowed her head, blinking against the tears, and moved toward the sofa that doubled as her bed. Why did the Quinters feel more like family than July had? He'd been her father for as long as she could remember. The sour taste of guilt filled her mouth. She should be in mourning, but grief over his death refused to grace her mind or heart.

Near the sofa was the large wicker basket Stephanie had given her to store her clothing. She lifted the lid to retrieve a night gown. A smile tugged on her lips at the memory of Snake asking if his mother used her stitching machine on him. He'd been right to wonder. His mother loved her sewing machine. Summer carried the gown to the water closet on the far side of the room, silently adding the woman was amazing when it came to the craft. Since arriving she and the children had received more clothing than they'd ever owned. Every day, Stephanie created one of them another outfit.

Shut in the room, Summer took her time removing her clothing and donning the gown. At first she'd refused the clothing Stephanie offered, it had been September who'd came up with a proposition. She'd said they'd all, she, Summer, and August, work for the clothing, doing chores and odd jobs. The children were upholding their end of the bargain without complaint. The security of living on the farm could also be part of their compliance, though to be honest, neither September nor August ever balked about helping out.

Summer gathered her clothes and blew out the lamp hanging on the wall before leaving the room. She paused for the briefest moment, the conveniences of the Quinter home—namely the indoor plumbing—made her feel like an imposter. She shook the sensation aside and closed the door.

Moving through the house lit only by the moonbeams shining through the windows, she concluded the reason she wasn't mourning July was because she'd thought of the day he would no longer be around for years. Not that she ever wished him dead, but the hope he'd just leave one day had been with her continuously.

After placing her folded clothes in the basket, she closed the lid and settled onto the sheet and pillow Stephanie had already placed on the makeshift bed. July had been more work than help for as long as she could remember.

She rested her head on the pillow and stared at the ceiling. Perhaps he was also the reason she never thought of marrying. It wasn't as if she'd had any offers, but then again, she'd have had to encourage a man to court her before they'd ask to marry her. Finding work that would provide enough money to keep food on the table didn't leave time for such things.

Her head turned, and she gazed at the door to Snake's bedroom. If she hadn't thought much about marrying, why did she have this urge to sneak in his room and lie down beside him? A warm, exciting tingle raced over her body, and she twisted her head, staring up at the ceiling. He was so handsome, and the thought that they were married—no matter how unconventionally—seemed dreamlike. She hadn't wished for a husband, but she had dreamed of having a secure home and plenty of food and clothing for the children. Her feelings had never played into her dreams, other than happiness at seeing September and August fit and fine.

Her marriage to Snake certainly entangled her feelings—to the point she was utterly confused. She closed her eyes, and listening to the crickets singing outside the open windows, she willed Jonas to offer assistance.

The next thing she knew, morning light had crept into the house, and the scent of coffee filled her nose. She threw the sheet aside and jumped to her feet.

"Whoa, slow down there, girl," Stephanie said from her stance near the stove.

Snatching her dress and rushing for the water closet, Summer apologized, "I'm sorry, I must have overslept."

"There's no rush." Stephanie kept her voice low. "The thrashing is done."

Summer ducked into the wash room. Minutes later, her nightgown in the basket and the pillow and blankets folded and put away, she walked to the table where Stephanie sat with two steaming cups.

"Have a seat, it's early yet," Stephanie offered. "I just couldn't sleep."

Summer sat and accepted the cup Stephanie slid across the table. "Are you ill?"

"No," Stephanie said thoughtfully. Her gaze was on the steam swirling out of her cup and both hands were wrapped around the thick white mug. "You know, for years after my husband died I wished I could have him back for just one night. I wanted to feel his arms around me one more time, sleep one last time with my head on his chest."

A single tear rolled down Stephanie's cheek. Summer reached over and placed a hand on one stooped, thin shoulder, wishing she knew what to say.

Stephanie gazed across the room. "He was here," she whispered. "Last night—" a tiny, raspy sob slipped out. "He came to me."

Summer's hand grasped on tighter, and she held her breath.

Stephanie wiped at her face with one hand and lifted the coffee mug to her lips with the other. After swallowing, she said, "You probably think I'm crazy."

"No," Summer admitted. "I don't think you're crazy." She eased her hold on Stephanie's shoulder and rubbed the spot consolingly. "Jonas loved you very much."

Stephanie's head snapped up, and her eyes narrowed into a serious squint. "How do you know his name?"

Locked air in Summer's lungs made her cough. "I-I-someone must have mentioned it," she lied.

"No, no one would have mentioned Jonas."

Summer bit her tongue.

"If anyone around mentioned him, they would have called him Jay. That's what he was known as in these parts. Jay, not Jonas." Stephanie stared as if she could see right into Summer's head. "Even his headstone says Jay."

Summer swallowed, shuffling her feet under the table. Stephanie's gaze didn't falter, just kept going in deeper and deeper. Summer lowered her eyes and drew her hand away. Picking up her coffee cup, she took a tiny sip. "Why? Why didn't anyone around here call him Jonas?"

Stephanie turned around and stared at her bedroom door for a few moments before she turned back to Summer. Her gaze was softer, and a tiny frown had settled between her brows. "Because," she started hesitantly, "he was known as Jonas in Missouri." She took a breath and continued, "After his first wife died, he left there to lead a wagon train west. My family was a part of that train. We were on the gold rush. The first one. The big one in California. Jay Quinter was the wagon master."

She took a swig of coffee and seemed to be more settled in telling her tale because she'd barely swallowed before continuing, "From the moment I saw him, I was head over heels in love. I was sixteen, and he was twenty-six." A wide smile flashed on her lips. "I tried everything I could to get his attention." The grin disappeared. "But he was crushed over the death of his wife and baby. He didn't let it rule his life though. He led that train through Indian attacks, hail storms, and blizzards that would have killed us all if not for him. He stayed on with my family that winter, and by spring, I knew I couldn't let him leave California without me."

Jonas hadn't told Summer any of this. She was in awe and needed to know more. "What happened?"

Stephanie rose and retrieved the coffee pot from the stove. While refilling their cups, she said, "He left." Plopping the pot on the stove, she added, "Without me."

"What?"

Taking her seat at the table, Stephanie laughed, "That's what I said when I woke up that cold spring morning."

Summer stared at Stephanie until the humor on the other woman's face tickled her insides. All of sudden Stephanie Quinter looked younger, happier. Grinning, Summer asked, "Then what happened?"

"I waited." Stephanie slapped the table hard enough to make Summer jump in her chair. "He didn't come back for two years." Stephanie giggled like a school girl, "I was so mad at him by then I could have shot him. Probably would have if he hadn't kissed the daylights out of me as soon as he jumped off his horse."

"Where had he been?"

"He'd gone back to Independence and led out another train."

Summer had never heard a love story, and truly wanted to know more. "Had he written?"

Stephanie gave her a skeptical look. "No." She cocked her head thoughtfully. "But he didn't need to. I knew he'd be back."

"Had he said so?"

"No."

"Then how did you know?"

Stephanie reached over and softly tapped Summer's chest with the tip of one finger. "In here. I knew he was the man for me. And I knew he'd be back. We were married the next day and a week later we left California to settle here."

There was so much more Summer wanted to know, but she didn't know where to start her questions.

Stephanie made it easy. "He said I was too young when we met. He also said he'd worried I'd find someone else before he made it back to California. Men can be so silly sometimes. I would have waited for him forever. If he'd have never made it back to California, I'd still be there, a grumpy old woman living alone."

Summer frowned.

"It's true," Stephanie said, "I'd never have married if he hadn't come back for me. In those days men out numbered women ten to one. I had an offer for marriage every week by men who'd struck it rich and those who didn't have a pot to spit in. But not one of them lit the spark in me that he did."

Something flared in Summer's chest, as if she knew what Stephanie referred to. She changed the subject, needing time to dwell on the warmth filling her insides. "How did you find this place?"

"He'd seen it on the way out. The Indian raids in Nebraska were wiping out whole trains, so his second trip out had been through Kansas. This route was harder because water isn't as plentiful as it is further north. One day he rode ahead of the train, scouting, and saw this basin. He said he pictured his family living here. It was tough at first, since there were no towns, hardly a neighbor within a day's ride, but we settled, built a cabin, and a year later, he went back to Missouri to get Kid."

"Kid?"

"Yes. Kid had been living with his mother's family. We wanted to go get him before then, but Jay wouldn't go until he was sure Skeeter and I had everything we'd need while he made the journey." Stephanie laid a hand on Summer's. "You never said why you called him Jonas."

Summer had forgotten that part. She bit her lip. A thunderous crash from the other side of the house saved her from having to come up with another lie. Simultaneously, she and Stephanie leaped from their chairs to race to Snake's room.

Chapter Seven

Snake managed to pull the blanket off the bed and cover his private area before the door flew open. Summer, followed closely by his mother, flew into the room like two hens—clucking and wings flapping.

His heart slammed against the walls of his chest as his eyes settled on Summer's face twisted with concern.

"What happened?" she asked, arriving at his side.

The erratic thuds in his chest made the pain in his leg and shoulder all but disappear. Guilt of causing her worry settled in his stomach. "I-uh..." Not a single comprehensive thought formed.

"Did you fall out of bed?" Her hands ran up and down his arms and torso.

He grabbed them before they caught the edge of the sheet. He wasn't about to tell her he'd thought he could make it to the water closet, nor did he want her to see what the sight of her did to him. She sat back on her hunches, and he balled the sheet, making sure it hid his desire. Using his good elbow, he wiggled and pushed himself up to sit against the bed frame.

"Yes, I guess I did." His cheeks burnt with enough heat to boil water. It was damn hard to be a man while injured from head to toe.

"Here," she offered, "let me help you get back in bed."

His hand tightened on the sheet. "No. No, I think I'll just sit here for a minute."

"Don't be silly," his mother demanded. "You can't sit there on the floor." None to gently her fingers dug into his arm. "Come on, we'll help you get back in bed."

"No." He shook off her hold. "I'm just fine where I'm at."

His mother would have grabbed his arm again, but Summer reached up and stopped her. "Would you mind getting him a cup of coffee?" Her big, dark eyes settled on him. "I'll check his wounds. Make sure the fall didn't tear out any stitches."

He swallowed the groan bubbling up his throat. Her closeness made the throbbing in his loins increase. Yet, he couldn't find the wherewithal to discourage her from touching him.

His mother turned and strutted out of the room, banging the door shut as she left.

Summer grinned, and Snake had to smile as well. "She's a little grumpy in the mornings."

Summer laughed. "Like someone else I know?"

He cast his eyes down. The balled sheet hid what he felt this morning, and he wouldn't necessarily call it grumpy.

She rose and walked to the dresser where she gathered bandages, ointment and other such supplies. When she settled on the floor beside him, she pushed the sheet off his lower thigh. "I'll start with the leg."

A zing ripped up his inner thigh, jolting his shaft. He bunched the sheet tighter, and tried to ignore the ache, which had very little to do with the wound Summer gently cleaned and prepared for a new bandage. Snake wondered if he'd live through the morning.

She talked as she worked. Her voice, songlike and gentle, explained how nicely the wound was healing and asked how he slept. He managed to eek out a comment now and again. When her fingers flowed over the inside of his thigh, wrapping the bandage around and around, he squeezed his eyes closed and tried to imagine she was as bald and old as Doc Sanders. His mind wasn't so addled that happened so he found himself wishing his mother would come back with the coffee, her arrival would surely dowse him like a cold rain.

Summer had finished with his shoulder by the time his mother arrived, carrying a tray with a mug of coffee and a plate of scrambled eggs—burnt. He grasped the edge of the tray as it landed on his lap. Summer glanced at his intake of breath, her brows furrowed.

He snatched up the cup of coffee. The liquid practically scalded his mouth and gullet. Who would have ever imagined healing was more painful than getting shot? He set the cup down and lifted the fork. Summer left the room with the old bandages, but his mother stayed with her hands braced on her hips and staring down at him with a deep, but not unfriendly frown.

"What?" he asked after eating the small amount of eggs that weren't scorched.

"Nothing," she said, but quickly added. "I just never realized how much you look like your Pa. I always thought Bug and Kid took after him more, but that's just their dark hair and eyes. You have his features and his build."

Ma never talked of Pa much, and the look on her face made him wonder if it was because she missed him so much. For years they all thought it was because she was mad that he'd got himself killed. Now, he wondered if she'd just been protecting her heart all these years. It was odd for him to think of such things this morning, sitting on the floor eating breakfast.

His mind took another route, back to when he'd been unconscious. His father had been there, he'd

71

swear his life on it. The fork fell from his fingers. While he'd been out, his father had told him to nod his head, and Summer had said he'd nodded in agreement of their marriage before the doc began surgery.

His gaze went back to his mother. She hadn't been the one to make him marry Summer. His father had. He lifted the tray off his lap, handing it toward his mother. "Here, help me get back into bed before Summer returns."

His mother set the tray on the table he'd toppled earlier when trying to get out of bed, and reached down to aid his rise. "Don't know why you're embarrassed. She's been nursing you for over a week now and has seen all you got to offer."

"Ma," he groaned, ears steaming.

"Well, she has."

He covered himself with the sheet. "Get me a pair of britches."

"Why, you ain't going no where?"

"Just get me some pants."

She did as asked, and helped him get them on before she made her exit.

Snake sat on the bed, with one suspender hooked over his good shoulder when Summer re-entered the room. The gaze on her face said she was surprised, but she didn't comment as she went about replenishing the medical needs on top of the dresser.

A strong, undeniable urge made him break the silence. "Thank you."

The long, black tresses flowing down her back swished as she twirled about. "For what?"

For coming into my life. He frowned, wondering where that thought had come from and said, "For nursing me."

She crossed the room, and his heart swelled. Was this beautiful creature really his wife? It was amazing how things happened. He'd thought he'd never marry. Well, not for a few years anyway. Yet, here he was hitched, and the thought wasn't all that bad. No siree, not bad at all.

Her smile grew. "What are you grinning about?"

Not willing to admit anything, he said, "Nothing."

"Oh? You look like a little boy with a big secret."

He held out a hand, and she took it. Tugging her forward until she sat on the edge of the bed, he whispered, "I might know a big secret, but I'm not a little boy."

She leaned over him, straightening the sling holding his other arm. "I know."

The air in the room grew enchanted as he examined her fine features—the graceful arch of her delicate brows and the fine lines of her high cheekbones, as well as the curves of her perfect lips. Her face hovered inches from his. She slipped her tongue out to wet her lips. The action enticed him to lift a hand and run it over her shoulder, beneath the veil of hair until his palm cupped the base of her neck.

She didn't move, just kept her gaze locked with his.

He applied pressure. They met in the middle, their noses bumping. He tilted his head so their lips could connect. The union caused a wave of satisfaction that started in his scalp and ended at his toenails and left him melting at the same time it fueled desire for more.

Her hand pressed against his chest, branding him more thoroughly than a hot iron. A rewarding moan rumbled in his throat, and he increased the force of his hold, demanding the kiss deepen. She complied, parting her lips for him to explore her honeysuckle sweetness. He was transported into a pain-free wonderful world he never wanted to leave, and used his hand to tug her closer.

The mounds of her breasts flattened against his chest. He eased into the pillow behind him, completely enjoying the pressure of her bearing down on him. Her lips played a precious game of tag with his, and Snake concluded he'd never been more content in his life.

"Summer!"

The sound startled them both, but it was another moment before Snake had enough sense to lift his mouth from hers. Blinking past the stars floating before his eyes, he saw her little sister standing in the doorway with a snarl on her face.

"Summer," September, openly disgusted, said, "your help is needed out here." With that she flipped around and stomped away from the open doorway.

August walked in the room in her wake, his nose wrinkled with confusion. "Were you two kissing?"

Summer groaned. Snake snapped his gaze to her as his heart leaped to his throat. Her eyes shone and a deep blush covered her cheeks. He kissed her forehead before glancing back to the boy. "Yup."

"Why?" August stopped near the foot of the bed.

Summer sat up and smoothed the skirt covering her lap. Snake laid a hand upon hers, stalling their movements. "Because," he said to August though he kept his eyes on her. "I-we like each other."

She tilted her head, and a tiny smile lifted the corners of her lips.

"I like people, too, but I don't go around kissing them," August declared.

Snake lifted his hand and brushed a finger along the fine line of her chin. "Someday you will," he assured.

Shaking like a dog with fleas, August said, "I hope not."

Summer turned toward her brother. "Have you finished your morning chores?"

"Yup," he said, and quivering again he pointed

toward the doorway. "September helped make breakfast." He stuck his tongue out with a mock gag.

"August Austin, you stop that," Summer demanded, grateful her brother brought her ability to speak to the surface. It was difficult with her head spinning in the clouds, and her body fluttering like a flock of birds. Control finally settled and she continued, "You should always be thankful for a meal."

"I am thankful for the food. It was the taste I ain't."

She didn't answer, mainly because it would be impossible over Snake's laughter. Letting out an exaggerated sigh, she glanced toward him. His sparkling eyes and wide grin took her breath away, along with the ability to muster up even a touch of annoyance.

His hand held hers, and he squeezed her fingers. "You can't blame him," he whispered. "You've tasted my mother's cooking."

The sounds of a wagon along with Stephanie bellowing from the kitchen that someone had arrived saved her from commenting. August tore through the room, and Summer rose from the bed. Snake's hold on her hand kept her standing there for a moment longer. He looked as if he wanted to say something, but when he didn't, she broke the connection and moved to the door.

The front door opened, and Kid strolled in along with two women. One was old and hunched over to the point Summer wondered how she walked, and the other was young with long brown hair and pale skin.

"Willamina and Eva want to help with the wheat," Kid said, nodding to the two women.

Summer had heard of the two women who lived a short distance away and were family friends, but had yet to meet them. She smiled a greeting, but instead of an introduction Kid pointed to the doorway behind her.

"Is he awake? Every wagon we own is full of wheat. I've got to find out how much he wants stored and how much we have to take to the mill in Garden City."

"Yes, he's awake," Snake shouted from behind her.

Summer stepped aside as Kid went into the room, closing the door behind him. The old woman, aided with a cane, maneuvered across the room.

"So, you're the one."

Summer stood stock still as the woman eyed her from head to toe.

A steely gaze from beady green eyes settled on her face. "Jessie said you were a pretty thing, but she didn't say you had Indian blood in your veins. What tribe you from?"

Summer's heart fell to the pit of her stomach where it beat with dread. It wasn't the first time someone had asked about her heritage, nor would it be the last, but since coming to live at the farm, she hadn't dwelled on it. For the first time in her life, she hadn't been reminded of it daily. Over the years she'd made up names and tribes and would use whatever one seemed to be most fitting at the time. Right now, not one of her dreamt up connections formed.

"I don't know," she muttered before realizing she'd done so.

A frown formed on the woman's face. "That's a shame. My husband had Osage blood. He was a good man, a damn good man. He got snake-bit many years ago." She let out a long sigh. "I still miss him. Anyway, I'm Willamina, this here is Eva. It's good to meet you."

Summer grasped the hand thrust toward her, and the old woman, stronger than expected, tugged her forward, wrapping her with boney arms.

"Welcome to the family." When she stepped away, Willamina added, "I'd say you're just what our Snake needed to get his mind out of the dirt. All he ever thinks about is growing something."

Not giving anyone else the opportunity to speak, Willamina turned to Stephanie. "Just got one left to marry off."

Both Willamina and Stephanie looked at Eva who turned beat red and lowered her gaze to the floor. Summer's mind, and gaze, leaped about like a grasshopper on a sunny day. September tossed a dish towel at her. She caught it and the look of hatred filling her little sister's eyes.

"I finished your morning chores, now I'm going out to do mine." Without acknowledging anyone else in the room, September stomped out the door, slamming it behind her.

The weight of the world became so heavy Summer wondered how she managed to move across the room.

Stephanie beat her to the door. She took the dish towel from her hands. "Let her be," she said, and holding Summer's arm, she added, "Time is what that girl needs."

Kid came out of the bedroom then, with Snake hanging on his side. After he deposited Snake in the water closet, he got himself a cup of coffee. "Snake says he has most of the grain sold to a man in Dodge. We'll send a couple of loads to the mill in Garden City for flour and unload the rest we cut yesterday in the granary. I'll ride to town tomorrow to send a telegram to Dodge. He said the man there will send wagons out to collect it."

Summer glanced about, wondering why he told her all this. She had an inkling Kid had more to say to her, or wanted to know more about her. It made her stomach stew. When no one commented, and for lack of anything else to say, she provided, "There's a storm brewing."

He nodded. "A haze is building to the southwest. I'm hoping we can get it all into the granary before it hits." He turned to Eva. "Would you mind taking a wagon to the mill in Garden? Bug's taking the other wagon."

Eva agreed. "We can send the telegram to Dodge from there, too."

"Good idea," Snake said, leaning against the door jamb of the water closet.

Summer moved, but again, someone was faster. Kid had Snake's arm over his shoulder and helped him to the table before she'd made it half way across the room. She pulled out a chair and hovered near Snake's shoulder after Kid lowered him onto the seat. The closeness gave her the hint of security she needed for some reason.

"I'll write out the message for you to send," Snake said to Eva, and then he turned to the rest of the occupants in the room. "Thanks. Thanks to all of you for helping out. I'm sorry I can't do more."

Willamina patted his arm. "That's what family's for. We're glad to help. We just want to see you healed up proper real quick."

Kid finished the coffee he'd left while aiding Snake and set the cup on the counter. "Actually, that new thrashing machine of yours is quite the invention."

"It's called a separator," Snake corrected. "I didn't invent it. I saw it in a magazine and converted my old thrashing machine by adding a few belts. I'm glad to hear it worked so well. I wish I could have seen it."

Summer laid a hand on his shoulder, feeling his disappointment.

"It works," Kid said. "The big reaper on the front cut the stalks off right at the top and the cleanest grain I've ever seen fell into the wagons we pulled beside it. Bug said you'd worked on it all winter."

"Yeah, I did," Snake agreed.

"Well, good job little brother. I gotta say, I'm really impressed. We cut that field in half the time it otherwise would have taken. We unloaded several wagon loads into the granary, but I wasn't sure what you wanted us to do with the rest. Now that I do, we'll have the harvest done by the end of the day."

Bug poked his head in through the door. "Got the wagons hitched up." He glanced toward Snake. "How you feeling this morning?"

A smile came over Snake's face as his gaze left Bug to glance up at her. "Good," he said.

Bug chuckled and pulled the door shut. Blood rushed to Summer's cheeks. There was no doubt August had mentioned the kissing he'd witnessed.

A swirl of activity happened as everyone prepared to leave and within minutes it was just her and Snake. Somewhat unsure as to her duty, she moved to the door. She counted ten wagons leaving the yard. Bug and Eva in one direction while the rest went another. The past couple of days, at least that many loads had already been delivered to the granary, a large building several miles away. Kid had been right when he said how well the thrashing machine worked. She'd never seen anything like it, and therefore, was thoroughly impressed.

August sat on the bench beside Willamina. The woman didn't seem nearly as feeble perched on the bouncing seat. The child waved, and Summer lifted a hand to repeat his actions. September, nose in the air, refusing to so much as glance toward the house, sat beside Stephanie. For a moment, Summer wondered who had decided she'd be the one to stay behind today, but then the twinkle in her mother-in-law's eyes said it all as Stephanie flayed the reins over the back of a team of horses and waved with her other hand.

Other wagons were driven by men who worked for Kid and neighbor men that had helped with the harvest. She watched until the last one left the yard. A question she'd had yesterday came to mind, and she turned around to ask it.

The way Snake looked at her caused her heart to leap to her throat and pound mercilessly. They hadn't spoken since the kiss. She wasn't embarrassed by what they'd done—matter of fact she'd give her right arm to have it happen again. It was all too confusing and so overwhelming.

She gave her head a clearing shake. "Why did you build the granary so far from the house?"

His look grew thoughtful for a moment. "Because grain storage attracts rats and other varmints. Besides, this is Ma's house. I bought the acreage next to here a few years ago. I plan on building a house there someday. But not near the granary. I wouldn't want rats around my house either."

"Will you store the wheat all year?" She kept the conversation going, mainly because it was a safe subject.

"No. Mr. Everest in Dodge said he'd buy all I wanted to sell. I'll keep enough to plant this fall and some to experiment with."

"Experiment what?"

"New crossbreeds. Winter wheat does well out here. The Russian immigrants know a lot about dry land agriculture and have had some success doing so here. I've combined their knowledge with a derivative of wheat. Winter wheat is hearty and when planted in the fall it establishes a deep root system as well as thick foliage above ground. When the ground freezes, the tops of the plants goes dormant, but the roots stay alive and absorb moisture from the snow. When spring comes, the

Guardian Bride

plants utilize the moisture they saved up and by early summer, it's ready for harvest. No irrigation needed. I've pretty much concluded it's one of the few plants that can thrive out here without irrigation."

She'd moved to the stove and busied herself by making a fresh pot of coffee. "What other seeds are you experimenting with?"

He chuckled. "Everything from trees to flowers. I'm hoping the irrigation system I created has kept everything growing while I'm laid up."

The land surrounding the farm yard came to mind. It had astonished her to see such a variety of trees and plants when she'd first arrived. Most of this part of the state was covered with little more than sage brush and soap weeds.

"Several years ago," he said, drawing her attention back to him. "I went to Garden City with Kid. It's only about twenty miles south of here."

She nodded, familiar the area.

"A few men who used to hunt buffalo out here had decided to settle down there." He paused as if just remembering something. "That's why my father chose this area to settle. He scouted for wagon trains, and then buffalo hunters. Even Royalties from England came out here to hunt in those days. After the hunting died out, he tried his hand at farming. Guess that's where I get it from."

He sat for a moment in silence, staring at the cup sitting on the table in front of him. When he lifted his head, he continued, "Anyway, I went to Garden, well at that time it was called Fulton, with Kid and some other men because the cattlemen didn't like the idea of a settlement sprouting up in the middle of the route they used to get the cows to Dodge. Kid and the others wanted to talk the folks into moving east a bit. The folks at the settlement didn't want to move. A rancher closer to Dodge told them they couldn't grow so much as weeds in the dry ground. The settlers disagreed, and thinking he'd prove them wrong, the rancher offered fifty bucks for every bushel of corn grown. I left town with the challenge in my head. A few weeks later, I went back to the settlement and told Mr. Fulton I could help him grow enough corn that the rancher would go broke paying him off."

Intrigued, she moved to the table and sat down. "What happened?"

His smile went from ear to ear. "A year later they renamed the settlement Garden City because of Fulton's bountiful garden."

"Really?"

"Yes, really."

"What had you done to make everything grow?"

"Irrigation."

She waited for him to continue.

"One windmill with a large enough reservoir can irrigate ten to twenty acres."

"How?"

"The windmill pumps the water out of the ground and into the reservoir which flows into ditches that carry the water to the fields from one end of the crops to the other. I put in gates to slow or increase the water as needed." He glanced up. "The water under the ground in this region is inexhaustible, and it's not far below the surface. I've also discovered several natural springs on my land and use those to irrigate some fields."

A frown formed between his brows. Summer held her breath, wondering what he thought about now. Was it the kiss? It wasn't far away in her mind. The coffee boiled over behind her, and she leaped to remove it from the heat. Once the frothing slowed, she filled his cup.

His fingers wrapped around her wrist when she attempted to move from his side. "You know." His gaze locked onto hers. "I haven't even told my brothers about how I helped Fulton."

"Why not?"

He shrugged. "We all have our interests. Kid has his cattle, one of the largest ranches in the state, and Skeeter has his dinosaurs." He winked. "That's a long story. Hog was always in the kitchen, so opening a restaurant seemed fitting, and Bug can sniff out rock tar from a mile away. He claims the oil seeps will transform America. They know about my gardening, but I never told them about Fulton."

She set the pot down and sat in the chair next to him. "Why? Did he ask you not to?"

"No. He offered to pay me for my help."

"Did he make lots of money from the rancher for his bushels of corn?"

"No, the rancher never made good on his bet."

He went silent again, and Summer's stomach churned, believing he must be remembering another bet. The hand holding hers moved. His thumb softly ran up and down the underside of her wrist, causing an array of tingles to zip up her arm.

"I told Fulton he could repay me by buying interests in the first flour mill they were opening in the city. He kept his word. I own one fourth of the mill that Bug and Eva took the wheat to."

"Does your family know that?" she asked. The fact he'd told her things he'd never told anyone else filled her with a sweet, heady sensation. No one had ever told her a secret before and it seemed like a very special gift.

"No."

"If you own interest in the mill, why did you sell your wheat to the mill in Dodge?"

His hand left her wrist, and she swallowed at the absence.

He took a swig of coffee before answering, "Because I don't believe in keeping all my eggs in one basket. The mill in Dodge is buying my wheat for seed, to sell to farmers. It's a hybrid I created, so therefore I can set my own price. The mill in Garden is a flour processing mill. The grain I sent there will be turned into flour for us to use, not for resale."

"Because you own shares in it, do they process your wheat for free?"

"No. I pay like everyone else does. The difference is I earn profits off processing my own wheat, as well as every other bushel they mill."

"Oh," she answered, rubbing her wrist that still fluttered from his touch.

"What about you?"

"Me?"

"You must have a secret or two."

She had enough secrets to fill a bushel basket twice over. Her bottom lip trembled as she wondered what one to tell him, figured it was only fair. She certainly couldn't tell him she knew his father—well Jonas' spirit anyway—and she couldn't tell him how July had killed his father. There were a million other small things she kept to herself, but nothing overly interesting.

His eyes had settled on her as he waited patiently. For some reason, the secret that ate at her like lye sprang forward. "I don't know who fathered me."

"You don't?"

"No. I don't know if I'm Osage, Arapaho, Wichita, or Pawnee. I don't even know if he was from one of the tribes in this region or some other."

"Why not?"

"My mother never told me." Tears formed in the back of her eyes, but she held them at bay. "She started to once, but July heard her. He hit her until she was unconscious. I never asked after that."

"Bastard," Snake muttered under his breath, but she heard it. He took her hand again. "You don't remember your father at all?"

"I only remember July. I don't know when nor where he and my mother met, if it was before I was born or after." She shrugged as if it didn't matter, but deep down, it did. It always had. "I used to make up tales to tell people when they'd asked, especially other children when I was young. But after mother died..." The lump in her throat made her stop.

"What? After your mother died..." He lifted her hand and rubbed her knuckles with the point of his chin.

The contact eased the gloom bearing down. "I guess it didn't matter anymore. I had September and August to take care of, which left very little time to worry about me and my past."

"I'm sorry," he whispered. His hold drew her closer.

"You're sorry? Why? None of it's your fault."

"I know, but I'm sorry you've been hurt by it. I'm sorry you didn't have a wonderful, happy childhood."

"Did you?" she asked. "Have a wonderful, happy childhood?"

"For the most part, I think I did. It was hard to lose my father, but"—he shrugged—"we had each other. We all got through."

A lump formed in her throat—guilt at knowing who caused the loss of Jonas. What would this kind and wonderful family do when they found out it was July? They'd hold it against her and the children. Who wouldn't?

He'd leaned closer. The warmth of his breath tickled her lips. Even tormented by the secrets filling her mind, a swell of excitement rippled from her toes to the top of her head. Her mind escaped to that wonderful place it went when he'd kissed her earlier. Where birds sang and breezes blew soft and sweet, and not a single, dark, gloomy concern darkened the world.

Her lids fluttered down when his warmth mingled with hers. The contact, his lips brushing against hers, was gentle and engaging. She leaned closer, to amplify the touch. Floating in the dreamlike ecstasy, she parted her lips, enticed by the way his tongue ran along the swell of her bottom lip. At that precise moment, when the tip of his tongue slid over the row of her bottom teeth, someone knocked on the door.

They turned to the sound, noses colliding, and ended up cheek to cheek, staring at the door as the sound came again.

Chapter Eight

Snake leaned back in his chair and squeezed her fingers. "Don't worry. Wainwright wouldn't knock."

Summer swallowed. The thought it was Wainwright hadn't entered her mind. Her gaze locked on the door. She had no idea who stood on the other side, but their knock caused a deep disappointment that had little to do with who it might be.

She stood but he kept his grip on her. "Hand me the gun belt hanging next to the door before you open it."

A quiver happened then, one that told her she'd better not let her guard down so easily in the future. Nor should she allow herself to be carried away so swiftly.

By the time she'd done as instructed whoever was on the other side of the door beat on it steadily and a feminine voice shouted, "Scott! Scott Quinter, open this door!"

Snake's face contorted into a pained look. "Open it," he advised. "She won't go away."

Debating if she wanted to open it or not, Summer walked to the door, knowing there was no choice. As soon as she turned the knob, the door flew out of her hands.

A whirlwind of pink and yellow flew past her, screeching, "Scott Quinter, why didn't you call for me?"

Summer caught herself from being knocked down by grabbing the wall. Once her feet settled beneath her, she turned to the table. A tiny woman, covered in ruffles and lace, knelt beside Snake's chair. A fierce rumble rolled across Summer's stomach. The nails of her fingers bit into her palms. It was all she could do not to stomp across the room and grab the creature by the back of her blond curls.

A tall man entered then, and seeing her next to the door, he removed his hat. "Hello," he said, extending a hand. "I'm Rodney Zimmerman. I don't believe I've made your acquaintance."

Snake batted Dora's hands away like a kid being chased by a bee. The tone of Rodney's silver tongue ran up his spine, intensifying the irritation of the disruption. He leaned as far away from Dora as he could get and glared toward the door. "Back off, Zim."

Rodney flashed him a shit-eating grin and lifted Summer's hand. Pain shot up Snake's leg as he pressed his feet to the floor, attempting to rise as the man brushed his lips over Summer's knuckles. Keeping his seat, he slid the pistol out of the holster. "You want to get yourself shot?"

"Scott!" Dora screeched, inches from his face. Her fingers patted his cheeks.

He tossed his head. "Knock it off, Dora."

By the time she pulled her hands away, to plant them on her hips, Rodney had released Summer and moved toward the table, hand extended.

"How you feeling?"

"Like shit." Snake dropped the gun on the table and shook the man's hand.

"Scott," Dora wailed, "You mustn't say such things in my presence."

He didn't respond, there was no use. Dora Zimmerman was the epitome of an irritating, screeching female, if there ever was one. With his hand he gestured to Summer.

Dashing uncertain gazes at both Dora and Rodney, she walked around the table to stand near his other side. He held in the regret he couldn't use that arm to wrap around her waist. With his good hand, he reached across his chest and found her hand, balled in a fist and hanging near her hip. Her annoyed gaze was on Dora. A sweet tickle flitted across his chest.

"Rodney, Dora," he started, remorseful that he couldn't stand up while making the introductions. Silently he cursed his injuries. This was his first opportunity to introduce his wife, and the fact made him want to strut like a rooster on Sunday. Rodney had to be the biggest womanizer in the state, and Snake had to admit, he and the other man had shared some good times. "I'd like you to meet Summer..." he paused to make sure he had everyone's attention. "Quinter. My wife."

"You're what?" Dora spat.

"I'd heard as much," Rodney said. "Congratulations, my friend."

"You'd heard?" Dora screeched. "I hadn't heard! Why didn't anyone tell me?"

Rodney ignored his sister and continued, "It is extremely nice to meet you, Mrs. Quinter. Your husband and I have been friends since I moved here from Dodge about ten years ago. My family owns the hardware store in Scott City."

"Hello, Mr. Zimmerman," Summer said, bowing her head slightly.

"Rodney!" Dora's voice was enough to make the hair on a boar stand on end.

"And this screaming"—Rodney glared at Dora— "pipsqueak is my little sister, Dora."

"Hello, Dora," Summer greeted.

Dora crossed her arms over her chest. She didn't acknowledge Summer at all, instead she glared at Snake. "You were supposed to marry me."

"Dora!" Rodney reprimanded.

"I never said I'd marry you, Dora," Snake

sighed. The girl had been chasing him since she'd been about thirteen, and it drove him nuts.

"I know *you* didn't say it. *I* did. Last year at the Fourth of July dance."

She was little more than a child, and Snake didn't want to hurt her feelings anymore now than he had last summer. "Dora," he said calmly. "You're a sweet girl, but you're just too young for me."

A loud huff flew from her mouth. Snake took a deep breath to continue, but his attention was drawn to his fingers. Summer's hand had opened, and her fingers curled through his. Renewed by his wife's actions, he asked Dora, "How old are you now? Fifteen?"

Dora nodded.

"I'm twenty-five. Much too old for you."

Dora's arms fell to her sides, and she let out a long sigh. "Well, you could have at least notified us that you were ill. Sheriff Turley only mentioned it in passing last night when he was in to buy bullets."

Snake wasn't sure if that meant she'd accepted his justification or not. Luckily Rodney spoke up, expanding on the subject she'd brought up. "So, you got yourself shot up pretty good, I see. What happened? Turley didn't offer much."

He turned to Summer. "Would there be some of that peach pie left from last night? Maybe Rodney and Dora would like a piece."

"Of course." Her cheeks grew pink. "I'll get it." She lifted her gaze to the guests. "Dora, would you prefer coffee or tea?"

"Oh, tea if you have it, thank you."

"Why don't you help her get it?" Rodney asked his sister.

"That's all right, I can manage." Summer moved toward the counter.

Rodney pointed to a chair, but before Dora moved toward it, she leaned closer to Snake's face.

"You married a squaw?"

His spine stiffened, and his gaze flew to Summer. Her slender back was to them, and he had no way of knowing if she'd heard Dora's question or not. Lips tight, he glared at Dora. If he had two good hands, he'd wring her scrawny neck.

Rodney, as fast as a whip, grabbed Dora's upper arm. "Mother and father may not paddle your bottom, but I will."

Dora's eyes grew wide. "What? It was just a question."

"If you don't want to walk all the way home, you'll sit your butt in that chair and not open your mouth except to eat pie and drink tea. Is that understood?" Rodney growled.

Dora quivered and nodded her head.

Snake looked over in time to see Summer turn back to the cupboard. Dread dripped off his shoulders. She had heard. A glob swelled in his gut. Only because he had no idea what to say to her, he didn't ask the Zimmermans to leave.

The visit with Rodney wasn't unpleasant, but whether it was because he'd already been up for some time, or if it was because his mind was conjuring up a million ways to apologize for Dora's words, Snake's strength waned. After serving their pie and coffee as well as Dora's tea, Summer excused herself.

He half listened to Rodney prattle about the latest incidents in town—something about a herd of cattle that stampeded down Main Street—while the other half of him was tuned into the sounds coming from his room. Summer reappeared now and again to refill their cups and offer more pie, but her gaze never met his, and she didn't settle on the chair beside him. It seemed like hours before she did finally sit down. By then he felt about as mighty as a kitten with its eyelids still welded closed.

Summer's eyes traveled his way, and a startled gaze overtook her face. She turned to Rodney. "Mr. Zimmerman, perhaps you'd help me get Snake back into bed?" The tips of her fingers massaged his shoulder. "I put fresh linens on your bed while you were visiting. I think a rest is in order."

Snake thanked her with his eyes, but his vision had diminished, too, because he swore he saw two of her.

"Of course," Rodney agreed. It sounded like he spoke from ten miles away.

The ache in his leg grew as Rodney practically dragged him into the bedroom. "Damn, I don't know why I'm so weak," Snake moaned.

"The way Turley talked, you lost enough blood for two men. He said you're lucky to be alive." Rodney helped him onto the bed. "But don't worry. In no time you'll be back to your ornery old self."

"Thanks," he muttered and dropped his head onto the pillow.

Summer pulled the covers up to his chin, and he wrapped his hand around hers. He wanted to pull her down for a kiss, distinctly knew that would make him feel better, but he didn't even have that much strength. She brushed her other hand over his forehead and whispered in his ear, "I'll be back in a minute. I'm just going to walk your friends out."

He nodded, or at least he thought he did before the black void sucked him in.

Rodney Zimmerman had stepped out of the room, and Summer took advantage of the opportunity. She touched her lips to Snake's forehead. Absorbing him with every facility she had, she willed him to heal quickly. It was somewhat startling, how deeply he touched her. If able, she'd give her very life for him.

She pulled her lips away and stood. His eyes were shut, and the fingers holding hers had gone lax. She ran a hand through his curls, wishing she'd checked on him earlier. The doctor had said he shouldn't be up for more than an hour or two at the most, and it had been much more than that.

A noise in the other room signified she'd forgotten the Zimmermans were still here. She slipped her hand away and walked across the room. Both Dora and Rodney stood near the table, and she pulled the door closed.

"Thank you"—she included Dora in her gaze— "both for coming to visit Snake today. It'll be sometime before he's well again, and I know he'd appreciate it if you have time to come again."

Rodney guided Dora toward the door. "Of course we'll come again, if you don't mind."

She opened the door and followed them out. "I won't mind in the least."

Dora hadn't met her gaze nor spoken since she'd asked Snake her question. Summer walked beside the girl to their black, canopied buggy parked in the shade. Shame hung over the girl like a dark cloud. Summer's heart went out to Dora.

"It's all right," she said, "I'm half Indian."

Dora and Rodney both stopped to stare at her. He spoke first. "She needs to apologize for that comment."

"Why?" Summer asked.

"I didn't mean it to be rude," Dora said solemnly. "It just surprised me is all."

Empathy for the girl made her reach out and rest a hand on Dora's shoulder. "I know, and I hope you do come out to visit again. I have a little sister, she's not here right now, she's helping with the wheat harvest, but I know she'd like to meet you."

"Is she—"

"No," Summer interrupted. "She's not part Indian. Just I am."

"How old is your sister?"

"Eleven."

"Why is she with you? Where are your parents?"

"Dora!" Rodney snapped. "Will you ever learn to keep your mouth shut?"

Summer accepted the apology in his eyes. "It's all right," she offered. "Our mother died years ago, and my step-father died a short time ago. Both my little sister and brother live with me-us."

Dora smiled, and despite the grown-up clothing, Summer saw the child still lingering.

"I am sorry. I really didn't mean to be rude. I'd like to meet your sister. If Rodney will let me ride with him again."

"As long as you behave," he insisted.

"I will." Dora's curls bobbed as she nodded.

Grinning, he flicked the end of Dora's nose with the tip of his finger. "All right, pipsqueak, I'll let you ride with me again."

Dora turned back to Summer. "Will your brother and sister attend school in Scott City? Once it starts back up that is. It's closed now since harvest will start soon."

The question caught her off guard. Not once since they'd arrived had she thought about school for the children. Which wasn't like her at all, each and every time they moved, the first thing she'd done was enter the children in the nearest school. A conclusion settled quickly. She'd enrolled them so swiftly before, not entirely for the educational benefits, but to keep September and August away from July.

"I'm not sure," she answered honestly, "what will happen for sure."

Dora nodded, but Rodney Zimmerman looked at her curiously, as if he mulled her answer. He then reached out to shake Summer's hand. "It was wonderful meeting you, and I guarantee we'll be back in a couple of days."

"It was nice to meet you, too, and I'm sure Snake will look forward to your visit," Summer replied.

Rodney helped Dora into the buggy, and as he walked around the front he turned to Summer. "I have to admit, I'm a little surprised he lets you call him Snake."

Confused, she asked, "Oh? Why?"

He shrugged. "Because he hates that name. Always has. He insists everyone outside his family call him Scott." His smile increased. "I answered my own question, didn't I? You are family. You're his wife."

Summer didn't respond. As if there weren't enough issues separating her and Snake. She had no idea he didn't like the name. It was what Jonas always called him. Hearing Dora and Rodney refer to him as Scott had been as out of place as a fish out of water.

With a wave Rodney and Dora drove away, and Summer, once again carrying the weight of the world on her shoulders, turned to shuffle back to the house.

The day became one that minutes barely crept into hours. She stayed busy, baking a cake and preparing a roast for supper, and checking on Snake every two to three minutes. He barely moved, and more than once, she rested a hand on his chest to make sure he still breathed.

He awoke only moments before wagons rolled into the yard. She was assisting him to the water closet, his arm looped over her shoulders and hers around his waist, when the front door flew open. September glared at them and then stomped toward the stairs that led to the loft.

August on the other hand, shone like stars filled his head as he raced across the room to hold the water closet door open. "Need me to help you with your britches?" he asked.

Snake ruffled his hair as they walked passed. "No, but thanks for asking, partner."

The grin on her little brother's face never faltered as he waited and then pushed the door closed, leaving Snake to his privacy. Summer wrapped an arm around August and tugged him toward the kitchen. "How was your day, young man?"

"Kid let me drive the wagon, Summer. All by myself!"

"He did?"

"Yup. He was sitting beside me. But I had both reins. He said I did a good job. Said I was a born wagon master."

"I never had any doubts." She pulled plates from the cupboards and carried them to the table.

"But you never let me drive."

"No," she said in agreement, "I didn't. But that's mainly because we never had too many places to go in the wagon."

"I guess you're right about that." He reached out to help with the plates.

She stopped him. "Not until you wash."

"Oh. I guess I forgot." He rushed to the sink and pumped enough water for ten people. When the water closet door opened, he threw the towel toward the counter. "I'll help you, Snake." The towel landed on the floor.

Summer helped, too, and the two of them settled Snake on a kitchen chair as September clomped her way down the stairs and across the room.

"August! We have chores to do."

"September," Summer said as the girl grabbed the door. "I would like to speak with you."

"I have chores to do."

Snake had had about all he could take from the young girl. "September," he stated in a way that reminded him much of his father. "Your chores can

96

wait. Your sister wants to talk to you."

Her faded blue eyes shot daggers at him.

"Now." He met her glare.

September folded her arms across her chest. Her lips puckered, and her eyes squinted.

He stared back, but instead of scowling, he grinned.

She gasped and her nostrils flared.

Summer's hand left his shoulder. Snake glanced up. Her expression was unreadable. "August," she said, "I'll be right back. Will you get Sn-Scott a glass of water, please?"

Taken aback, Snake reached out and took her hand.

"Who?" August asked.

"Sco—

"Snake," he interrupted her. Glancing quickly toward August, he clarified, "Me." He settled his gaze on Summer. "Snake."

Her only reaction was a slight nod before she moved to follow the still fuming September out the door. Snake didn't have time to dwell on why she'd called him by his given name because August was full of questions and began firing them faster than a repeating rifle.

"Why'd she call you that? Is Scott your middle name? I got a middle name, too, it's Milton. August Milton Austin. That there's my name. So is your name Snake Scott Quinter?" His questions didn't slow down his ability to follow orders. After he set a glass of water on the table, he kept on talking. "Does Kid have a middle name too? He let me drive the wagon. You gonna let me drive the wagon someday? Kid says I'm a natural born wagon master. Yup, that's what he called me. A wagon master. Are you a wagon master, too?"

Snake set the now empty glass on the table. "No, it's not my middle name. It's my nickname."

"Nickname?"

"Yes, my father gave it to me. He gave all us boys nicknames. Kid's real name is Kendell and Bug's is Brett."

August tapped his lips with one finger, as if he deeply contemplated nicknames. "Do you got a middle name, too?"

"Yes. It's Andrew."

His little hand slapped the table. "Aw, shucks. I was hoping it was Milton."

"Sorry, partner." He liked this kid more and more every day. For years his nickname had irritated him, after all, what grown man wants to walk around being called Snake? But, when Summer had called him by his given name, a power deep down inside him rose up. He liked the way she said Snake. Hell, if August could go around being named after a month, who the hell was he to complain? Besides, his father had given him the nickname, and right now, that made pride swell in his chest. It was a gift, that's what it was, one his father had given him, and no one could take it away.

"So, you think you'll let me drive your wagon someday?" August, off to his other questions, asked again.

"Sure," he agreed, partial to the idea of riding around with the kid. "As soon as this leg heals up, we'll go for a wagon ride. And you'll be the driver."

The door opened as August was ya-hooing. Ma and Kid entered. "What you so fired up about now, August?" Kid asked, grinning.

"Snake says I can drive his wagon as soon as his leg's healed. I told him you said I was a natural born wagon master. That's what you said, Kid. Remember? A natural born wagon master."

"Yes, that's what I said." Kid chuckled as he made his way to the table. He leaned a wooden crutch against the table.

"You need a glass of water, Kid? I already got one for Snake. Oh, it's empty. I'll get you each one." August leaped from his chair, glass in hand. A matter of seconds later, he set two on the table. "You two don't mind me none, I'm just gonna set out these here plates that Summer left."

Snake looked at Kid and felt a kinship as they shared their enjoyment of the boy.

Ma had finished washing up, and as she patted August's blond curls, she asked, "You staying for supper, Kid?"

"No, Jessie will have mine on the table when I get home." He turned back to Snake. "I need to talk to you. Feel up to a trip back into the bedroom?" Wrapping his hand around the crutch he added, "Joe's been staying back at the ranch, and he nailed this together for you. It looks kind of crude, but should get the job done."

"Tell him thanks," Snake offered as he pushed off the table to stand. The crutch was crude, but Joe never claimed to be a carpenter. Kid's ranch foreman was getting up in years. "How's Joe feeling lately?"

Kid slid the crutch under Snake's arm. "He says he's fine, but Jessie makes him take it easy. His rheumatism is catching up with him."

Snake did his best to hobble to the bedroom. The crutch helped, and by the time they got to the room, he'd almost mastered the uneven gate the wooden aid provided.

He plopped onto the bed. "Be sure to give him my thanks, this thing really works."

"I will." Kid closed the door. "I saw buggy tracks."

Chapter Nine

Snake took a deep breath as the memory of the visitors filled his mind. He'd damn near slept the day away. The oblivion had stolen Dora's question and his worries. Irritation returned with the speed and control of a runaway train. "Rodney and Dora Zimmerman were here to pay a visit," he growled.

Kid walked to the window. "You don't sound happy about it."

"Dora's an irritating little snipe if there ever was one."

"She's spoiled rotten, that's for sure," Kid offered neither in agreement or denial.

Snake wasn't about to tell Kid what Dora had said, it was Summer he needed to talk to about that. The visit continued to fill his mind. "Rodney said there was a stampede through Scott."

"Yeah, some drive making its way up to Ogallala. They didn't do much damage, but you can bet you'll see more barbed wire being put up."

He could tell Kid was just making small talk, so he continued, "The cattle drives are coming to an end, aren't they?"

"Yes, but that's not a bad thing. The railroads are safer and less expensive anyway." Kid moved away from the window. "The harvest is done."

Snake took a minute to gather his thoughts. He'd practically forgotten the harvest. It was his livelihood, not Kid's and he was amiss to forget that. "Thanks, again, Kid. I'm sorry to be laid up during this time."

"You're welcome. We finished just in time.

Something's brewing out there. An odd storm."

Snake agreed with a nod. The sunshine and blue sky gracing the window didn't guarantee a thing. It could go from sunshine to thunderclouds in less than a minute in western Kansas. Storms cropped up as the air fell over the mountains in Colorado, often bursting over the plains with a lightning show that outdid the last.

"It's in the air," Kid said. "I've never seen one like this. It's like it's trying to make up its mind if it wants to hit or not."

"You'll want to head home then, before it decides."

Kid sat down on the edge of the bed. "Yeah, I will. I have to show you something first."

"What's tha—" he started, but Kid was already holding something up. The gold shimmered before his eyes, as did the engraved initials. *J.Q.* Flabbergasted, he could do little more than whisper, "That's Pa's pocket watch."

"I know."

Snake took the watch and rolled it between his fingers. Heavy emotions that had renewed themselves lately coated his insides. "Where'd you get it?"

Kid remained silent for a few minutes. He pulled his hat off and twirled it between his fingers. "George Hinkle gave it to me."

"George? Where'd he come across it?"

"The undertaker found it in July Austin's pocket. He recognized it from the description we gave when Pa died."

Snake grew colder than ice. He searched his mind to remember if Austin had pulled it out during the card game. Snake hadn't noticed a watch, but then again, he hadn't been looking for one, either. "You think July had something to do with Pa's death?"

101

"I don't know. It's been a long time. I'm sure Austin played a lot of poker since then. I suppose he could have won it off someone over the years."

Snake opened the front and stared at the tiny hand ticking its way around the numbers. "The whole territory knew we were looking for this. Knew about the reward you offered."

"That was a lot of years ago. People forget." Kid replaced his hat and stood. "Pa's isn't the only murder to go unsolved."

"Every paper in the nation had a picture of Pa and that Prince from England when he gave Pa the watch for scouting his Buffalo Hunt. Ma's even got a copy of the *New York Times* with the picture."

"Like I said, that was a long time ago."

Snake snapped the watch face closed. "Ma seen this?"

"No. I haven't shown anyone else. I don't know if I should."

"Why not?"

Kid's gaze was solemn. "Because your wife is July's daughter."

Thunder struck in Snake's head. He planted his feet to rise, but pain shot up his leg. Grabbing the crutch, he said, "You can't believe she had anything to do with it."

"Of course I don't." Kid caught his arm and helped him settle his weight on the crutch. "And I don't want Summer or September or August to think we do. That's why I haven't shown anyone else. It would bring up too many questions, and a good portion of them would be directed at Summer. I wanted you to know in case Hinkle mentions it next time he's out."

Snake handed the watch back to Kid. "You better keep it at your place."

Kid slid it into his hip pocket. "I haven't even shown it to Jessie."

That meant something coming from Kid. He shared everything with Jessie. Snake rested a hand on Kid's shoulder. "Thanks for telling me. For showing me." The loss of their father rolled in Snake's stomach close to how it had ten years ago, but this time it was mingled with hatred toward the man responsible. Seething, he vowed, "We'll get to the bottom of it, Kid. We'll find out why July Austin had that watch in his pocket."

Kid nodded but didn't speak. He walked to the door and held it open for Snake to hobble through.

Summer spun about as Snake exited his bedroom. Nervousness quelled. It wasn't a stomach pitch, or a shiver, but something odd stewing inside her. Perhaps due to the uneven pattern the crutch caused to echo off the floor, but Kid hovered nearby incase Snake stumbled. Furthermore, Snake seemed comfortable and in control of the walking aid. She pulled out a chair as they grew near.

Kid walked around the table, ruffling August's hair along the way. "Thanks again for your help today, August. You did a great job." He smiled across the table. "You, too, September." Then he hugged his mother. "I'm heading home now. You best batten down the hatches. I've a feeling we're in for some nasty weather."

"You, too, and kiss those grandbabies for me," Stephanie said as they separated.

"Thanks again, Kid." Snake laid the crutch on the floor.

"Any time, little brother." He nodded toward her. "Take care of him, Summer." Winking he added, "But, don't let him fool you into pampering him too much."

Her hand fell to Snake's shoulder. "I won't. Thank you for all you've done."

"No problem. We'll see you all in a few days."

The door shut behind him, and Summer let her

gaze roam the table. August had said good-bye of course, but September had remained silent, just as she'd done while Summer tried talking to her.

September had never been overly friendly, but the past few days she'd been downright rude, especially to Snake. Perhaps if she didn't look so much like mother, being angry at her would be easier. With eyes the color of a winter sky and hair the same shade as the petals of a sunflower, September was the spitting image of June Austin. Sometimes Summer did a double take when she came up behind her sister, for a split second she'd believe it was their mother, especially now that September had grown taller.

September hadn't offered any excuses, nor had she denied her behavior of late, and she certainly hadn't provided an apology or a promise to cease her actions. As if she knew Summer contemplated what to do, September turned and met her gaze with a cold, almost insufferable stare.

A warm hand fell atop hers, and Summer glanced down to where her fingers rested on Snake's shoulder. His palm cupped the back of her hand. He glanced to September, who quickly averted her eyes, and then back to her.

"Sit down," he suggested, "it's time to eat."

"Where's Bug?" August asked as he passed the plate of bread.

"Eating over at Willamina's and Eva's I suspect," Stephanie supplied. "He took them home earlier."

"Do you think he'll kiss her?"

The bite she'd just taken caught in her throat. Summer dislodged it, and after several coughs into her napkin, she admonished, "August! That is none of your business. And don't you be asking Bug about it either."

August grimaced, but his smirk readily

returned. Summer caught the way Snake winked at him and had to contain the grin it ensued. The meal passed without much ado, the conversations mainly came from August, who had questions about everything from driving a wagon to how Stephanie's stitching machine worked. Snake and Stephanie answered affably and quizzed him a little in return. Summer piped in when needed, but September didn't. She pushed her food around on her plate, remaining seated only because she knew Summer wouldn't allow her to leave the table until everyone was finished.

September's behavior grated on Summer. As if there wasn't enough to worry about with Snake's injuries and Wainwright on the loose. Why couldn't September be more like August? Summer laid her fork down and sat back in her chair. It wasn't fair of her to ask that. September was her own person, just as August was, and she shouldn't expect them to be alike. Moreover, she shouldn't want it. Everyone had the right to be who they were. She stared across the table. However, that still didn't give September the right to behave poorly.

"I cleaned my plate, Summer. Can I have a piece of cake now?" August held his plate up for all to see.

"That's about the cleanest plate I ever did see," Stephanie proclaimed. "September, why don't you help me get cake for everyone?"

"I'll help," August offered, jumping from his chair.

"You can pick up the dirty plates and set them in the sink." Stephanie pointed to the pot of stew in the center of the table, but her eyes were on September. "Summer worked all day cooking us this fine meal, the least we can do is clean up and serve her some cake."

September mumbled something, and Summer turned, trying to catch what it was.

"We didn't work, we rode around in wagons all day," August justified. "I call that fun, not work." He gathered Snake's plate on top of his. "What do you think, Snake?"

"I think you've all worked very hard lately, and you each deserve a cut of the harvest. As soon as I'm able, we'll ride to town and get the money out of the bank."

"Can we take the wagon? I'll drive!" August juggled the plates as he skipped with glee.

"Sure, we can take the wagon." Snake chuckled good-naturedly.

"Can I drive?" August asked.

"Well, I don't know." Snake glanced to September as she set a plate with a large piece of cake on the table. "Maybe September wants to drive."

September twirled around without commenting, August on the other hand had his answer ready. "No, she doesn't. She hates to drive. Ask Summer, she'll tell ya. September hates to drive, doesn't she Summer?"

Summer smiled at August, she couldn't help it, but she felt inclined to explain, "September does a fine job driving, August. She's driven the wagon many times."

"But she didn't like it, and that was only Maisy. Not horses. I drove horses." He spun around to face September as she carried another plate to the table. "You ever drive horses, Sissy?"

September sidestepped and set the plate down, not in front of Snake, but within reaching distance. He reached over and slid the first one in front of Summer and then the second one in front of him. "Have you ever driven a wagon with horses, September?" he repeated August's question.

"No," September snapped.

"Would you like to?" he asked.

"No," she answered.

"No, thank you," Summer reminded.

"No, thank you," September stiffly repeated. She took her place at the table along with Stephanie and August, who carried a plate with an overly large piece of cake on it.

Snake's grin was quite captivating as he glanced from August's plate to Summer. "This cake looks mighty fine."

Her cheeks sizzled with heat. "Thank you."

"It sure does," August agreed. "Chocolate cake, yum, yum." He forked a large piece in his mouth. "Chocolate's my favorite. Is it your favorite, Snake?"

"August, don't talk with your mouth full," Summer reminded.

"Sorry," he mumbled between chocolate crusted, but closed lips.

Snake leaned over, and loudly whispered to August, "Yes, chocolate's my favorite, too."

August giggled, and the happiness she'd chosen to make this particular cake today made Summer smile. She lifted her face to find September glaring across the table again. It was like a shower of cold rain.

"What about you, September, what's your favorite?" Snake asked.

September shrugged.

Summer took a breath, ready to remind her sister of her manners, but under the table, Snake's knee bumped hers. She pressed her heel onto the floor, the connection setting her leg afire. He was trying so hard to be nice to September, which fueled her ire at the girl even more.

Stephanie Quinter piped in. "I like spice cake. My son, Hog, he makes the best spice cake. I bet I got the recipe around here somewhere. There's a whole book of his recipes that Jessie wrote down. Maybe you'd like to make one, Summer."

"Certainly," Summer agreed.

"Do I like spice cake?" August asked, frowning.

"I don't know," Summer answered. "I've never made one."

"Well, if it's anything like chocolate, you should bake one."

The adults laughed while August cleaned his plate and September scowled. Bug opened the door just then, and glancing around, asked, "What's so funny?" while shutting the door.

Mouth full, August answered, "I dunno, a minute ago we was talking about spice cake."

"Spice cake? It looks like you're eating chocolate cake to me, kiddo." Bug ruffled August's hair as he walked toward the counter. "I think I'll have a piece, too."

"Do you want some stew?" Stephanie asked.

"Nope, cake'll do just fine." He pulled out the chair beside Summer. "I ate in town."

"In town?" Stephanie asked. "I thought you took Eva and Willamina home."

"I did, and then I went into Nix—Scott. I'll never get used to the name change." He ignored the frown covering his mother's face and pointed his fork at Snake. "I ran into Zimmerman. He said he'd been out here today."

"Yeah, he was," Snake answered.

"He tell you about the stampede?"

"Yes."

"What stampede? Can I go see it? Where's it at?" Excited, August climbed onto his knees and practically leaped across the table. The napkin tucked in his plaid flannel shirt caught the top of his glass, tipping it.

Summer caught the glass before the milk spilt. A toppled glass was an often affair with August, and her reaction was pure instinct. Her mind, on the other hand, was anywhere but on the conversation.

Stephanie's frown had increased, and she'd stopped eating her cake. Summer doubted the other woman's behavior was because of the stampede. It appeared to be because of Bug—not that he'd gone to town, but that he hadn't eaten supper with Eva and Willamina.

"Sit down there, bud, before you fall," Snake instructed kindly, holding the back of August's chair as he followed orders. "The stampede was a few days ago."

"Oh, rats. Can I see the next one?" August asked as he lowered onto the chair.

Summer replaced his glass once he was properly seated.

"Stampedes are dangerous, stupid," September snapped.

"September," Snake said before Summer had a chance. "That's no way to talk to your brother. He's not stupid. You need to apologize."

Lips puckered, September glared at Snake. Summer held her breath, along with everyone else. Silently, she begged her little sister to mind. She didn't want to cause a scene, knew it wouldn't help the situation, but at the same time, September's behavior couldn't continue. The tick-tock of the mantle clock over the fireplace made the silence thicker.

Snake didn't back down. "Apologize to him." His tone was stern, but his eyes soft.

September bowed her head. "Sorry."

Summer let her breath out slowly, and believing she needed to step in, she added, "Sorry, who?"

Letting out a disgusted sigh, September pushed her plate aside and repeated, "Sorry, August."

August, in his good-natured, nonchalant way, shrugged. "It's okay, Sissy." His eyes landed on her half-eaten cake. "Are you gonna eat that?"

"No," September groaned dramatically.

"Can I?"

"I don't care."

He grabbed the plate and scooped the frosting off with one quick swipe of his fork. Chocolate oozed through the tines. "Thanks," he managed to emit as the fork disappeared between his lips.

Summer shook her head. Perhaps she needed to focus more on August's table manners. The chuckles from Bug and Snake made August's grin grow. September's head hung so low her chin sat on the ruffles around her neckline. Sadness welled inside Summer. There was more behind September's behavior—much more, and Summer wished with all her heart she could discover what it was.

The scrape of chair legs sounded. Bug carried his plate to the counter. "I don't know about the rest of you, but I gotta have a bath. I even got wheat dust in my pockets." He turned one pocket inside out in demonstration and shook it. A cloud of dust formed. "See?"

August jumped off his chair, this time Snake caught the empty glass before it clattered to the floor. "There's no dust in my pockets. They're as clean as a whistle." His hands were buried in his pockets.

Snake glanced to Summer. A deep connection entered her soul as a knowing grin covered his face. If there was one thing August didn't like, it was taking a bath. Snake hadn't said it, but nonetheless, she knew his thoughts. She nodded, telling Snake he'd hit the nail on the head.

He grinned, as if acknowledging her silent communication, and then glanced toward August and let out a loud sigh. "I need a bath, too. But I don't think I could climb into the one outside."

"No—" Summer started. She'd seen the huge tub behind the woodshed. Stephanie said Snake had built it a few years ago for the brothers to use. He

110

couldn't possible think he was going to hobble all the way out to it, let alone climb in it. There was also a large, hammered-brass tub in the lean-to, she, September, and August had used it a couple times already.

Bug, interrupting her protest, gave Snake a stern stare. "If you think I'm carrying you all the way out there, you got another thing coming, big brother," he said. "But, I'll carry Ma's into your room."

August crept up beside Snake. "Summer can't make you take a bath if'n you're too sick. She done told me that."

Her cheeks grew warm.

"She did, did she?" Snake asked.

"Ah-ha, when you were sleeping, and she made me take one. She said you was the only person who didn't need to take one, 'cause you were too sick." August turned his somber face to her. "Ain't that right, Summer? You just washed him with a rag, didn't ya?"

It was the truth, and a simple fact, but for some reason she was mortified.

"I'm feeling a whole lot better now, buddy, and I think a bath will make me feel even better," Snake said. His gaze had settled on her cheeks, which were blazing.

"A *bath* will make you feel better?" August was clearly horrified. His little body shivered from head to toe.

"Yup, and when I'm done, you can jump in." Snake caught August by the waistband of his britches.

Trying to escape, August's arms pumped at his sides. "I got chores to do. Don't I got chores to do, Summer?"

"None that I can think of, August," she answered, rising from the table.

He wasn't about to give in that easily. His worry encrusted face went to September. "We got chores to do, don't we, Sissy?"

The girl cracked the first smile Summer had seen in weeks. "Not that I can think of, August," September said.

The activity in the room flew into high gear. While she and September cleared the table, Stephanie set water on to heat, and Bug carried in the tub. August followed Snake into the bedroom, and though she couldn't hear what he said, Summer had no doubt he was attempting to convince Snake just how awful baths really were.

"The boys are going to put in a tub like Hog has in his hotel in Dodge, complete with hot and cold running water." Stephanie, helping September dry the dishes, sounded breathless. "They already ordered it, and I'm itching for it to arrive. No more hauling buckets, you just climb in, turn on a handle, and low and behold, your tub fills up with hot and cold water. Afterwards there's a little plug you pull, and the water just drains away."

"Beth Timmer told me about those tubs," September said. "She and her sister Mary were at the big party there."

Summer rinsed another plate and handed it to September, not commenting. It was good to hear her sister talking. September hadn't willingly conversed with anyone lately—not that she knew of anyway.

"Oh, yes, I met them. They watched the children that night," Stephanie remarked.

"Yes, Mary said a woman stole one," September said. "And that the hotel caught fire."

Stephanie's face puckered, then relaxed. "Yes. Yes, there was a very mean woman there that night. She stole little Winifred. You've met her, Kid and Jessie's baby. But we got her back, and she's just fine and dandy."

"Did the hotel catch fire, too?"

"Yup, but the boys put it out. There was no real damage done."

Summer recalled the event—the party that is— all of Dodge was in attendance, except for her of course. She never attended social gatherings. She'd heard of the fire, and the arrests of Thurston Fulton, the man running for Governor, and his wife. It was more news than the cow town had had in ages. Yet, it had slipped her mind.

"So, you used those bathtubs, the ones with hot and cold water?" September asked.

"Yup," Stephanie answered.

"Mary said they were made of gold."

Stephanie laughed. "No, they aren't made of gold. But they sure are nice. You'll see. After the boys put it in, you can be the first one to take a bath."

September's eyes sparked. "You mean it? I could be first?"

"Sure."

Bug entered then, carrying the big tub from the lean-to on the back side of the house. The empty tin clanged and banged as he shouldered it across the kitchen to Snake's room. Summer was sad his entrance had interrupted the conversation between her sister and Stephanie. Maybe there was something September liked besides reading—baths. She'd never complained about taking them like August did, but then again, up until recently, September never complained about anything.

"You best go make sure he gets it situated." Stephanie bumped her hip against Summer's. "September and I will finish up here."

Chapter Ten

Snake sank into the hot water. He wasn't covered in wheat dust, but he did feel as grubby as an earthworm. Must be all the sweating from lying in bed so long. The temperature of the water caused his skin to sting at first, but as he grew accustomed to the heat, the aches and pains of sore muscles and injuries dulled. He rested the back of his head against the rim, sighing with contentment.

"Don't get too comfy, I ain't got all night." Bug sat on the edge of the bed, tapping the toe of his boot. "There's a storm moving in, and I want my bath before the rain commences."

Snake closed his eyes and exaggerated another sigh.

The tapping increased.

"Go take one then."

"I can't. You heard Summer. I can't leave this room until you are safely out of that tub and lying comfortably in this bed."

Snake didn't bother to open his eyes, but a smile did form on his lips. That was exactly what Summer had said. Safely and comfortably. He could get used to all the pampering she gave him. There was something to be said about being fussed over by a beautiful woman.

The bed springs squeaked. "I suppose you want me to wash your hair, since you only got one arm."

"I've still got both arms. And no, I don't need you to wash my hair."

"Hoping that wife of yours will come in and do it?"

Snake's grin grew. His mind conjured up how fun it would be to wash her hair, and every other inch of her sweet body. The clomping of boots—Bug pacing the room—played havoc with his visions. "Go take your bath."

"Can't."

"Go."

"Can't."

"Tell Summer I said you could. Just don't take all night. I'll probably need your help when I'm ready to climb out."

"Probably?"

He kept his eyes closed but pointed to the door with his good arm. "Go."

The door banged shut, and voices sounded on the other side. A cooling breeze said the door opened again. He lifted one lid.

August snuck in and shut the door behind him. "Hi," he greeted nervously.

"Hi," Snake repeated in-kind.

"I'm supposed to sit in here and holler for Summer if'n you try to get out before Bug comes back." His back was pressed against the door as if the tub full of water could snatch him up like a frog does a pesky fly.

Snake grinned and pointed to his dresser. "In the bottom drawer, there are a bunch of magazines."

August frowned.

"There's neat pictures of thrashing machines and windmills and horses and dogs and—"

"Dogs?" The kid scampered toward the dresser. "I like dogs."

By the time Bug reappeared, August, stretched out on the bed, was surrounded by a good dozen magazines, and Snake wondered if the wrinkles on his fingers and toes would be permanent. The boy had helped him rinse the soap from his hair, but other than that, he'd managed just fine.

"It's about time," Snake said between clenched teeth. The wound in his leg protested against climbing out of the tub.

"It takes a while for a man to get this good-looking," Bug recanted, jutting across the room. He grabbed a clean sheet off the dresser top and held it open for Snake to wrap around his dripping loins. "I had to shave and comb my hair, and—"

"Just help me to that chair," Snake interrupted. Bug did, and after a few deep breaths that helped ease the torture tearing at his leg and shoulder, Snake rearranged the sheet and held out a hand. "Get my shaving stuff. I feel as wooly as one of Gustafson's sheep."

Bug gathered the supplies from the top of dresser. He wet the soap block and stirred up a good froth. Lather hung off the brush as he asked, "Want me to shave you?"

Snake glared at the teasing glint in his brother's eyes. "No. I've spewed enough blood lately. Just hold the mirror."

"I could hold the mirror," August offered, climbing off the bed. His wary glance went to the bath tub. "That way Bug can haul that out of here."

"Why don't you take a quick bath while Bug's holding the mirror?" Snake swirled the foamy brush over his face. "There's no sense in wasting good water."

"No, that's all right." August inched his way back onto the bed.

Scraping the long blade over the curve of his jaw, Snake kept his gaze on his reflection. "Suit yourself. I was gonna give you some of those magazines. If you took a bath."

"The ones with dogs in?"

"Whatever ones you want."

"Why do I have to take a bath?"

"Cause it would make Summer happy. She

116

works real hard and anything we can do to ease her load would be a kind thing to do."

"I don't see how my taking a bath would ease her load. Or be kind."

Snake wiped the blade on the towel hanging over Bug's arm. His brother's eyes glistened with merriment. Snake's reflection proved his were just as shiny, but he didn't want August to see his cheerfulness, and hid a smile behind the shaving suds on his face. "Well," he offered as he scraped the other side of his face. "Don't you think Summer would be surprised if you took a bath without her having to force you to?"

"Yeah."

"Well, then, that would ease her load. I bet she'd be so downright happy, she'd give you another piece of cake before you went to bed."

The bed springs creaked, and the magazines fluttered against one another. "You think so?"

"I do. Don't you Bug?"

"I surely do. I'd say chocolate cake and dog magazines are a fair trade for one old bath."

The splash sounded so quickly Snake wondered if the kid jumped in with his clothes on. He wiped the blade again and glanced toward the tub. August scrubbed the bar of soap over one tiny arm so hard bubbles exploded in the air. A haphazard pile of clothes sat beside the tub, catching droplets of water now and again.

"Do I gotta wash my hair?" August asked.

"Yes," Snake and Bug answered in unison.

Another splash sounded, followed by spits and spatters. By the time Snake was done shaving, August was done bathing and had pulled on his britches. He looked like he'd just walked in out of the rain.

"Don't you want to dry off before you get dressed?" Snake asked, running a comb through his own disheveled hair.

"No, that's all right."

"Here, at least sop up the river running off your head." Bug tossed an extra towel at the boy.

Giggling, August pulled the towel from where it landed on his head and chaotically wiped his head and tiny chest. "Can I go get my cake now?"

Snake checked his reflection one last time in the mirror. Would Summer even recognize him? "Sure," he answered August's question before nodding for Bug to take the mirror away.

Half-way to the door, August did an about face. "I almost forgot my magazines." Scooping up several, he asked, "How many can I have?"

"Go ahead and take them all."

"Gosh! That was worth a stinking old bath!" The door slapped against the wall as August made a swift exit.

Bug laughed and walked across the room, putting the shaving supplies away. "I like that kid more and more every day."

"Me, too," Snake agreed, his voice fading. Summer stood in the doorway, lips slightly parted as she stared at him. Her taken aback gaze hit a bull's eye on his heart. Time shattered, giving him an everlasting moment that linked him to her for the rest of eternity. If he lived to be as old as the hills, he'd forever remember this moment—for it was the exact moment he realized that at some point during the past few days he'd fallen in love with Summer Austin.

Something tugged on his arm. He broke the connection to see what it was.

"Come on, I'll help you into bed," Bug said, pulling him to his feet.

Snake grabbed the sheet before it slid off his lap and turned back to Summer. She wiped her hands over her flushed cheeks and twisted. "August, come get the rest of your clothes."

"I'm coming, Summer," sounded from some far off space in the house.

Bug's fast movements didn't provide Snake with enough time to cover his backside with the sheet. Pushing his brother aside, he wound the thin material around his hips best he could. "I can do it," he grumbled and jumped one-legged to the bed. Heat ate at his cheeks, and he pushed Bug's hand aside again. "I can do it," he repeated, landing on the bed like a rock hitting water.

"Fine," Bug moved away. "I'll haul away the water. Next time, you can take a bath all by yourself."

"It'll be a pleasure," Snake sneered, flopping onto his back. He blushed again when he realized Summer now stood beside his bed.

Snake wanted to cuss, curse, spit, yell, and hit something all at the same time. It was bad enough being injured, hobbling around like a cripple, and putting up with his smart aleck brother, but knowing he'd done the last thing he'd ever imagined—fall in love—was enough to make a grown man throw a tantrum. He sunk deeper into the mattress.

Summer laid a hand on his shoulder.

He flinched at the sting.

She pulled her hand away and empathy filled her eyes. "I just need you to lift up a bit so I can pull the covers out from beneath you. I'll be gentle."

Bug laughed. "Don't be too gentle. A good, swift kick is more what he needs."

Snake bit the curse leaping on the tip of his tongue.

She acted as if she hadn't heard Bug. "I was afraid a bath would be too much. I'll just bandage your wounds and then you can go to sleep. Some laudanum will ease the pain."

Bug cackled again, like an old witch on a broom. Snake ignored it and lifted his backside. In a matter of seconds, Summer had the blankets over him instead of under him, and as soft as her shadow danced on the ceiling, her fingers applied salve and then a bandage to his shoulder. His wounds dulled in comparison to the way his body reacted to her nearness.

When she lifted the edge of the blanket, he held the covers against the mattress. She frowned. "I need to bandage your leg."

"It's fine," he croaked. The injured leg was not what was throbbing.

"No, it's not. It needs to be covered."

He shook his head. "The air will do it good."

"It's not getting any air under the covers."

"It's fine, Summer, trust me." His ability to speak was being hampered by her closeness. If Bug hadn't been taking his time getting rid of the dirty water and tub, Snake would have pulled her onto the mattress and shown her just how fine his leg was.

She let loose of the covers. "I'll get the laudanum."

Regret pelted him like sleet in November. He snatched her hand. "I'm sorry."

Her hand rolled beneath his and clutched his fingers firmly.

"I don't need any laudanum," he assured. "I just need to relax for a minute. That's all."

Concern and compassion covered her face. He lifted her hand and brushed his lips across her knuckles. "Leave the bandages on the table. I'll wrap the leg in a few minutes."

The tub banged against the door jamb. Bug cursed but made no apologizes for the scraping noise. Summer ran her other hand over the side of Snake's face, the warmth and softness of her touch singed his freshly shaven skin.

"All right," she said. "I'll just clean up the floor and leave you be."

Snake bit his lips together, afraid his plea for her not to leave would escape. If love is what made him go from a grown man to a babbling weakling in mere seconds he didn't want it. But hell and damnation if he didn't want her. He closed his eyes and felt her move away, sensed her cleaning up the water splattered floor. It wasn't until he heard the door click that he opened his eyes to gaze at the ceiling above.

Summer carried the wet clothes and towels to the back porch and carefully draped them over the railing to dry, reducing the opportunity for mold to form before wash day arrived. She eased her way down the steps, holding the railing lest the quivers racking her from the inside out caused her to stumble.

Seeing August, sparkling clean, bounding out of the bedroom had been a shock, but nothing in comparison to the clean shaven, handsome man sitting in the chair wearing nothing but a very damp sheet.

She'd wiped the sheen of fever from his body, bandaged his injuries, and combed back his thick hair while he slept, but none of that had prepared her for the emotions that ripped through her when their gazes connected moments ago. The event had left her winded and exhilarated at the same time.

Snake was remarkably handsome, she'd known that from the first time she'd seen him back in Dodge, but this time, it was as if she saw his inner soul, which was beautiful and pulled her in like a whirlpool of sorts. She lowered onto the bottom step and rested her head against the solid rail post. The swirling storm of emotions inside her slowed and calmer, more intuitive thoughts emerged.

Love. She loved him. It wasn't just because Jonas had provided a mysterious connection to Snake—or the rest of the family—for all these years, nor because he was injured and needed her assistance. It was her. Somehow she'd let down her guard and fallen in love with Snake. Up until now, she'd accepted her fate—the marriage, the aid from all of the Quinters, even the warming of her heart whenever he was near—as what simply had to be in order to provide for August and September. But that had been a ruse on her part. Truth be told, she was now discovering that secret no one knows until they find that one person in the world who makes them complete. Standing in the doorway of his room she'd felt their souls unite.

The door behind her creaked, and Stephanie said, "You all right? Need some help?"

"No, yes." She shook her head. "Yes, I'm all right, and no I don't need any help. I was—" She glanced around, looking for a plausible excuse. "Just wondering when the storm's gonna hit."

The other woman sat next to her. "It's odd, isn't it?"

"What?" Summer swallowed the lump in her throat. Stephanie must sense what was going on inside her, and knowing the other woman, would most likely share her take on it.

After a long pause, Stephanie waved a hand. "This weather. The haze to the southwest. It say's there's a storm brewing, but it's hanging there. That's usually what happens in the winter, a few days before a big snow—not summer time. Summer rains fly in and out without any warning. This one has the hair on my neck twitching."

Summer scrutinized the horizon. Night had fallen, and moonlight shimmered off the haze hovering the curve of the land. "I've never seen one like this either. Signs of a storm have been in the air for two days, but it doesn't seem to be getting any closer."

"I know. It's too strange." Stephanie patted her shoulder. "Well, there really ain't no use in worrying about it. There's nothing we can do. Maybe it'll miss us completely."

"Perhaps."

"I gave August another piece of cake. He's a growing boy and needs it."

Summer couldn't help the smile that formed. August had taken to the family like a rabbit to a cabbage patch. He'd always been a friendly, likeable child, but the lack of attention from male figures had subdued his natural enthusiasm. Not so here. All of the Quinter men lavished him with such open and honest interest; he literally beamed with eagerness every moment.

"September's a good girl, too. She just ain't figured out if she's coming or going yet."

Summer frowned, deciphering the meaning of the statement.

Stephanie rose. "I'm turning in now. Don't sit out here too long. We don't know when or how hard that storm's gonna hit."

Summer nodded, but felt inclined to say, "Thank you, Stephanie, for all of your kindness."

A firm hand patted Summer's head. "You're welcome. But I sure do wish you'd call me Ma. I'd feel right honored."

The woman's gaze held a pleading hint that sucked Summer's breath away. Her eyes stung and accepting the love simmering deep inside, Summer nodded. "Good night, Ma."

"Good night, sweetie."

Summer sat there long after the door closed. The storm didn't move any closer, yet the heaviness of the air grew suffocating. The eeriness of it drove her inside. Nighttime silence filled the house. She prepared for bed, but before lying down on the sofa, she snuck into Snake's room, intent to see if he had bandaged his leg.

Before she arrived at his bedside, he whispered, "Hi."

Happiness created a smile. "Hi."

"I was hoping you'd come say good-night."

"You were?"

He took her hand and pulled her to sit beside him. "Yes."

"Why?" The mattress dipped, and her hip bumped his thigh.

"Because I like whispering with you in the dark."

A warm stirring of her insides caused her breath to shake. "Oh?" was all she could manage.

"Yes, don't you?" His hand left hers, slipping its way across her lap to cup her side. The husky sound of his voice shrouded her with a misty and fascinating temptation. A calm, yet inspiring silence hovered between them, and a bonding happened. Their minds and bodies, silently and naturally, communicated with a private and mutual understanding.

After a few minutes, Snake's hand tightened on her waist. "Lie beside me."

Chapter Eleven

Summer's mind didn't conjure up an excuse before her body accepted the invitation. Stretched out on the mattress, she settled her head upon his shoulder and closed her eyes, reveling in the experience.

His arm curved around her shoulder, and his hand stroked her upper arm. The warmth and hardness of his palm penetrated the thin material of her nightgown, and she found herself wishing the gown was sleeveless.

"I've been lying here wondering how to apologize to you."

She eased her face upwards to scan his profile in the faint moonlight. "For what?" Her hand brushed along his jaw, tugging his face her way. "I thought the bath might cause you too much pain."

"No, not that. I needed a bath. I was getting as rotten as week old eggs."

Her fingertip edged along his chin. "No you weren't."

His gaze roamed her face before stalling on her lips. She ran her tongue over the way they pricked and tingled. Her back arched as his arm tightened its hold.

Perfectly, without hesitation, their lips met.

The tangy, musky sent of his shaving soap filled her nose as his soft warm mouth floated over hers so gently she moaned with sweet pleasure. His lips hardened, and hers followed suit, securing against his with a demand that raced to her toes. She gasped and he reacted by kissing her bottom lip, and then the top one. The action made her want more. Stretching, plastering her breasts against his chest, she buried her lips into his.

His mouth opened, and his tongue tasted her lips before it slipped into her mouth. Welcoming, she accepted him and explored and tasted as long and feverishly as he. Suddenly, he withdrew, kissing her nose, then eyes and forehead, he forced her head to rest upon his shoulder again. His fingers were buried deep in her hair, massaging her scalp. She ran her hand along his forearm, and then realized it was his injured one.

"Your arm. It should be in a sling."

"It's fine," he said against her hair. "It's fine."

Worry crept into her mind. "Did you bandage your leg?"

"Shhh, it's fine, too."

She lifted her head. His eyes slowly opened. "It'll be sometime before they are both fine, and you know it."

A contented grin formed on his lips, but it faded into a frown.

"What's wrong?" She wiggled, afraid her weight on the bed caused him pain.

His hand held her still. "I'm," he sighed and started again. "I'm sorry about what Dora said."

"About marrying her?"

"No." His lips brushed over her forehead. "About what she called you."

"Oh, that." She hadn't completely forgotten the incident, but had hoped he had. "There's no reason for you to be sorry," she whispered, while believing there was plenty of reason for him to be sorry he'd married an Indian.

"She's a spoiled brat and shouldn't have called you that."

"Why? It's true. I'm half Indian."

"So? That doesn't give anyone reason to call you

names."

She shrugged, hoping it would ease the gripping of her heart. "I'm used to it."

"I'm not. And I won't stand for it."

Summer eased onto her elbow to see him more clearly. There was conviction in his tone. "Why?"

"Why?"

She nodded.

"Because you're my wife."

"I'm also part Indian."

His hand cupped her cheek. "I don't care what nationality you are. You're my wife. From this day forward. To have and to hold. For richer for poorer. 'Til death do us part." The calluses on his hand rubbed the side of her face. "I didn't hear the words the other night, but I know them. I believe in them. And I promise, I won't let someone, anyone, hurt you ever again."

No one had ever stood up for her so ardently. The tears slipping from her eyes made speaking impossible. He brushed aside the droplets and then pulled her toward him.

"I mean it, Summer. I'll die protecting you if need be." He kissed her then, forcing the sob in her throat to turn into a moan. Infatuation filled her, and their kissing went on until she was throbbing and wet in places never awakened before this moment.

Their lips parted and heavy breathing filled the room. His arms, wrapped around her like steel bands, didn't grow slack. He rested his chin on the top of her head, and whispered, "Sleep with me, tonight. Just like this. All night."

Summer couldn't have moved if she wanted to. Walking would be impossible since her muscles had turned into limp ropes. She snuggled beneath his chin, closed her eyes, and let the worries of the world completely disappear.

****

Flames flashed in every direction. Something held her tight, wouldn't let her run from the fire. Summer twisted and tugged from the confines. The moment she burst free, her eyes flew open.

"What's wrong?" Snake whispered.

Gasping for breath, she glanced beside her and then around the room. The darkness and silence of night still cloaked the room.

Snake, propped up on one hand, asked, "What is it? Did you have a bad dream?"

"Yes," she started to nod, but her sleepy senses awakened fully. Leaping from the bed, she asked. "Do you smell that?"

"Wha—" he started before acknowledging the scent surrounding them, "Fire!" He threw the covers aside. "Get me my britches."

"No, you stay here. I'll go—"

"Summer! Get me my britches!"

The smell intensified. "No—"

"Go get the kids!" He grabbed the crutch and hopped toward the dresser. "Now, Summer, go get the kids."

She flew from the room, but not toward the stairs. It wasn't wood burning. The smell was sharp and smothering. Throwing open the front door, a bright orange glow filled the landscape to the south. The wind whipped smoke in every direction.

"Good Lord, it's a grass fire!" Ma screamed behind her. "Everyone to the root cellar!"

Never one to panic, Summer didn't understand why her feet wouldn't move, why her gaze couldn't be pulled from the red blaze eating a wide path across the land—straight toward the house.

"Don't just stand there, girl, get the children!" Ma tugged on her arm. The action was effective. Summer flew back into the house, nearly colliding with Bug who had a child under each arm.

He planted them on the floor. "Get to the root cellar!"

Snake rushed past, grabbing Bug's arm. "We gotta get the animals out of the barn." His crutch clattered against the floor.

Summer grabbed it. "Snake!"

He twisted in the doorway. "Leave it. Get the kids and Ma into the root cellar."

Chaos abound. The flames were already gobbling at the trees planted along the driveway, and the smoke had grown so thick breathing made her lungs burn. Summer towed August and September in her wake, but halfway across the yard, September broke loose.

"I gotta get Maisy!" the girl shouted.

"No, Snake and Bug will get her!" Summer insisted.

"She won't budge for them!" her sister's voice faded into the colossal snaps and crackles filling the air.

It was like a train bore down upon them. "September! No!"

"The boys'll get her," Ma insisted, pulling on Summer's arm. "We gotta get in the cellar.

August stumbled. Summer reached down and hefted him on her hip. His sobs filled her ear. "We're gonna burn, Summer. We're gonna burn."

"No, we aren't," she promised. Heat made her believe flames scorched the back of her gown and sticks and stones dug into her bare feet as they raced around the tool shed toward the hill that held the door of the root cellar. Bug arrived moments before them and threw the wide door open. "Quick! Get in!"

Ma raced in and Summer paused briefly. "September!"

"Snake has her. They're coming!" Bug shouted above the roar.

Half falling down the steep steps, they all landed on the dirt floor seconds before blazes raced over their heads. Summer dropped August to his feet, staring at the underside of the flames consuming the door in record time. "NO!" she screamed. "No. No. No."

She was dragged backwards and planted on the ground. A tarp fell over the top of all of them. It felt as if the fire was inside her. Summer tried to push the heavy material aside.

"No!" Bug said. "We got to stay under the tarp."

"But Snake and September!"

Bug grabbed her face. His nose was inches from hers. "August is right beside you, Summer, and we need to stay under the tarp."

His words weren't for comfort, they were for survival. She squeezed her eyes shut and growled at the pain consuming her insides. When her lids lifted, the pain in Bug's eyes was crystal clear.

He patted her cheeks and said, "August."

She twisted and gathered her little brother close.

****

Through the dark, swirling smoke, Snake wondered if he truly saw Bug ushering everyone into the cellar or if it was a vision of his imagination. His leg and arm screamed, and he knew he'd never make it up the hill in time. September clung to his side, and though slight, the extra weight was more than he could handle.

Survival instincts took over where doubt flashed, and he shouted to the girl, "Hold your breath!"

He thrust with both legs, and the pain made him shout with agony as he dove over the top of the large bathing tub. They sank beneath the water. Seconds later, he tightened his hold on September and tugged her head above the water line for a breath of air. Smoke filled his lungs. The canvas tarp they used to cover the water to keep debris out when not in use partially hung over the edge. He snatched it and pushed it beneath the water. "Grab a corner!"

September did, and moments before the flames caught up to them, they plunged beneath the water again. Once the wet tarp was over their heads, Snake pulled September to the surface again. With just their heads sticking above the water, they stared at one another. Thuds and indentions of sparks landing on the canvas surrounded them.

Snake wondered what he'd do once the flames ate the wooden barrel holding the water they sat in, but chose assurance instead. "We'll be fine."

"Did—" Cry filled hiccups snatched the rest of her question.

"The rest of them made it to the root cellar. I saw them go in."

She wiped at the water running down her face.

"And Maisy flew out the back door along with the rest of the horses." He pulled her closer as a hole flamed in the canvas beyond her shoulder. "Let's dip the tarp under the water again. On the count of three?"

She nodded. He counted off, and as one they ducked beneath the water. Spitting and sputtering, they surfaced again and settled the tarp over their heads. He sat on the bottom of the tub, but she being much smaller balanced on her knees.

"Are you doing all right?" he asked.

With eyes sad enough to make a grown man cry, she answered, "Yes, thank you."

Her answer, calm, as if she wasn't in the depths of peril, made him grin. He hugged her miniature shoulders. "That's the girl."

"How long will we be here?"

He was about to say he had no idea when a new

sound happened. For a second he thought it was the barrel collapsing around them. But as the sound came again, he recognized thunder rolling overhead. Moments later splatters hit the canvas with deafening force.

"Not long! It's raining!"

September's gaze shot up to the canvas. Shock quickly turned into joy.

"It is!" she exclaimed. Little arms looped around his neck. Her smile stretched from ear to ear. "It's raining, Snake, it's raining."

"Yes, sweetie, it is!" He threw back the tarp, and they both lifted their faces to the blessing being sent down from above. The downpour of rain smothered the smoke, leaving the air entering their lungs fresh and clean. They sat, together for a few moments, just breathing.

Snake helped September rise to her feet, and she in turn helped him. "Here, give me your hand," she said. "I'm stronger than I look."

He held her hand, but also used his other arm to push off the side of the tub. Not even the pain tearing his shoulder in two slowed his rise. Small fires blazed around them, but the rain, pouring straight down dowsed them before his eyes. Beyond the cellar, the once raging line of flames was little more than a trickling stream, shrinking every second.

September climbed out first. "I'll help you," she offered.

He once again accepted her aid and was just lifting his bad leg over the edge when Bug walked out of the hillside. "You two all right?" he shouted.

"Yes! We're fine!" September yelled in return.

It was Summer who arrived at their sides first. She hugged September and then threw herself in Snake's arms with enough force they would have toppled into the tub if the sides hadn't been so sturdy.

Her lips, wet and hot, kissed his face over and over. The salty taste told him her tears flowed as hard as the rain. His grip on her tightened, and he returned her kiss, long and hard.

"Oh, good Lord, the house is gone."

The agony in his mother's words broke the kiss. As one, he and Summer turned to the smoldering structure that had been the Quinter home for decades. The barn, tool shed, and chicken coop, had damage no doubt, but they hadn't been completely consumed by the flames. Not like the house. As they stood in the rain, staring with disbelief, the stone chimney tumbled.

Chapter Twelve

The sun was barely up when people started to arrive. Sheriff Turley was first, he nodded to her as he rode in, but didn't stop his horse until he was beside Snake, who, despite the fact she'd told him over and over he shouldn't be, was helping Bug pull down the few standing house timbers.

Summer wrapped the old coat Ma found for her to wear tighter around her chest, and followed the path the horse and rider made through the debris. She stopped beside Snake before the Sheriff had dismounted. Snake leaned against the plow horse hitched to the charred beam, now lying amongst the mass of others, and she wondered which pained him more, his injuries or his heart.

"Anyone hurt in the fire?" the Sheriff asked.

"No, luckily we made it through just fine." Snake twisted, his gaze following that of the sheriff's to the burnt homestead.

"How many other places did it hit?"

"None." Sheriff Turley shook his head. "Took out some grassland, that's how I heard about it. The train engineer saw it around two this morning."

"Did the train start it?" Summer asked.

Snake reached over and took her hand, pulling her closer to his side.

"No," Turley answered. "It was full blown when he saw it."

"Lightning?" Snake asked.

The sheriff shrugged. "I haven't checked it out yet. Wanted to ride along its trail first, see if anyone was injured."

"It died out just east of the hill." Snake nodded toward the cellar hill. "The rain came."

The sheriff pointed at the plow horse. "I'll take over for you. You can't be healed yet."

Snake shook his head. "Sometimes there ain't time to be sick. And this is one of them. I can't let you take over for me, but I'll let you help."

"Good enough." Sheriff Turley slapped his horse on the romp, and as the animal ambled away, he rolled up his sleeves.

Snake brushed a quick kiss across her lips before he asked, "Can you set another plate for breakfast?"

"Yes, your mother keeps hauling stuff out of the barn like it was a mercantile."

"It's all the stuff we used in Dodge while helping Hog build his restaurant."

"She explained that." Summer couldn't help but voice her concerns. "You need to rest a bit. You've been up since the fire hit."

His hand that had been resting on the back of her neck slipped forward, and he tugged on her earlobe. "Like I told Turley, sometimes there just ain't time to be sick. Don't worry about me. I'll be fine."

"I can't help but worry about you. You certainly don't."

The pad of his thumb caressed her cheek. "That's because I have too many other, very important people to spend my time thinking about."

The clink and clank of a wagon caused them both to turn to the road. It was Kid and Jessie, who were soon followed by Eva and Willamina, and then wagonloads of people Summer had never met before rolled in. The crowd quickly organized themselves. Summer, after feeding the ones who were hungry with the few provisions Ma gathered, began to worry about a lunch meal.

The Zimmerman's, Rodney and Dora, as well as their parents arrived before noon. As if her worries had been heard, their wagon held a buffet of foods Summer had never imagined.

Rosalie Zimmerman, though dressed in white seersucker, was as no nonsense as Ma. Within minutes of pulling in, she had tables arranged and people eating in shifts so the clearing of the house ruins wasn't interrupted. Even Maisy helped tug the charred wood away, and not once did Summer see the animal sitting on her haunches.

Summer was washing another load of never ending plates when August tore across the yard, shouting at the top of his lungs, "Grandma! Grandma! You gotta come see this!"

Ma stopped him before he plowed into the table of eating workers. "What is it August?"

"You just gotta come see. You, too, Summer." He waved a hand at the crowd. "All of you, come look!"

A haphazard crowd formed behind August who pulled Ma's hand. Summer walked beside them, wondering when August had started to call Stephanie Grandma. Though she knew the woman didn't mind, she couldn't help but consider how appropriate it was, and what the others must think of it.

"Careful!" Bug shouted as they drew nearer the shambles that had been the front porch. "Watch where you step."

They climbed over and around unrecognizable piles until they stopped near Bug, Snake, and Kid. Grinning from ear to ear, the men stepped aside. A white sheet of canvas, with barely a dusting of ashes came into view. It's cleanliness amongst the charred black heaps stood out like a beacon on a stormy sea.

"Oh, my." Ma's hands went to her chest. "My stitching machine." She swooned, but Jessie on her far side, and August still clutching her hand, kept her upright.

An arm wrapped around Summer, and she met the sparkling green eyes of her husband. A swirl let loose in her insides. So many people had asked about her husband's health today, she'd started to think about him in that manner as well.

Bug on one end and September on the other, lifted the white canvas and revealed a remarkable sight. There wasn't a mark or scorch anywhere on the sewing machine. Ma stepped closer, running her fingers over the wooden cabinet. She turned then and hugged August against her bosom.

Tears popped in Summer's eyes. Her little brother hugged Ma back. The love August had found expanded Summer's heart. Snake tugged, and she let her head fall against his shoulder. She sensed more than felt the kiss he planted on her hair.

"It was the last gift she got from Pa. It was right after the grasshopper plague. The little beasts had left our blankets and curtains little more than rags, and Ma needed to sew new ones."

Summer lifted her head as he continued, "It was delivered a month after he died. He'd gone to Dodge to order supplies and died on his way home."

A shower, colder than last night's storm, poured over her. Snake's gaze was still on the machine. The crowd around them chatted and congratulated Ma on the finding, but Summer's ears heard nothing but the silence that lingered after his words.

Swallowing, and afraid because she already knew, she asked, "How?"

"How what?" he asked, still gazing at Ma's joyous behavior.

"How did your father die?"

"Murdered. Someone shot him in the back and robbed him." His gaze was now on her. "Over near Cimarron."

Her heart, wrapped around her throat,

threatened to strangle her.

"Summer! Summer come take a look! It's as good as new. Not a burn mark to be found!" Ma waved a hand.

"Go on," Snake lowered his hand to the middle of her back and gave a slight shove.

"It's a miracle to behold," Ma said, grabbing her hand and pulling her closer.

"Yes, yes it is," Summer agreed. The smile on her face was as false as fool's gold. Inside, she was as cold as snow. The dread bubbling in her stomach said Snake knew. Somehow he'd discovered July Austin had killed Jonas Quinter.

The crowd closed in on them, fawning over the sewing machine as if it was brand new. Gobbled up in the moving and placement of the find—in the barn where it would be safe—and then the feeding of workers, it wasn't until the sun hung low in the sky that Summer caught a glimpse of Snake. Half of her wanted to go to him, to say how sorry she was. The other half—full of shame—wanted to hide in a place where he'd never find her, assuring she could never hurt him again.

The crowd cleared out. Shouting promises of returning in the morning, wagons left the yard in a long trail. As the last one rumbled down the driveway, Bug took one of Snake's arms, and Kid the other. The brothers assisted Snake's hobble toward the big water tub that had saved his and September's life.

Again, Summer had the desire to go to him, to assist him, but the fear wouldn't allow her legs to move.

"We have his bed ready," Jessie said, placing a hand on Summer's shoulder. "And I have bandages laid out. I noticed blood on his shirt and pants. I'm sure he tore open his stitches."

"I tried to make him slow down this morning."

The pain Summer held made her voice squeak.

"I know. We all did. Sometimes it's just too hard for men to listen." Jessie took her elbow. "I'll show you where I put everything." Walking across the yard, she continued, "For now, I'm afraid, it's boys in one tent, girls in the other. I tried to convince Ma that you all should stay at our place, but she refused. Kid tried the same reasoning with Bug and Snake, but they refused, too."

For lack of anything to say, Summer nodded. Her mind had been a fuzzy mess all day. Though busy, keeping the food and coffee plentiful and hot, she'd barely comprehended all of the work happening in the front yard. Not far from the barn, Jessie led her into one of the two tents set up. Three cots filled the area.

Jessie moved to a small table near the furthest one. "Here are bandages and ointment, and some pain powder. It's all I had at home. I wasn't sure what to bring this morning."

"This is fine. Thank you for thinking of it."

The wail of a baby had Jessie moving to the doorway. "That will be Winifred telling me it's time to eat. Dora Zimmerman has done such a wonderful job of watching the children today. September, too, the two of them seemed to have hit it off."

Summer followed Jessie out of the tent, not commenting because, wallowing in self-pity she'd barely noticed where September and August were all day.

"Hey," Jessie patted her arm. "Don't look so sad. In no time a new house will be built, and Snake will be as healthy as that plow horse he loves so much."

"Plow horse?" Summer asked.

"Yes, Gunter, the lead horse that pulled the thrashing machine."

Summer didn't know he loved his plow horse. There were a zillion things she didn't know about

Snake—but there was one thing she did know. Her father killed his. There was no hope for the two of them to even be friends with that between them.

****

Aching from head to toe, Snake let his brothers lower him into the tub of water. He'd refused at first, but Jessie had insisted he take a bath before bed. And whatever Jessie said, Kid did. Snake loved his sister-in-law and appreciated her concern, but he'd rather it had been Summer insisting his wounds were cleaned before bed. If there were any stitches left, which he doubted since the trickle of blood had oozed down his chest, arm, and leg for most of the day, he wanted Summer to be the one to bandage them.

He sank beneath the water, letting the depth not only take his breath away, but kick his self-pity in the ass. She'd worked as hard as he today. Every time he caught a glimpse, she was cooking or washing or doing some other task to keep the dozens who'd came out to help fed.

He surfaced and glanced about. The fire was devastating, no doubt, but the comrades that descended upon the farm to help was more than any man had a right to hope for. Friends and family alike had not only pitched in, but promised to be back tomorrow. And they would be. He had to be grateful for that and not wallow in how the incident pulled he and Summer apart. The remembrance of falling to sleep with her head on his shoulder and inhaling the sweet delicate scent of her had lingered in the back of his mind all day. It was a memory to cherish, and he would until it could be repeated night after night. He grinned then, realizing they'd have a lifetime to make up for a few weeks of inconvenience.

Somewhat renewed, he scrubbed the soot from his body and then let Kid and Bug help him out. He tugged on his britches and boots and though he tried to walk, his brothers more or less carried him to the tents.

"You get some sleep, little brother," Kid said. "I'll be back first thing in the morning with some house plans." He paused near the door. "Or do you want to talk to Summer first? Some women may not like to live with their mother-in-law."

Snake lay against the pillow, feeling about as lively as a slug.

"There's plenty to do before we start building, so don't worry about talking to her tonight," Kid said.

"Talking to whom about what?" Summer asked as she entered the tent.

Snake sought energy deep inside, but he was as empty as hollow log.

"You, about the new house," Kid said, and then with a wave, he disappeared out the flap.

Summer frowned as she stepped closer.

It seemed to weigh fifty pounds, but Snake lifted his hand, encouraging her to step closer. "Hi."

"Hi." She sounded guarded.

He took her fingers when she was close enough, and gritting his teeth, found the ability to scoot his hips over to make as much room on the narrow cot as possible. "Sit down."

She set a lantern on the table. The tiny flame behind the glass globe flickered. "I need to check your wounds."

"I know, but you can do that sitting down." She carried a hesitancy he'd never seen before. Worry splattered his insides. "It's going to be all right. I know the fire was scary, but no one was injured, we have to be thankful for that."

Her fingers shook beneath his. He pulled, off balancing her enough that she landed on the cot. The movement caused shoots of pain, but he ignored them. Wrapping his hand around the back of her neck, he tugged until their faces met nose to nose.

"I don't even want to imagine how awful it could have been if you hadn't smelled the smoke when you did."

She nibbled on her bottom lip as if she tried to keep herself from speaking.

"Aw, sweetheart," he whispered, and kissed her—several times before she relaxed and her lips moved in unison with his. The action spurred a rejuvenation of his energy reserves. Despite the fact he didn't want to, he stopped their kisses before either of them grew too overheated. His reserve wasn't that deep.

A flush covered her cheeks, making her look healthier than when she'd entered the tent. "There," he said, kissing the tip of her nose. "That's better. And now I'll let you look at my wounds."

A smile parted her lips. "You'll let me?"

He nodded.

She gave him a haughty look. "Do you honestly think you could stop me?"

"Do you honestly think I'd ever want to stop you?"

Careful of the lit lantern, she pulled the table closer, but to his delight, didn't move off the cot. She leaned closer, examining the wound in his chest before dabbing the area with a small square of cotton. "You tore open almost every stitch."

"I know. Just bandage me up, I'll be fine."

"Sometimes things aren't fine. No matter how hard we wish they were." She smoothed ointment over the healing bullet hole. Her touch was soft, gentle, and caring.

"Why do I have a feeling you're not talking about my injury."

She shrugged and laid a piece of material over the wound. He lifted his shoulder and arm so she could wrap a strip around his back to keep the bandage in place. After she tied it off, she rose to her feet.

He caught her hand. "Where are you going?"

"Nowhere, but you need to take off your britches so I can bandage your leg."

"No, it's fine."

Her look said his protests were useless. He glanced about. "Give me the sheet off that bed."

"No, you have your own sheet."

He doubted he could stand long enough to take off his britches, let alone climb back into bed quick enough for her not to get a glimpse of how his body reacted to her. It may be more worn out than a twenty-year-old work horse, but his lust was as hearty as a stallion in its prime.

"Lift up," she said. "I'll pull the covers out from beneath so you can cover up as you undress."

He had the feeling it was she who was now doing the teasing but didn't quite know for sure. If he was certain that Bug or August wouldn't come barreling in, he'd not only drop his britches, but entice her to shed her clothes as well—exhausted or not.

"Up," she said, gathering a corner of the blankets. He arched and in one swift movement, she had the blanket and sheet out from beneath him and floating down to rest upon him.

He had no choice but to wiggle out of his pants, and hold the sheet tight over his mid-section as she bandaged and wrapped his thigh. When she finished and flipped the blanket back over his leg, he grabbed her waist and pulled her down. She landed on top of him and instantly pushed her hands in the mattress, lifting her weight off his leg.

"Snake, let me go. You're gonna make your wounds start bleeding again."

"I don't care." He kissed her lips. "I won't bleed to death." His tongue ran along the open space between her top and bottom lips. "I've got a wonderful, beautiful doctor at hand."

"I'm not a doctor," she whispered, keeping her lips on his.

Her nearness had remarkable energy and healing power. He plunged his tongue into her mouth. The need, the want, building inside could no longer be sustained. The vibrations of her belly pressing into his groin overcame any pain her slight weight caused his leg.

He settled his hands on the small, firm mounds of her backside. Squeezing and caressing them, he pressed her deeper onto him. She moaned and wiggled her hips. Their kisses went from hot, merging tongue lashes to soft pecks and back again several times. Heat swirled and his blood pounded, growing excited and begging for the ultimate.

A small voice shattered their connection.

"They're kissing again," August said.

"Oh, yeah? Well the rest of us need some sleep," Bug declared.

August's words had made Summer giggle, but Bug's had her leaping from Snake's arms so fast he couldn't stop her. He did manage to grab her hand before she flew to the door. "Give us a couple more minutes, will ya, Bug?" Snake asked, increasing the hold he had on her wrist.

"All right, but someday, you're gonna owe me. Big."

"I already do," Snake said, never taking his eyes off Summer. "Sit down."

She shook her head. The way her chest heaved with each breath told him she was as heated as he.

"I won't kiss you, I promise. There's something I have to ask you."

Wary, she looked him up and down.

He chuckled. "I take it back. I can't promise I won't kiss you, but I do need to ask you something.

Sit down."

She sat. "What is it?"

"I've been planning on building a house for sometime but kept putting it off because I figure one day soon Bug will be going off in search of oil seeps and that'll leave Ma alone. I know she can take care of herself, but I never liked the idea of her being out here all by herself. Now that the house burnt, I'm thinking about building one that's large enough for all of us, you, me, August and September, and Ma."

Her stunned looked caused more than a touch of apprehension. He squirmed. "I know living with your mother-in-law may not be ideal. But if you agree to it, I'll talk to the other boys and maybe once in a while she can go stay with them for a bit."

She shook her head.

He nodded. "I understand."

"No," she said with quivering lips. "No, you don't understand."

"I do," he assured. "And I'm sorry. It was foolish of me to ask."

Tears trickled from her eyes. She pressed a hand against his mouth when he attempted to speak. "No," she said. "You don't understand. It wasn't foolish of you to ask. It was admirable. It's just that I'm the last person who should have a say in who lives where."

He pulled her hand from his lips, kissing the fingers as he wrapped them in his grasp. "The last person? How do you figure that?"

"It's your house. It's Ma's house. It's not mine."

"Yes, it is. Well, it's ours. Yours and mine and August's and September's and yes, Ma's—if that's all right with you. Kid and Bug think it's a good plan, and they think Hog and Skeeter will be happy knowing Ma won't be alone once Bug leaves."

"I think it's a wonderful plan."

He let out a long sigh. "Then it's all right? You

Lauri Robinson

won't mind having your mother-in-law living with you?"

Tears fell from her eyes faster than he could wipe them away. This is exactly what scared him—how a woman could confuse a man to the point he didn't know if he was going north, south, east, or west.

"Honey," he said, somewhat exasperated, "I don't know if you're crying 'cause you want Ma to live with us or if you don't want her to live with us." He quit trying to wipe away the tears and cupped her cheeks. "Can you help me out here?"

She sniffled and rubbed her nose with the back of one hand. "I'd love to live with you and Ma in your new house." Her sniffles turned into sobs again, making her voice squeak and crack. "And I'm sure August and September would love it, too. But are you sure you want us?"

"Want you? Yes, I want you. I want you to live with me. All of you, forever and ever." He kissed her forehead. "It's settled then. I'll tell Kid to bring over some house plans for us to look at."

"Are you still kissing?" August asked from the other side of the tent flap.

"No," Snake answered. "Summer will be out in a minute, buddy."

She rose and he couldn't stop her from slipping off the bed. He smiled when she did stop, halfway across the tent, and turned around to face him. The seriousness of her face made his grin fade. "What is it?" he asked, wondering if she'd already changed her mind.

"What if...what if there's something about me or August or September that you can't live with? What then?"

For some odd and unexplainable reason, the image of his father's watch formed in his mind. He could almost hear the faint tick-tock it made. "Has

146

Kid said something to you?"

She shook her head. "Kid? Like what?"

"Nothing," he said. If Kid had said something, she wouldn't have to ask what it was about. "You worry too much. Go on now so August and Bug can come in and get some sleep." He smiled, and if he didn't think he'd fall flat on his face, he'd have walked across the tent for one more kiss. "You get some rest, too."

Despite the fear wrenching inside her, Summer nodded and turned to flip open the tent flap. She patted August's head as he ducked under her arm in his rush inside. He'd been ecstatic to hear about the boys and girls tents. It was surprising he'd held out as long as he had to claim his spot beside Snake and Bug.

The cool night air, though fresh, still held the acrid scent of fire. She didn't go to the tent she'd share with Ma and September, instead Summer made her way to the water tub. The dress she wore was one Jessie had brought, along with things for everyone else, including the children. She had no idea how or where the woman had found things to fit everyone. At the time, she'd been too thankful to ask.

The outfit wasn't overly dirty, but beneath it, she felt as soot covered as the ground. After laying the dress beside her borrowed boots on a nearby bench, she climbed into the tub and started to scrub. It wasn't until her skin started to burn that she realized she'd never be clean. For the dirt and grime wasn't on the outside. It was on the inside where July Austin's actions left her too filthy to live.

With a force that left her gasping, tears burst from her eyes. She rarely cried, years ago she learned tears didn't help. The force of the gush was so hard she wondered where all the water came from.

"You doing all right in there?" Ma's voice sounded from behind.

Summer sucked in a breath. "Y-yes." She attempted to disguise her tears by splashing her face.

"Crying's not a sign of weakness, Summer. It's a sign of strength. It's the body's way of getting rid of old, no-good feelings and giving room for new, healthy ones to grow." Ma stared off in the distance, as if contemplating what she said. "Sometimes we have tears of joy, like I did when I saw my stitching machine. But you know what? Those tears do the same thing. They release happiness so there's room for more happiness to grow." The woman patted the side of the tub. "I brought you a towel. But take your time. I'll leave a lamp on for you."

Chapter Thirteen

Long days filled with hard work and nights made short from pure exhaustion where he thought of little more than dropping on the bed made the weeks fly by. Snake now walked with barely a limp since it had been close to a month since the shooting. He set the last bundle of shingles on the ground and waved to the driver. "Thanks, Able."

The man slapped the reins across the horses. Turning the wagon in a wide circle, Able Turner shouted over his shoulder, "I'll see you tomorrow."

September, no longer madder than a wet hornet, ambled over. Snake patted her shoulder and chucked little Winifred, who was propped on the girl's hip, under the chin.

"Looks good, doesn't it?" he asked, noticing September's blue eyes scanning the new wood framing in the large, modern home rising from the foundation of Ma's old one. Progress was happening five times faster than expected for there were now five Quinter brothers working on the home. Skeeter and Lila, along with their children, Kendra and Charles, and Hog and Randi had arrived a couple of weeks ago. They helped with the building every day but spent the nights over at Kid and Jessie's.

"Yes, it does, but..." September let her words flutter off.

"But what?" he asked. There had been a change in September, but still he sensed something deep down inside her wasn't quite right.

She shrugged. "It just seems like an awful lot of charity to me."

"Charity?"

"Yes, the way everyone's bringing us clothes and food."

"That's not charity, September, that's being neighborly. You treat others as you want to be treated. These folks know we'd do the same for them if they needed it."

Her little eyes scanned the people mingling about. "In Dodge they call it charity, and people aren't nice about it."

The sadness of her tone stabbed him. "My leg's hurting a bit. Want to sit down with me for a minute?"

She shrugged but followed as he made his way to the shade of a weeping willow. The grass beneath was as soft as a rug, and he encouraged, "Why don't you let Winifred crawl around a bit?"

September giggled. "She's not old enough to crawl yet."

"Oh?" He accepted his ignorance. "I didn't know that."

"She might like to sit on the grass though." The girl lowered the baby to the ground, setting her on her plump bottom and tickling Winifred's tummy when she flayed her chubby little arms and legs.

"I think she likes that," he said.

"Yeah, she does."

"She likes you, too."

"I hope so, I sure like her."

Snake knew Summer loved her siblings, but the kids most likely hadn't received love from anyone else in their rough lives. He ached for their sadness and hoped someday it would be a thing of the past they never found the need to recall.

"You know what I think about charity? I think true charity comes from the heart. It's when you have something you know someone else needs and you give it to them. You don't hem and haw, or even wonder if they'll like it, you just give it and don't ask for anything in return."

September kept tickling Winifred's tummy, but her slow movements said she was listening and thinking.

He continued, "If folks are mean about giving something away, then they'd be better off not to give it. The good book says we shouldn't boast about our charitable deeds, so in my mind, those people in Dodge who were mean about charity, they're gonna have a lot to answer for when their day comes."

"You think so?"

"Yes, I do."

"Molly Henderson says people who accept charity are like stray dogs who scrounge the streets for food."

He balled a hand until his knuckles burned. "Between you and me, even though I don't know Molly Henderson, I think she needs her mouth washed out with soap. Her mother does, too, for letting her say such things."

A shadow of a smile touched September's lips. "Mrs. Henderson oversees the church donation program."

"Really?"

"Yup."

"Well, then, she needs to listen better when the preacher talks."

"You don't go to church on Sundays. How do you know what the preacher says?"

Snake chuckled. "You know my mother. Do you really think I'd need to sit in church every Sunday to know what the good book says?"

She giggled aloud. "She's even got August reading out of it."

"I hope he sticks it out. I'll be sure to let him know it eases up when you turn sixteen."

"Why sixteen?"

"Don't know. That's just one more of Ma's rules." He reached over and let Winifred wrap her little fingers around one of his. "You okay with that? With Ma's rules?"

September nodded.

"You okay with living here with Summer and me, and August and Ma?"

"Yeah." Her little eyes grew serious. "I'll work, too, for everything you give us, I'll work for it."

Hadn't she been listening? He looked deep into her faded blue eyes. "September, I'm not asking you to work for anything."

"I know, but I want you to know that I will. I'll do my chores, and—"

"Honey," he interrupted and placed a finger beneath her chin, holding her gaze. "Chores are things you do because you're part of the family. Everyone has to work to make a household run smoothly. That's not charity. That's love."

Her face scrunched with confusion.

He glanced down to Winifred, happily entertained by her own feet. "Are you watching Winifred right now because Jessie asked you to?"

"No, I asked if I could. Why do you need me to do something?"

"No, I don't. Watching Winifred is doing something. By watching her you give Jessie time to help Summer or Ma or Kid or let her do something else she needs to. In a way, it's charity that you give to Jessie."

"Charity? I've never given to charity."

"Yes, you do. Every day. Charity comes in many shapes and forms. Not just clothes and food. There's many ways to be charitable." He wiggled his finger and Winifred giggled. "Is watching Winifred a chore to you?"

September shook her head. "No, I like watching her."

"Even so, it is a chore. Someone has to do it. Just like feeding the chickens or taking in the laundry. Someone has to do all those things, too." Snake tugged his finger from the baby and ran his hand through his hair. He was making a jumbled mess out of his explanation. "I'm sorry, September, I've probably confused you more than helped. I just want to see you happy and thought if I explained charity, you might not feel so bad about things that happened back in Dodge."

Her gaze went to the house, where men and women looked like a colony of ants the way they rushed about. "I think I do understand what you said," she offered softly.

"You do? Then tell me, because I confused myself."

She giggled. "Everyone helping us out...they're doing it because they're nice people and when people are nice, others are nice to them."

He nodded. "That's right."

"And those people back in Dodge, they talked bad about people because they're just mean."

"That's right, too." He thought for a moment. "Has anyone been mean to you since you arrived here?"

"No." She shook her head and then glanced to him. "Dora even asked if I would like to spend the night at her house sometime."

"Really?" That did surprise him, but then again, Dora was a good kid, she just wanted to grow up too fast. "You should. It probably would be fun. Her family is good people."

"I said I'd think about it, but that I was needed here right now."

He touched the tip of her nose. "You'll always be needed here."

Her expression grew serious. "I'll do my chores, including watching Winifred, not because I expect

153

something in return, but because it's what I should do to be part of the family." She tickled the baby's tummy. "And because I want to."

He let out a sigh of relief. "Maybe that's how I should have said it in the beginning. No more worries about charity?"

She giggled and shook her head, but then grew serious again. "I haven't been very charitable to you."

Emotions flooded his heart. "Yes, you have. More than you know."

"What do you mean?"

"Remember the night of the fire, when you and I were in the tub?"

She nodded.

"When it started to rain, you smiled and hugged me. That hug was one of the most charitable things you could have ever done."

"It was?"

"I thought you hated me. Your hug that night gave me hope that someday we'd be friends."

Tears welled in her eyes and she blinked. He blinked as well—for the same reason.

"You are my friend, Snake. And I'm sorry for the way I acted. I was so afraid you'd hate Summer because of all the things we needed. The food and clothes. I guess I thought if I was mean first, you'd hate me instead of her." Little tears trickled down her cheeks. "No one should hate her. All she's ever done is love me and August. She can't help she has Indian blood, and it wasn't her fault Pa gambled and drank away the money she earned."

He pulled her close, patting her blonde curls as she laid her head against his chest. "Shh," he comforted. His heart bled for all the confusion the child had lived with over the years.

"I told her I'd go with Wainwright. I said she could sell me instead of coming out here and marrying you."

Snake set her away so he could stare into her eyes. Summer had never told him this. "September, don't you ever, I repeat, ever, think that again. Nothing in this world is worth selling yourself to someone. Especially someone as downright nasty and dirty as Wainwright. Do you understand that?"

She nodded. "But, in a way, Summer sold herself to you for the same reasons."

He couldn't respond right away, it took a moment for the shaking in his insides to ease. "It might have seemed that way at first. But I can honestly say it's not. I didn't marry Summer to turn a profit. I love her. Just as I love you and August. Do you understand the difference?"

The look on her face held shock and disbelief. "You love us? All of us?"

The admission had fluttered out before he had time to contemplate it. But it had taken root, and grew to encompass his chest faster than bind weed takes over a freshly plowed field.

"Yes, I do. All of you."

"I didn't think anyone would ever love us." She nibbled on her bottom lip. He had to wonder if it was because she tried to keep a smile at bay.

"Well, I do." He kissed her forehead before he stood up. "And don't you ever forget it."

His eyes scanned the homestead. Now he had to find Summer and tell her the same thing. Surely, she didn't think marrying him and selling September to Wainwright were in the same category. She'd been acting weird lately—kind of unreachable. He'd put it off to all the commotion— and perhaps his behavior, but now he wondered.

A trim form with long black hair entered the barn. He winked at September. "I gotta get back to work. Thanks for the visit."

"You're welcome, anytime," she said, more

confident than he'd ever heard her sound.

Chuckling he strolled toward the barn.

****

Summer made her way to the hayloft ladder and hitching her skirt, began to climb. She was out of sorts again today. Had been since the fire. No matter what she did, she couldn't shake the invisible, but dismal weight dragging her down. It wasn't like her, and over all, very exhausting. She propped her elbows on the loft floor and gazed through the dust motes floating in the stream of light shining through the open end doors.

Four large trunks sat in one far corner. She let out a heavy sigh, climbed the remaining rungs, and rose to walk across the thin layer of hay covering the floor. Ma needed another thimble. Even though the house hadn't been built yet, the woman had already sewn curtains, quilts, pillows, and of course, clothes for everyone. Lila was helping with the sewing, and Ma thought there might be another thimble in one of these trunks. Summer—relishing a moment of solitude, had offered to retrieve it. Her sisters-in-law were wonderful people, and an extreme amount of help. They were all witty and smart...but there was something about Lila...She was beautiful, and nice, and caring.

Summer paused near the trunks. She couldn't put her finger on what it was about Lila that was odd, and no one had said anything. At first she thought maybe Lila was from England or somewhere outside the United States, since her behaviors and mannerisms were so unique, but she'd learned Skeeter's wife had been born and raised in Kansas.

Shaking her head to send the thoughts away, she knelt and unhooked the heavy brass latch of the first trunk. She had enough of her own worries; taking on another set was the last thing she needed.

The hinges creaked, rust fighting against her as

the lid lifted. Careful of the worn, old metal, she eased the brace bar up and used it to prop the lid open. Moving aside a stack of old papers, looking for the small box Ma described, her fingers stalled.

She slipped the rest of a wooden frame out from under the papers. The breath she held pressed against her lungs. As it eased out, she wiped a hand over the glass covering the picture. With a casual grin, Jonas stared at her. Her finger stopped near the top of his head. Ma, young and pretty, stood beside him with a serious look on her face. All five Quinter brothers were also in the picture. Kid, looking much younger, stood on Jonas's other side. Skeeter wasn't even as tall as Ma. He, Hog, Snake, and Bug stood in front with skepticism tugging on their brows. Bug couldn't have been but three or four years old.

Her gaze locked on Snake. A rapid pitter-patter filled her chest and something deep in her stomach swirled. Even then, with his hair flat against his head and dark instead of golden, he was by far the most handsome of the brothers. A flutter of happiness tugged on her lips.

When Skeeter and Hog, along with their wives and Skeeter's children, had arrived by wagon a few days after the fire, the reunion of brothers had been a festive event despite the reason behind it. The five men reminded her of a batch of puppies the way they greeted one another with playful punches before they hugged one another. There hadn't been any embarrassment amongst the men and their joy at seeing each other.

Her gaze went back to Jonas's image. "Is this what you wanted?" she whispered. "A family reunion?" Closing her eyes she stilled her mind, making space for Jonas to visit. After several empty minutes, a warming sensation climbed her spine.

She sighed. "Where have you been?"

"Right here."

An explosion happened inside her, like a flock of birds taking flight. Her eyes snapped open as she twisted around.

His stroll across the straw included a stiffness in one leg. It was slight, but she recognized it, and gloom swallowed her again. She'd damaged this family in so many ways. Snake lowered to his knees beside her, and his gaze went to her hands.

Summer thought about stuffing the picture back under the newspapers, but it was too late, his fingers had already wrapped around the edges.

"I'd forgotten about this picture." A wide grin covered his face as he slipped the frame from her fingers. "Ma must have used a gallon of grease to flatten all of our hair. Except for Kid, he refused and she didn't force it on him. Pa was leading a buffalo hunt for some Prince from overseas. A man with a camera followed them around like a whipped pup."

He grew silent as he stared at the picture. Summer buried her fingers in her skirt to hide the way they trembled. The silence built until she felt swollen and stretched.

"Good thing it was here in the barn so it didn't get burnt." Before the final word left her mouth, she bowed her head. She might as well just shoot him again. Reminding him of all the troubles she'd caused had to have the same effect.

"Yeah, that was a good thing," he said. "What are you doing up here?"

She glanced up, worried he thought she was snooping. "Ma needs another thimble."

Chuckling, he replaced the picture in the trunk. "I should have known. Have you found one?"

She shook her head. It was all she could do. For the past few weeks, ever since that night in his tent when he asked her if it was all right that Ma lived with them, she'd been avoiding him. Actually, it had been easy, since the next day a man arrived from Dodge to buy the wheat they'd harvested. The following week he'd spent his time between cleaning up the burnt homestead and overseeing the wagons hauling the wheat from the granary several miles away. He'd bandaged his injuries himself since then, and the loss of that connection with him left her starving to touch him. His closeness right now had her screaming with need.

"I'll help you look," he offered, twisting to lift the lid of the next trunk.

Summer dug her hands below the picture, grateful to give them something to do. "Ma says it's in a small metal box."

"I remember it." He rustled through the contents of his trunk. "Ma packed all this up right after Pa died. I think she just couldn't look at it. His death was hard on all of us. I know now if Ma hadn't been as tough and strong as she is, she wouldn't have survived."

Her eyes stung as if her tears were made of real flames. She fought to keep the droplets behind her eyes.

"There it is." His hands brushed over hers. He lifted a box out of her trunk. "Good thing it didn't have teeth," he said teasingly, "or it would have bitten you."

She hiccupped.

He set the box down and then closed both trunk lids. The click of the last latch hung in the air. She should pick up the box and run as fast as possible, give the thimble to Ma, and find something else to do. Anything besides sitting here next to him.

Summer tried, but the tug to glance his way was too strong. Sitting cross-legged, his arms were folded across his chest. His fingers drummed on his opposite elbows.

"Are you ready to talk to me?" he asked.

159

She almost swallowed her tongue.

"You can't ignore me forever."

Dry mouthed and sweating, she shook her head. "I—" she swallowed again. "I'm not ignoring you."

"Like hell you aren't." His words were harsh, but his gaze was soft, concerned.

"I—" She let the gust of air out of her lungs, unable to deny the truth.

He took one of her hands. "I'm sorry, Summer. I shouldn't have gotten so carried away that night. I shouldn't have pulled you onto the bed and manhandled you like I did that night after the fire."

Heat swirled her insides. The remembrance of lying atop him and his hands caressing her bottom, pressing her against his hard, heated body filled her senses until she started to tremble.

He wrapped her hand with both of his. "I didn't mean to frighten you. I won't do it again."

Fear of never being kissed or touched by him raced in her veins. "I wasn't frightened," she blurted.

He lifted a hand to cup the side of her neck. "Well, then, I didn't mean to rush you. We'll take it slow. One day at a time."

His thumb slid back and forth along the side of her jaw. The touch turned her body into warm candle wax. "I wasn't rushed," she managed to whisper.

"You weren't?"

She bit her bottom lip, shaking her head.

"Then what's wrong, sweetheart? Talk to me." His eyes pleaded, and he renewed his caress of her face. "I've missed you sitting on the edge of my bed, whispering in the dark." His face inched closer to hers. "Kissing you."

An eruption of sorts happened in her insides. With a tiny squelch, she wrapped her arms around his neck and pressed her lips to his with all the grace of a wingless bird attempting to fly. His

160

reaction was as hot and hungry as hers, and within a matter of seconds they were gasping bits of air in between open mouth, deep consuming mergers.

She'd missed him, too. The absence of the light of hope and happiness his touch filled her with had allowed the menacing gloom of July's actions to take over and leave her drowning in the quicksand filling her insides.

Snake pulled her, laying them both down on the carpet of straw covering the floor. She melted against him, her curves fitting flawlessly with his. She dug the fingers of one hand deep into his hair, while the other knotted the material of his shirt against her palm, holding on and half afraid he'd let go. His arm around her tightened, while his other hand roamed her from hip to shoulder. She arched her back, pressing firmly into his chest. His palm molded over one of her breasts. The fiery pleasure made her moan and arch her back.

His lips left hers and created a route down her neck and then back up to her ear. She wished time would stop, so she could stay right here, enjoying his touch forever. He nibbled on her earlobe before kissing her cheek. She twisted and took his mouth in hers, again, unable to restrain the desire swelling her insides.

"Sheesh! You two are kissing, too!"

August's shout was like a cold shower. Summer pulled her mouth, wet and throbbing, from Snake's. Her breast begged his hand slipping away to come back. Gathering her wits, she sat up, brushing at the hay clinging to her blouse.

Climbing off the ladder and onto the loft floor, August continued, "Everywhere I go folks are kissing. Uncle Kid and Aunt Jessie. Uncle Skeeter and Aunt Lila. Uncle Hog and Aunt Randi. Sheesh! A man can't get away from it."

"What you need, buddy?" Snake asked,

chuckling and sitting beside her.

"Grandma sent me up to help Summer find a thimble. Aunt Lila's bleeding from the needle again, and Uncle Skeeter is kissing her boo-boos."

Snake lifted the little box next to his knee and held it out to August, who was kicking up straw dust as he walked. "Here, take this to Ma."

"I sure hope Skeeter's done kissing her fingers," August said quite disgustedly.

It wasn't until August's blond curls disappeared through the square opening in the floor that Summer grew coherent enough to attempt to push off the floor. Snake's arms wrapped around her. "Where do you think you're going?"

Chapter Fourteen

"I—" Summer started, squirming against his hold.

Snake merely increased it. A tremendous ache claimed his body, one that had nothing to do with his past injuries. The want of laying her back down on the straw and claiming her—body and soul—was a bitter sweet pain.

He reached up, intending to gently brush the hair from the side of her face, but the opportunity was too rare. He kissed her again. Serenely this time. Her lips quivered beneath his, and he pulled back while he still could.

"Why have you been ignoring me?"

She averted her eyes, gazing across the hayloft with an empty stare. Dust motes danced a lively tune in the sunlight. Far off, the pounding of hammers and muted voices hung just as delicately in the air. His insides churned. Helplessness was not something he regularly felt, therefore dealing with it was foreign.

He tugged her chin until their eyes met. "I can't help if I don't know what's wrong."

A heavy sigh made her shoulder's droop. Her slight weight seemed to increase and he shifted, pulling her onto his lap and gladly accepting the burden.

"Nothing's wrong." She squirmed again. "You're leg must be hurting."

"No." He wasn't about to release her so easily. "My leg is just fine. So is my shoulder. The only thing that's not fine is us." Brushing the long strands of shimmering hair off her shoulder, he continued, "I know it's hard, staying in the tents, and I know my family can be a little overwhelming, but I promise it won't be forever."

She slumped against him, as if her resolve deflated. "I've lived in worse," she said, "much worse."

He eased his hold so she could more comfortably lay her head on his shoulder. Brushing his lips over the top of her head, he offered, "The house should be done in a week or so. Maybe sooner."

"Why do you have to be so nice?"

He frowned at how hopeless she sounded. Kissing her hair again, he rocked slightly, gently swaying them both back and forth. "Would you rather I was as grumpy as a cornered badger?"

Her arms wrapped around him. "I don't know what I'd rather. I just don't know anything anymore." Her sigh was so weighted he felt it—in an odd and deep way.

His mind tumbled, twisted, and leaped about like a flea on a dog but came up empty no matter what. He continued to rock her. "Honey, I sure do wish you'd tell me what's wrong. That's the only way I can help."

"There's nothing you can do. There's nothing anyone can do." She sniffled, which struck his heart like a long, sharp needle.

"Hey, nothing's that bad. Tell me what's bothering you. Please." He almost flinched at how he sounded. August didn't whine that hard over a bath.

She sat up abruptly. "There's nothing bothering me." Her lie was completely unconvincing. "I'm sorry I've acted so. I'm just sad your family lost so much in the fire."

The reason he'd sought her had been sitting in the back of his mind, waiting for the right time. It wasn't now, he decided. Telling her he loved her wasn't what she needed. Then again, he had no idea what she did need. Wishing he did, he said, "We didn't lose anything that can't be replaced. That's the only thing that matters."

She stood, and whether it was real or disguised, she smiled.

"You're right. I am thankful no one was hurt. Extremely thankful." Her hand stretched toward him.

He took it, pretending to allow her to aid in his stance.

"And you shouldn't be climbing ladders with that leg, yet."

He used his grasp to tug her forward. They stood face to face. "Every day, in every way, I get better and better."

A glimmer of a smile sparked in her eyes. "I've noticed that." Her free hand ran up his arm.

Her touch, soft and loving, sent a bolt though him. He wrapped both arms around her waist, tugging her closer yet. "You have?"

She nodded, her nose practically touching his chin. The temptation was too much. He leaned down, offering the kiss she clearly asked for. It started out slow, just a soft, sensual connection, but when she stepped closer, pressing her torso against his, he had no control over his reaction. Their correlation was like a match thrown against dry kindling, going from calm and quiet to alive and raging within seconds.

"I bet they're still kissing!" filtered up the small hole in the floor.

Snake eased out of the kiss, and by the time August's head popped out of the hole, Snake was leading Summer across the hay. The way they stumbled, both he and Summer, made Snake wonder if getting caught kissing in the hayloft for the second time would have been easier than walking.

****

Lauri Robinson

"Excuse me?" Summer, once again daydreaming while washing the supper dishes, glanced to the woman standing beside her.

Lila had the brightest green eyes Summer had ever seen, and they sparkled with a devilish hint as her sister-in-law giggled.

"Is your head still in the hayloft?"

It had been hours since the hayloft incident, but the statement caused heat to rush into her cheeks—and other parts of her body. And, yes, that's exactly where her head had been.

"Don't be embarrassed," her other sister-in-law, Hog's wife, offered. "The rest of us know how irresistible they are." Randi's attention was on the house, where the brothers, all five of them stood, conversing with one another. "From the moment I met Hog, a constant thought has hung in my head." She let out a dreamy sigh.

Summer waited, wondering if Randi would share her thought—even though she knew what it was. Summer's mind trailed down a familiar road. It relived every moment she shared near Snake including each time they'd touched or kissed with such clarity she found herself trembling in her shoes.

After another sigh, Randi said, "Every day I wonder when is the sun going to set so we can be alone?"

Lila giggled. "Ain't that the truth."

Summer didn't answer, didn't need to since the other two women were staring at their husbands like August stared at chocolate cake. Besides, what could she say? She most certainly couldn't deny she had the same thoughts—about being alone with Snake. There was no way she could admit it either.

On cue, Skeeter and Hog turned around. Smiling, their gazes landed on their wives. Summer averted her eyes, feeling somewhat like an intruder, but her movement stalled. Snake's eyes had settled on her. A stirring happened in her stomach. The swirling heat caused her breath to catch. There was no doubt how strongly the Quinter brothers loved their wives. Anyone with eyes in their head could see that—probably even a blind man would pick up on the love that hovered between the couples. But that didn't include her and Snake.

Her heart pounded. Or did it?

The men began walking across the yard. Her nerves jolted and water splashed over the sides as Summer plunged her hands back into the dishpan. Her fingers searched, but besides the tepid water, the pan was empty. Almost panicking, she searched the makeshift cupboard for more to wash. Anything to keep her busy. Not a cup, nor spoon, nor pan was anywhere in sight.

"They're all done," Randi said, hooking the towel she'd used to dry the dishes on a nail left sticking out for that purpose. She was a petite woman, and when Hog, who was the largest of the brothers, walked up behind her and engulfed her in a hug, she looked even smaller. Randi embraced his hold lovingly, and Summer turned away again—only to catch a glimpse of Lila folding herself into her husband, Skeeter's arms. The two of them were closer in height, and Lila openly grasped Skeeter's backside as their hugging grew closer.

Summer spun about and ended up chin to chest with Snake. Swallowing her heart, she tipped her head up. Air swooshed out her lungs, and she spun back to the dishpan. Hands shaking, she grabbed for the sides of the pan. The gaze of Snake's eyes, as he'd looked down at her, was the same as Hog's had been to Randi, and Skeeter's to Lila. It held that unmistakable shine—like sun reflecting off a pool of water—of fresh, pure, devotion.

Someone else caught a hold on the dishpan. "I'll

empty that for you, Summer," Bug said, lifting the pan. Summer had no choice but to let loose of the edges as the man tugged the pan away.

"I'll help you, Bug," August, forever near the brothers, offered.

"Where's Kid and Jessie?" Skeeter asked, "It's time to get the kids back to their place."

"They're kissing in the barn!" August shouted over his shoulder, his little legs hop-skipping as he kept pace with Bug walking across the yard.

Summer didn't have the gumption to reprimand the child. It wouldn't have mattered anyway; the people surrounding her were all laughing.

Moments later, Kid and Jessie exited the barn. Grinning as they approached, Kid acknowledged, "That kid doesn't miss anything does he?"

"No, not much," Snake said, wrapping an arm around Summer's waist. His hand flayed out over her side, and his fingers squeezed, tugging her until their hips and thighs collided. A flock of butterflies took flight in her insides. An urge erupted. She wanted to wrap her arms around his waist and hold on for dear life. She quelled the want, forcing her hands to stay at her sides.

"See what we have to look forward to?" Hog asked Randi, resting his hand on her abdomen.

"What?" Lila asked, lifting her head from Skeeter's shoulder. Her eyes grew wide, and her smile increased, brightening her face with glee. "Is there something you haven't told us?"

Randi covered Hog's hand with both of hers. "No." She glanced at her husband, blushing. "He just thinks it should have already happened."

Skeeter slapped Hog on the back. "Maybe you aren't trying hard enough little brother."

The hoots, laughter, and jesting in general lasted for several minutes. Summer watched and listened with interest. She'd grown accustomed to the brothers—and their wives—and their playfulness and teasing, but a piece of her remained aloof, making her feel like the outsider. Not a single family member made her feel so, but just the same, she did—for she was an outsider. She certainly didn't belong with this loving, caring family. Soon they would all hate her—the moment they learned the truth.

Jessie put a stop to the hooting when, still giggling, she said, "We best head home. The kids are tired."

The others agreed and as the couples moved toward the tent where Ma and September had taken the children—less August of course—Jessie touched Summer's arm. "We were wondering if you'd mind if September came home with us for the night."

August as usual, appeared out of nowhere. "I'll go, too! Can I, Summer? Please?"

Snake's hand, gently rubbing her side—along with the turmoil racing up and down her spine—made thinking difficult. "What?" Summer asked. "Why?"

"So I can see the puppies!" August hopped up and down. "I can see the puppies, can't I, Kid?"

"Sure can, bucko, you can even feed them their supper," Kid answered, ruffling August's blond curls.

"Please, Summer?" her little brother repeated. "September wants to see the puppies, too, I heard her ask Jessie."

Summer lifted her gaze to the other woman. Jessie nodded. "She asked me this afternoon if she could come over and spend the night sometime. I told her I'd ask you."

"Pleeeease?" August had his hands folded beneath his chin as if praying to the Lord Almighty.

She really couldn't say no. August and September rarely asked for anything. The children had blossomed the past weeks. The sight of their

169

constant grins and glowing faces was something that had been absent in their lives up until now. The children were not only healthy, they were happy.

Summer knelt down in front of August. "You'll have to be extra good."

"I will." His head bobbed. "I promise. I'll be as good as gold."

"And go to bed when asked."

August nodded faster. "I will."

The love she had for her siblings swelled in her chest. Summer leaned forward and wrapped her arms around August. "I know you will. You always mind."

He hugged her briefly before he stepped back. "So I can go? I can go see the puppies?"

"Yes," she agreed. "You can go."

His grin faded slightly. "And September, too?"

Words tried to lodge themselves in her throat. Other than the night she'd followed Snake, she'd never spent a night away from the children since they'd been born. She swallowed her own anxiety. "Yes. September, too."

With a hoot and a holler, August took off toward the tent. Snake took a hold of her arm and unnecessarily assisted her stance. When her knees quaked, she realized she did need his assistance. It felt good to lean on someone. That, too, was something she'd never experienced before.

Jessie stepped forward and looped one arm gently around her neck. After a quick hug, which touched the inside of Summer's chest in a new and unique way, Jessie said, "Don't worry, we'll take good care of them."

Unsure and a bit confused by all the emotions spewing inside her, Summer nodded. Snake's arm was back around her, and he tightened his hold. She closed her eyes, and just for a moment, let his caring, affectionate touch fill her. While she was lost in that wonderful world, his lips brushed over hers.

It all happened in a blink of an eye—or at least, that's what it felt like to Summer. Still recovering from the quick kiss Snake had bestowed upon her lips, she was caught off guard when September raced over and gave her a quick hug before running back to the wagons the rest of the Quinter families loaded themselves into. Their departing greetings made the fog lift inside her head. She spied Ma holding one of the babies, either Kid's little girl, Winifred, or Skeeter's infant boy, Charles, the swaddling didn't allow her to determine which one.

Summer turned to Snake, who once again—or maybe still—occupied the space beside her. "Ma's going, too?"

"Looks that way," he said, waving to the departing troop.

"Why?"

"Maybe she wants to see the puppies, too."

The sparkles in his eyes held her attention. The jingle of harnesses, the stomp of hooves, and the gay chatter of those in the departing wagons faded like a ghost in the wind. His hands wrapped around the backs of her upper arms. "They'll be all right. Don't worry."

Her ability to speak had been stolen. She wasn't worried about the children. It was a new realization that had her choked up. They were alone. Completely alone. And heaven knows what entered her mind then.

She spun about. "Where's Bug?"

"He rode out." Snake's one hand still held an arm.

Her stomach flipped and flopped, and then repeated the action. "Where to?"

"Don't know. Why?"

Snake waited for her to answer until it was clear she wasn't going to. He stepped around to face her again. His family knew he and Summer could use some time alone, and he was thankful for their consideration, but it appeared she didn't feel the same way.

"Are you afraid?"

She shook her head, but the way she bit on her bottom lip belied the action. The emotions that flooded his body for this woman were amazing, more so now that the love he felt for her had grown all consuming. The want to ease her burdens, heal her injuries, and make her happy for all the days to come were all new to him, yet he relished the desire. He'd strive to his dying day to make all her dreams come true. If only she'd let him.

His hand floated down her arm until his palm found hers. Interlocking her small fingers with his, he turned and led her toward the bench beside the outdoor table. They sat and used the edge of the table as a backrest. Snake's mind searched and doubled back, looking for something witty and charming to say.

"Do you think August will ask Kid if he can have a puppy?" Summer asked, gazing at the sun kissing the earth with a rainbow of crimsons and burnt-oranges and flashing yellow streaks into the navy colored sky.

"Well, I kind of already told him he could pick one out," Snake admitted.

"You did?"

She hadn't turned his way, and her tone didn't give him a sense of how she felt about a puppy. He drummed his fingers on one knee. "Yes. I hope you don't mind. We talked about it once before the fire."

"I remember."

When she offered nothing more, he asked, "Do you mind?"

"No. I'm just afraid of how attached he'll become."

"Of course he'll get attached. A boy and his dog have a special relationship."

She twisted her neck, glancing his way briefly. "Did you have a dog when you were little?" The sadness in her eyes hadn't lifted. Dark circles hung beneath her lower lashes, making him wonder again what more he could do to lift the burden she carried.

"Yup, a couple of them. Roscoe was my favorite. We had him for years. Having a dog around again will be nice." He rolled his hand to thread his fingers through hers. "What about you?"

Once again staring at the sunset, she shook her head. Her depression had grown deeper and deeper. The fire must have affected her more strongly than he'd thought. Right now, he'd gladly let someone shoot him again just so he could see that proud and righteous woman who'd stomped into his room and declared they were married. A smile tugged at the corners of his lips. That was probably the minute he fell in love with her. The knowledge that he loved her had settled deep in his chest, and along with it came honey-kissed satisfaction. The kind that made a man want to cheer out loud. Yet, he couldn't—not when she seemed so distraught.

"Pets are good for kids," he offered, searching for something to say. "August will like it. September, too. They both love Maisy, despite her orneriness."

"Mmm hmm," she mumbled.

His attempt at humor, referring to the hat wearing mule had failed. He glanced around, wishing for something insightful, delightful, or significant to say. The fading evening light bounced off the building frame. "You want to take a look at the house? The rooms are framed in."

She turned and the despondent look on her face sunk his heart into the deepest pit of his stomach. It was as if he was on a rickety bridge, made of worn boards and frayed ropes with a raging river flowing below, and she was on the other side. He wanted to rescue her, but the frail bridge was collapsing faster than he could traverse it.

He reached out a hand. She avoided his touch, and then rose to her feet. "Why?" she asked, shaking her head and scrunching her face.

"Why?" he repeated, unclear what she asked.

"Why do you have to be so nice? So wonderful?"

He stood and took a step closer. She backed further away, still shaking her head. Snake stopped and let out the sigh that had built to mammoth proportions in his lungs. "Summer, I don't know—"

"Stop," she said. "Just stop. Don't say anything." Her hands flayed up and down at her sides like the wings of a frustrated hen. "Why can't you just hate me?"

"Hate you?"

Her face grew crimson. "Yes! Hate me." She puckered her face as if pained. "Why can't your entire family just hate me? It would make everything easier if they would. If you would. I could pack up the kids and be gone."

"Gone?" His stomach landed somewhere near his heels. "What are you talking about?"

She made a growling noise and flipped around. Stomping away, she shouted, "Everything. I'm talking about everything."

He caught up with her. She twisted her arm out of his grasp and kept moving. "Just leave me alone." Her words were heated, angry, but sad tears dripped from the corners of her eyes.

Snake didn't try to touch her again, knew she'd oppose it, but he did keep up with her fast pace. "Why?"

"Why?" Her breath came in short gasps, as if she was winded.

"Yes, why should I leave you alone?"

"Because."

His patience was running thin. He wasn't about to leave her alone, and she sure as hell better never plan on packing up the kids and leaving. He'd hogtie her to the chair if need be to stop such an event. Grabbing her arm, he held on and forced her to stop.

"That's not an answer. Tell me what you're talking about. Why you want me to leave you alone? Why you want everyone to stop being nice?"

She was mad now, the darkness of her eyes glowed as she tried to tug out of his hold. The fact he wouldn't let go made her lips form a tight line.

"Because I'm not worthy!"

Instinct, and anger, made his hold tighten. He forced his fingers to relax, but still kept her captive. "Not worthy?"

"Yes!" She twisted and tugged.

Now thoroughly frustrated, he growled, "What the hell are you talking about?"

"Let go of me!"

"Like hell I will!" He tugged her forward.

She thumped his chest with both fists. "Let me go!"

"No!" Her fists pounded harder. The frustration in her actions caused bits and pieces of his anger to diminish. "Not until you tell me why you think you're unworthy."

"Because I am!" Her body trembled beneath his touch. "All I do is cause pain."

He attempted to rebut her, but she broke free and continued before he could say a word. "That's all I've ever done. Pain and heartache. Loss and misery. Trouble and destruction. Mayhem and murder. That's all I'll cause your family."

She was on a roll, and not likely to stop. Her stomping feet led her to the bathing tub. He kept pace, searching for the right words to stop her self-loathing.

"I'm a half-breed. A squaw. I'm no good. Ask

175

anyone."

That did it. Something inside Snake snapped. If she were badgering him, saying disgusting and degrading things about him, he could have taken it, but he couldn't stand the way she was demeaning herself. Before he quite contemplated his actions, he'd picked her up and hoisted her over the edge of the bathing pool. Realization hit as his fingers let loose. He reached forward, but she was already dropping beneath the water. The splash along with her screech cracked as loud as a thunderbolt.

"Ooooh!" bubbled in the water as she went under.

"Summer!" He plunged his hands into the water. "Summer! I'm sorry!"

Her head surfaced, spitting and sputtering. Her long, glossy hair flipped over her head as she snapped her neck back. The ends landed with a smack and then floated around her shoulders as she sat on the bottom of the tub—stunned, water swirling around her shoulders.

"I'm sorry," he repeated, feeling about as sheepish as August looked at times.

Her eyes lowered, and she stared at the rippling water as if she had no idea how to get out of it. He climbed over the edge. Water instantly filled his boots and soaked his britches as he moved through the knee high water. Kneeling down in front of her, he cautiously touched one cheek.

"Summer?"

The image before Summer's eyes dissolved into the ripples. Jonas, disappearing as fast as he appeared, whispered inside her head, *Don't fight it any longer. Trust me.*

Summer closed her eyes, wanting to keep him talking. It had been so long since he'd come to her. She needed his guidance. Needed his council now more than ever. His voice, fading, yet echoing, continued, *Live, Summer. Live. Laugh. Love.*

She shook her head, silently begging him not to leave.

It was to no avail. The emptiness following his words made her want to cry. Jonas was gone again. She willed, eyes closed and heart aching, for him to return. He didn't, but something warm and gentle, and solid and real on her cheek made her eyelids lift.

Snake's face, close enough she could feel his breath, was filled with worry lines. The heart in her chest galloped, forcing a hot and somewhat excited stirring to race through her veins. Live. Laugh. Love. A smile tickled her lips, and she bit down on the bottom one, refusing to let the grin emerge.

"Summer?" he asked tentatively.

She met his gaze. It was as if a dam had broken within her and washed the gloom that had been hovering about away. Maybe by her dip in the water, or by Jonas' visit, she wasn't quite sure, but either way, dread no longer filled her inner being. She'd never been a grim and dismal person, and truly didn't know why or where the depression had come from. Now that it had lifted, she wondered how it had been able to consume her so thoroughly the past weeks. Before her was more than she'd ever had. Pure, real love, from a man more handsome and sincere than all the others she'd ever met combined.

Snake cupped the side of her cheek. "I'm sorry. I—"

Glee filled her insides, but she downplayed it and interrupted. "You're sorry?"

He nodded.

"So am I." Before he had a chance to stop her, she planted both hands on his shoulders, and shoved.

The force of his weight hitting the water made waves slosh her shoulders as he went over backwards. The tips of his boots broke the surface before his head bounded upwards. Splaying droplets from his hair, and gasping for air, he landed on his knees before her.

An outlaw with a pearl handled six shooter couldn't have stopped the laughter rolling up her chest. It burst from her lips like a stick of dynamite. Snake's eyes widen briefly before he, too, started to laugh.

Brushing his wet hair off his forehead, he declared, "I deserved that."

Summer brushed her hair back and rose to her knees to face him nose to nose. "Yes, you did."

"I just wanted to shut you up." His cheeks glowed red.

More bold and brazen than she'd ever believe herself possible of, she grabbed the sides of his face. "I know a better way." While the shocked looked covered his face, she planted her lips on his.

Chapter Fifteen

The emotions that had been buried deep in gloom rose up like the water surrounding them. The love that Jonas spoke of, like the warm bathwater, seeped into every crook and crevice of her being. Summer wrapped her arms around Snake and pressed her body against his until she felt their hearts beating in unison. She parted her lips and kissed him with the force of a freight train roaring down a mountain.

The beating, tasting, and soul merging continued until she was dizzy and breathless. When Snake pulled his mouth from hers, giving them both a chance to catch air, she flung her head back and laughed. Merriment and delight rushed through her like the summer wind, hot and welcomed.

Snake grasped her cheeks, bringing her face forward to meet his. Softly, gently, he kissed her hairline before his gaze met hers. His eyes smoldered, yet held a hint of question.

She kissed the tip of his nose, giggling. His gaze grew serious, but it didn't daunt her joy. "What?" she asked, placing a small peck on his warm lips.

"Well," he started as his hands moved around her neck and his fingertips massaged the back of her head. "I was just thinking that if we weren't already married, I'd ask you to marry me right now."

The sincerity of which he spoke took her breath away. It was a moment or two before she could speak, and then it was somewhat of a squeak. "You would?"

"Yes, I would."

If a person could die from love, she'd have keeled over right then and there.

His fingertips, working their way through her hair to rub her scalp, were the first things to penetrate the numbness that had overtaken her. Softly spoken, his words were the next. "What would you have said, if we weren't already married, and I asked you?"

Her body was alive again. The blockage in her throat gone. "I'd have said yes."

She hadn't realized he'd been tense, holding his breath, until she felt him relaxing beneath the hold she had on his shoulders. The happiness she felt was mirrored in his face.

"I not only love you, Summer Quinter, but I'm in love with you. And I want to be in love with you for the rest of my life."

"I'm in love with you, too, Snake. And I want to be—forever. Oh, how I want to be."

The kiss he bestowed upon her made the tears stinging the backs of her eyes with pin prick sharpness slip forward. She'd heard of tears of joy, but until this moment, had never believed in them. The merger of their lips, their souls, was as delicate as the petals of a flower, yet as strong and binding as the railroad ties that bound the East and West. When he pulled her closer, the last bits of hesitation lingering in her mind fluttered away on the gusts of the summer breeze whizzing past.

Their coupling grew more intense with each passing moment. As if they were twins, thinking exactly alike, they rose from their knees without parting. Water sloshed between them and dripped from their sopping clothes, but the distraction wasn't enough to break the kiss.

A startled yip, when he caught the backs of her knees and lifted her into his arms, escaped her lips, but he absorbed it, and continued to taunt her lips and tongue with his as he carried her out of the water tub.

They were halfway across the yard before his injuries came to mind, and she tugged her mouth from his. "Your arm and leg. You should put me down. I can walk."

"My arm and leg are just fine." He tried to recapture her lips.

She couldn't resist completely, but after a brief merger, added, "You might re-injure them."

"I could climb a mountain right now."

The energy surging through her system allowed her to admit, "Me, too."

He kissed her again, but had to pull away when they arrived at the tent to see how to pull aside the flap. "I think I need to get you out of these wet clothes before you catch cold."

"It's August. In Kansas," she reminded. "Night's don't get any hotter than this."

"I know the feeling," he said as the flap fluttered behind them.

While the sun set and the prairie grew calm and peaceful, blanketed with a night sky and decorated with twinkling stars that found a way to penetrate the heavy canvas and tease the inside of the tent with a clandestine glow, Summer found herself engulfed in a world so wondrous and precious, she completely forgot her worries and fears. With divine tenderness, yet intense passion, Snake led her on a journey that had her reeling and releasing the hidden hopes and dreams she'd secretly cherished the past weeks.

Summer's heart burst with newfound joy. At this moment, they were the only two people on earth and nothing mattered except that they were together, uniting as one.

****

Hours later, something rousted her sleep.

Drawing her awareness from a deep, pleasurable dream world, Summer stirred. The smooth warmth of skin beneath her cheek enticed her to snuggle closer. Arms as strong as bands of steel pulled her close.

"Good morning, sweetheart," Snake murmured above her head.

Remembrances flowed into her mind and happiness enticed a smile to crest her lips. "Morning," she offered, kissing the hollow of his neck.

"Sounds like we have company." The jingle and jangle of harnesses and clopping of hooves on dry ground accompanied his words.

Too content to care, she ran her hand up and down his side, caressing the warm skin as she had during the hours they spent exploring one another. "Maybe they'll go away."

He chuckled. "You know my family better than that."

"I guess I do." She kissed the bottom of his chin and rubbed her nose along the line of his jaw. "But a girl can dream, can't she?"

He flipped her onto her back and hovered over her, staring down. Happiness made his eyes bright green. "Dream?"

She wrapped her arms around his broad shoulders, and squirmed deeper into the feather tick below. Welcoming his weight to settle upon her, she slid her hands beneath the blanket to roam down his back. His flesh molded against hers, and she pressed her palms against his hips, inviting the union.

"Do your dreams include me?" he asked.

"You're all they include," she admitted.

"Then I hope you dream forever." He started at her hairline and kissed the entire side of her face. When his wandering mouth found her lips, he added, "You're all I'll dream about for the rest of my life."

Her body, now fully awake began singing the dreamy and exciting tune he'd taught it the night before. Heart drumming and nerve endings strumming, Summer closed her eyes and let the outside sounds fade as the internal music and his kisses carried her away.

Unexpectedly, Snake rolled off and something else began to lather her face. Summer pulled her eyes open, and half batting away the unknown, she reached for Snake to return.

His deep chuckle entered her ears at the same time a little voice said, "He likes you, Summer. I knew he would."

She grabbed for the cover, and finding it snug beneath her chin, her fingers then wrapped around the golden-yellow ball of fluff romping on her chest. A tiny, pink tongue kept trying to lick her face. She lifted the puppy. Its little legs squiggled as she touched her nose to the dog's.

"Well, hello."

The pup let out a tiny ruff, and then its tongue went wild again.

"Yup, I'd say he likes her all right," Snake said, propping himself on his elbow. He rubbed the dog's fuzzy head.

August, standing beside the bed, leaned over Snake. "Kid said I could keep him, if'n you say I can. Can I keep him, can I?"

Summer set the dog down, and it instantly snuggled in below her chin. Burying her fingers in the soft fur, she glanced to her brother. His little face glowed with love as he gently patted the puppy.

"A dog's a lot of work," she warned.

"I know. I promise to do everything myself."

She glanced to Snake. He winked at her. The gaze in his eyes was as deep and loving as August's. A wave of happiness flooded her system. She turned her eyes back to her brother.

"You can't be letting him get underfoot."

August shook his head. "I won't." A tiny frown formed. "Can I keep him?"

"Yes, you can keep him," she answered. Denying him such pleasure had never entered her mind.

With a whoop and holler, August snatched up the pup. "Thanks, Summer!" he managed to exclaimed as the puppy's tongue lathered his face. "I'm gonna name him Jerome."

Snake rolled onto his back. His one arm slid back beneath her neck and held her close. "Jerome? Why Jerome?"

August shrugged. "It's a nice name. Don't you think it's a nice name, Summer?"

The interruption of the puppy surprise had stifled their love making, but it hadn't drowned the feelings floating in her veins, and snuggled, flesh to flesh beneath the covers, had her mind roaming in several directions—the last of which was focused on the new pup's name.

"Don't you like Jerome, Summer?" August asked again.

"Yes," she said quickly. "Jerome is a fine name."

August gave Jerome a bear hug, and then, growing serious, turned to frown at her and Snake. "Why are you two still in bed?"

Heat rushed into her cheeks, but Snake, calm and gentle, said, "Because we were tired. You and Jerome go on, now. We'll be out in a few minutes."

"All right," August readily agreed, but halfway across the tent, he slowed, glancing at the pile of clothes on the floor. "How'd your clothes get all wet?"

Summer swallowed a groan.

"Never mind, August," Snake said.

"Even your boots are wet," August declared.

"There you are!" Ma stuck her head in through the flap. "Come on, you get out of here." She caught the back of August's shirt collar and tugged him outside without a glance toward the bed.

August's voice, asking questions, faded as Ma undoubtedly hauled him across the yard. Summer kept her eyes on the doorway, an inkling of embarrassment at the way she'd stripped off her wet clothes the evening before kept her from glancing to Snake, who was gently rubbing her arm from elbow to shoulder. The caress had the ability to turn her blood into warm honey. She let out a sigh that was half full of pleasure, half full of regret, and glanced up.

"Jerome?" Snake said, grinning from ear to ear.

His twinkling eyes made her giggle. "Yes, Jerome."

"He's quite the kid."

There was reverence in his whisper, but more than that, his eyes spoke to hers, sharing his love and respect of her younger brother. She'd never have imagined how much that meant to her if she hadn't experienced it at this moment in time. The fact she'd not only found someone she loved, but someone who loved her siblings threatened tears to trickle from her eyes. She held them in, and tilted her face upwards to brush a soft kiss over his lips.

"Thank you."

Summer felt the smile that curled his lips beneath hers. After a deeper, more passionate kiss than she'd intended, Snake held her tight in his arms.

"You're welcome, even though I don't really know what you're thanking me for."

Head once again tucked beneath his chin and savoring the scent and feel of him, she admitted, "Just for being you. Thank you."

He was silent for a few cherished moments, before saying, "As much as I wish we could lie here all day, I think we better get up. It sounds like everyone has arrived."

As if she'd been deaf and just regained her hearing, the sounds of activity filtered into her senses. People laughing, talking, and the steady, repetitive pounding of hammers jolted her.

"Oh!" She wiggled to push away from his hold.

"Just one more kiss." He grasped her face before she had a chance to protest, and by the time he lifted his face, she'd once again forgot a world happened outside the tent.

Snake eased his way off the mattress, wishing he didn't have to, but knowing he did. The sooner the house was complete, the sooner the day would come when he and Summer could dally in their bed on quiet, simple mornings. He flipped open the lid of the trunk that held his clothes and quickly tugged out fresh garments. Once his britches were on, he turned to the bed.

She sat on the edge, wrapped in the blanket and gazing at the wet dress in her hands. They were in his tent, and her clothes were still in the girl's tent. Snapping his suspenders over his shoulders, he tossed his shirt on the bed and took the dress from her hands. "Wait here. I'll go get your trunk."

"Thank you." A pink blush covered her cheeks. The sight made his heart, already overflowing, swell again. A more beautiful, wonderful woman didn't exist, and he wondered just what he'd done in his life to deserve her. He took a moment, remembering the day she sat beside Ma on the wagon bench with Maisy sitting on her plump mule rump in the middle of his wheat field. Funny thing, just when a man thought he had it all figured out—what he wanted and what he didn't—something happened to prove him wrong.

Tickled pink, as Ma would say, he leaned down and kissed the soft hair at one of Summer's temples.

"I'll be right back."

A Kansas summer-morning sun met him with

all her heat and glory. The homestead was alive with activity, and though he knew the others witnessed him leaving the tent, no one turned to acknowledge him. The grin on his face remained. His family, for all their teasing and joking, knew when a little discretion was needed, and he appreciated it.

In the next tent, a trunk had been pulled near the door. Ma no doubt, letting him know which one was Summer's. Snake hoisted the trunk and made his way back to his tent where he found Summer wearing his shirt and tucking the blankets in neatly around the edges of the bed.

He set the trunk down, and unable to control the urge, wrapped both arms around her middle. She stood but didn't pivot about; instead she leaned back against him. Nuzzling the side of her neck and nibbling on her ear lobe, he stated, "I love you."

"I know," she giggled, scrunching her neck as if his teasing tickled. "I love you, too." She spun then.

The way she looped her arms around his neck made her breasts tease his chest right through the material of the shirt she wore.

"And it's wonderful," she said, her breath floating over his lips. "So very, wonderful."

He slipped his hands under the long tails of the shirt, and cupped the firmness of her backside with both hands, wishing it was evening instead of morning. The night they'd spent in each other's arms was so exhilarating, he could barely wait to repeat it.

"We really need to get dressed."

"I know," she answered, growing still in his arms.

He leaned back, looking down. Her big, dark eyes glimmered, and he noted a hint of apprehension. A chill tickled his spine as he recognized fear mingling in her gaze.

"Hey," he coaxed. "There's nothing to be afraid

of."

She nodded.

"We are married."

"I know," she said, slipping out of his arms. "It's just..."

"Just what?" He followed her to the trunk he'd hauled in.

She opened the lid and lifted clothing out. "I don't want the spell to break."

"Spell? What spell?"

Her gaze was on the tent flap. "Once we walk out that door, we'll enter the real world again."

"We've never left the real world." He stepped in front of her and cupped her cheeks. "What we shared here is real. We are husband and wife."

"I know." She patted his hands and then tugged away, setting her dress and other garments on the bed. "I'm sorry. I'm just being silly."

Against his better judgment, he didn't push her for a deeper answer and gathered his socks and boots while she dressed. The leather of his boots was still wet, but there wasn't anything he could do about it. He gathered up the shirt she'd removed, shrugged into it, and then kept busy with menial tasks while she completed her dressing. He knew his family, no one would comment on their sleeping together, nor would they do anything to insult or cause Summer embarrassment.

"They all love you, you know." He nodded toward the tent door.

She finished buttoning her boots and then glanced up.

He couldn't read her expression, so he walked over and offered his hand to assist her to stand. When she wrapped her fingers around his, he asked teasingly, "Are your boots as wet as mine?"

A hint of a grin formed on her lips. "Yes."

"Sorry." He engulfed her into a hug.

"I forgive you." Summer laid her head on his chest, hugging his solid frame close. It helped to ease the fear working hard to fill her mind. The beautiful night they'd spent together wouldn't prevent the inevitable from happening. Maybe she should just flat out tell him about her part in Jonas's death. It would be a chance, a gamble if he'd forgive her, but anything would be better than the heavy weight hanging around, threatening to engulf her again. Or would it? Could she stand losing him? Losing all of the Quinters?

"Come on." Snake broke the hug and took her hand, tugging her toward the doorway. "I've got a lot of work to complete today. If we're lucky, we could be moving in by this weekend."

Despite the dread building deep in her soul, excitement bubbled. "Really?"

"Yes, really." He flipped open the doorway and led her into the bright sunshine.

The yappy-yap of the puppy instantly drew their attention. August ran in a wide circle with the yellow ball of fluff right at his heels. September sat nearby with baby Winifred sitting on her lap. Both of them clapped at the show. The brothers, along with a few men from town, worked away on the house, and the women, her sisters-in-law and Ma, were busy near the makeshift, outdoor kitchen. Everything looked normal, yet at the same time, it all looked different. The clarity was impeccable. As if her vision had been blurred and now crystal clear.

Summer turned to Snake. He winked and then kissed her cheek before letting go of her hand and making his way toward the house. She watched for a moment longer. There was barely a limp in his swagger. The wide brimmed hat covered the golden curls she'd ran her fingers through last night. Her belly stirred at the remembrance.

A carefree giggle drew her attention, and eyes,

from his departing shape. Turning, she witnessed September playfully fighting off kisses from Jerome. Hitching her skirt, she quickly made her way across the yard to rescue Winifred from September's lap. Jerome instantly took the baby's place, and September stretched out, letting the puppy romp on her stomach as he licked her face. The wholesome, genuine, laughter rippling the air was contagious, and Summer sat down, rubbing the pup's back with her free hand, giggling right along with her little sister.

"Isn't he wonderful?" September asked. Her blue eyes sparkled brighter than Summer had ever seen them.

"Yes, he's wonderful."

"He was the biggest of the batch," September continued. "And took to August right away."

Summer spotted August carrying a bowl. Water sloshed over the edges as he carefully picked a pathway back to the pup. "He seems to have taken a liking to you, too."

September grinned. The sight was breathtaking. "August said he asked and you said we could keep him," September said while still dodging Jerome's tongue.

"He did, and I did."

"Thank you, Summer. He's the best present we ever got." September sat up and settled the dog in her lap. Panting, Jerome rested his head on her arm. "Life sure has gotten good for us lately, hasn't it?"

Summer's attention automatically went to the house, where she instantly found Snake climbing a ladder, hammer in hand. "Yes, it has."

"It's not going to change, is it? We aren't going to have to leave, are we?"

The worry that overtook September's face stabbed her chest. Repositioning Winifred who was contently snuggled in her arm, Summer wrapped her other arm around September.

"I'll do everything I can to make sure we don't have to leave." Kissing the air above her sister's head, she silently vowed, *Everything I can to make sure they never learn the truth.*

If it was just her, she'd take the chance and tell Snake the truth, but when it came to the children—came to seeing they never again went cold, hungry, or unloved—she'd hold her secret until the day she died.

Chapter Sixteen

The work accomplished in the next two days was astonishing, and the love she found in Snake's bed each night, even more so. Bug had moved his belongings into the barn and created himself a palette to sleep on in the hayloft. Summer tried, though half-heartedly for she didn't want to return to Ma's tent, to convince him the move wasn't necessary.

August, on the other hand, was more than happy to join Bug in the barn, for there he didn't need to worry about Jerome leaving a puddle in the middle of the night. The pup seemed to grow every minute—at the rate he was going, he'd catch up to his paws within a week—and his connection with August multiplied as quickly as his size. The two were practically glued to one another.

The now common sound of puppy paws on the new floorboards of the house echoed behind her. Summer paused in sweeping the sawdust off the floor of the kitchen caused by the construction of the cupboards lining one wall to let the pair race past her. Together, the boy and his dog bound out the doorway. Bug, carrying the door for the framed in area, hoisted the large planked wood over his head and spun about as August and Jerome dashed under his arms.

"Sorry, Bug!" August called, "Jerome has to puddle."

"No problem, Buddy. Can't have an accident in the new house," Bug replied cheerily while he finagled the door back down and carried it across the porch deck. After propping it against the house, he walked in the space, each footstep echoing off the newly built walls. "So? What do you think?"

"I can't believe how big it is." Summer pointed around with one hand. The kitchen walls had been covered with lath and plaster, and one entire wall held upper and lower cabinets. "I watched it rise from the ground, but until I started sweeping, I didn't realize its true size."

Bug pulled the hammer out of his back pocket. "Yeah. I bet we could fit our old house in the kitchen and dining room alone." After grabbing a handful of nails from the bucket on the counter, he walked back out the doorway.

"Don't forget the indoor plumbing."

Snake's voice had her pivoting. The broom handle slipped from her grasp and clattered to the floor. He moved from the arched doorway that led to the front rooms of the house and picked up the broom before she gathered enough sense to bend down to retrieve it.

"I thought you went to town," she said.

"I did," he answered, leaning the broom against one of the cupboards. "I'm back." His hands cupped her elbows, and her knees quivered, as they took to doing every time he was near. She wasn't afraid of him, but the fear of losing him was something she thought about regularly.

"Did you miss me?"

She locked her knees, guaranteeing she wouldn't topple like the broom had, and met his gleaming eyes. "If you must know. Yes, I missed you."

His laugh ricocheted about the empty room. "I missed you, too." Drawing her closer, he added, "Come here, so I can show you how much."

Her heart thudded faster and harder than the hammers had the past weeks. His lips, soft and warm, touch hers briefly, and she, wanting more, slipped her hands around his waist and clutched onto his shirt.

"Mmm..." His lips vibrated against hers. "You did miss me."

She pressed her mouth against his, needing a deep, thorough kiss as badly as a wilted plant needed water. He teased her, dodging her lips and nuzzling her neck and ear lobe. His hands trailed down her sides and then back and forth across her back.

Heating up, from tip to top, she moaned.

He chuckled.

Her control snapped. She leaned back and grasped his cheeks with both hands, but when she stretched on her toes to meet his lips, he tilted away. "Do you want me to kiss you?" he teased.

"Yes," she groaned.

His lips touched the tip of her nose. "Why?"

"Why?" she managed to ask without screaming.

He continued to tease and tempt, brushing his lips over her eyebrows, cheeks, and the tip of her chin. "Yes, why do you want me to kiss you?"

She moaned as his lips fluttered over the top of hers to land on her other cheek.

"Is it because you like me?"

"Yes," she muttered, trying to catch his lips as they slipped over hers again.

"You do?"

"Yes, I do." He was stronger, no matter how hard she tugged on his head he pulled away from her lips. "Or at least I did." She dropped her hands.

He continued to grant little kisses, here and there. She forced herself to stand as stiff and cold as stone. After a few other touches, he leaned back to stare at her. Summer knew her glare looked more like a pout, but didn't care. She was pouting.

His eyes sparkled brighter than fireflies. "Come here."

It took every ounce of willpower she had to dodge his lips. "No."

"No?"

"No."

His brows arched. "You don't want me to kiss you?"

"Nope." She swallowed. If he could play this game so could she. But it was hard. Big, familiar and, oh so wonderful hands, were still working their magic on her back, making her skin quiver beneath her dress.

"Okay." He shrugged and pivoted on one foot.

Dumbfounded, but not dumb, she snatched his arm before he stepped away. His gaze sent the smoldering fire inside her loins into flames. The smile on his face grew serious as he pulled her close and kissed her with all the passion she'd wanted in the first place. Her hands couldn't find a place to rest. She squeezed, caressed, clutched, and kneaded, all the while smothering herself in his kiss, and molding her shape to his.

It wasn't enough. Fire consumed her, and his hands readily stoked the flames like dry oak in an open pit. "Snake," she pleaded between kisses, begging him to satisfy the want encompassing her.

He grasped her backside and forced her hips against his. It helped but didn't begin to satisfy. When he eased his hold, she lifted her head, wondering where he'd lead her to so they could complete their union. But he wrapped his arms around her shoulders and tucked her head against his shoulder.

She squirmed. He whispered, "Shhh."

"Wh—"

"Summer! Didn't you hear me yelling?" August's voice hit her like icicles falling off a roof top. "Bug's got that door in the way. I had to run all the way around and come in the front. I was hollering and

195

hollering, and—"

"You're inside now, August, there's no need to yell," Snake instructed calmly.

Summer trembled too hard to speak, and clung to Snake's side as he turned them to face August.

"What did you need?" Snake spoke her thoughts.

"Summer, you gotta come see this guy!" August exclaimed.

"Who?" she asked, gaining a touch of control.

"The guy Snake and Skeeter brought home."

She looked to her husband.

Snake grinned. "He's a friend of the family."

Friend or not, she really had no desire to meet someone new. She wanted to shoo August on his way, and resume her position in Snake's arms. Since that wasn't about to happen, she asked, "Oh? Who is it?"

Keeping his arm around her, Snake guided her through the unfinished house and around piles and crates of furniture stacked in the front room.

"Buffalo Killer. He lives out by Skeeter and Lila."

The soles of Summer's boots grew spikes, causing both she and Snake to stumble to a stop.

"Buffalo Killer? He's an Indian?"

Snake eased his hand from her shoulder to gently hold her upper arm. She quivered beneath his fingertips. Concern replaced the pleasure that had been singing in his chest.

"Yes," he admitted. "Buffalo Killer is an Indian. But more importantly, he's a family friend. He and Skeeter have been friends for years. There's nothing to fear."

Her eyes had grown wary, and a frown wrinkled the normally smooth space between her delicate brows.

He brushed a few stray hairs away from her cheek, tucking the strands behind one dainty ear, before pulling her closer. "As long as I live, I promise you'll never have anything to worry about. Nothing to fear."

The top of her head brushed the underside of his chin as she shook it from side to side.

"That's an impossible promise to keep." Her voice held anguish.

He set her a few inches away, so he could look deep into her dark eyes as he swore a solemn oath, "It's a promise I'll do everything within my power to keep." His words settled deep in his soul. He'd never spoken a more true or genuine statement.

August, who had dashed out the doorway earlier, darted back in. "Ain't you coming?" His blue eyes flashed between Snake and Summer. "You two ain't kissing again, is ya?"

"Yes, we're coming," Snake answered. Upon seeing the faint blush on Summer's cheeks, a touch of mirth rippled his chest. He couldn't contain the chance to tease her just a bit.

"And yes," he said, tugging her forward. "We are kissing again."

"Sheesh!" August declared. The echoing departure of footsteps said the child must have left. Snake didn't bother to glance that way. He was much too busy once again reveling in the honeydew sweetness of Summer's mouth.

When they parted this time, it wasn't the heated want of bedding her filling his system, but the dreamy warmth of contentment swirling from head to toe.

He took her hand. "Come on, you'll like Buffalo Killer. I promise."

She fell into step beside him. The pride he felt every time he introduced her swelled his chest. Someday the buttons might pop right off his shirt. It would be worth it, a few lost buttons. Having her at his side was worth more than all the buttons, gold or silver, this side of the Mississippi. With one hand on her elbow, he guided her across the large front porch and down the steps of their new home.

Buffalo Killer stood amongst the crowd, gesturing as he spoke to Kid, Skeeter, Bug, and Hog. The man's movements and voice stilled as he caught sight of them. An eerie sensation tickled the back of Snake's neck. The look in the Indian's eyes made him recall how Buffalo Killer had wanted Skeeter to share Lila when they'd first met. Snake's jaw tensed, and he glared at the Indian, clearly stating he wasn't any more willing to share than his brother had been. However, Buffalo Killer's gaze never left Summer.

When they arrived near the group, Snake was ready to declare his property, but Buffalo Killer didn't give him the chance. The man stepped forward, a startled look filling his black eyes.

"Summer Dove?" Buffalo Killer sounded astonished.

Summer stumbled. Snake caught her, and she clung to his arm as if unable to stand on her own.

Buffalo Killer shot an expectant and somewhat excited glance around. "Silver Bird? Where is she?"

Just then September walked out of the barn, carrying Winifred on one hip as usual. Buffalo Killer took a step forward then paused. He spun back to stare at Summer. "Where's Silver Bird?"

Summer's hold on his arm lessened, and Snake, feeling about as disorientated as a jackrabbit in a stampede of cattle, turned to question her. The flesh on her face had grown chalky white. As he reached for her, her eyes rolled back. He caught her as she crumpled.

Hoisting her limp body into his arms, he turned to Buffalo Killer. "What the hell is going on here?"

The man's answer was lost in the crowd. Ma shouted to carry Summer to the tent. September screamed, which caused Winifred to start crying. Jessie took the baby while Randi wrapped her arms around the girl.

And August, crying, clawed at Snake's pant leg. "She ain't dead, is she Snake? Summer ain't dead, is she? You can't let her die, Snake. You can't let her die!"

"She's not dead, August," Snake managed to say when the child took a breath. "She just fainted. Let go so I can go lie her down." He glanced to Kid, who stepped forward to tug August off his leg.

Summer came to before he got her to the tent. She lifted her arms, looped them around his neck, and hid her face in the crook of his shoulder. He gestured the others away from the tent and carried her in. Rather than lay her down, he sat, cradling her on his lap. The bed sank beneath their weight. A sigh, as gentle and light as a leaf falling from a tree, slipped between her lips, brushing his skin exposed by the open buttons of his shirt.

He repositioned her and tugged his arm from beneath her knees to use his fingers to tenderly encourage her chin to tilt up so he could look at her. Blinking due to the muted light of the tent after the bright sunshine outside, he stared at her still face. The long lashes of her eyelids fluttered, but didn't lift.

Ma, her face contoured with worry, entered the tent. Without a word, she handed him a damp cloth and then left again. He laid it over Summer's forehead. A million and one thoughts raced across his mind, but only the one, which was concerning her welfare, took root. The possibility she could be ill—seriously so—scared the dickens out of him. What would he do if something happened—if she'd acquired the fever and couldn't be saved?

No. Snake shook his head, dismissing the thought. She wasn't ill. No one had had the fever in ages. She was just frightened by seeing Buffalo Killer. The Indian, with his buckskin britches and fringed moccasins, could be scary if you didn't know him.

Snake ran the cloth over her cheeks and chin, and then back up to her forehead. Buffalo Killer needed to learn to wear clothes around the women. He'd talk to the man about it.

Summer sighed again. The unreadable depths of her dark eyes made a tight band squeeze his heart. Snake swallowed, trying to relieve the pressure.

"Are you all right?"

She nodded. "I'm sorry-I—"

"Shh," he encouraged, kissing her brow.

Shaking her head, she pushed herself upright and onto the edge of his knees. "I know him."

"Buffalo Killer?"

She nodded.

"You've met him before? Where? When?"

"I don't know. But I know him."

An uneasy and peculiar sensation, not unlike a being stabbed by a dozen porcupine quills, developed on every inch of his skin. "What do you mean?"

She closed her eyes, sheltering her face with both hands.

The quills dug in deeper. "Summer?" he asked, not knowing what else to do.

It was a long, quiet, and forlorn moment before she dropped her hands.

Damn, he had a lot to learn about women.

"Summer," he repeated. "Talk to me. I can't help if I don't know what's wrong."

She turned, looking at him with a sober gaze.

"Why do men always think they can help? Sometimes there's nothing to be done."

He tucked her hair behind her ear again. It was a simple thing, but he enjoyed doing it. The silky strands flowed beneath his fingers as he smoothed the hair in place.

"There is always something that can be done."

She shook her head.

"Why do I have the feeling we aren't talking about Buffalo Killer?" he asked, feeling the quills again.

This time her sigh was weighted with tension. She leaned back. He gathered her closer, gladly shouldering any worry she was willing to let go. It was obvious she wasn't going to answer, so he changed the subject.

"When did you meet Buffalo Killer before?"

"I don't know. Honestly, I don't know."

He held her, letting the silence filter around them like water filling up a bucket. The shaft of light that entered the tent was like a welcoming beacon. Snake lifted his gaze to the tent flap. Skeeter poked his head in.

His brother glanced between the two of them cautiously. Summer opened her eyes, and her slight nod gave Snake the approval to acknowledge his brother.

"Come on in."

"You doing all right, Summer?" Skeeter asked.

"Yes, thank you." She sat up, but Snake kept her from scooting off his lap.

"Buffalo Killer is really worried. He didn't mean to frighten you," Skeeter offered.

"He didn't frighten me. It was more like a shock."

Skeeter sat down on the trunk beside the bed. "So you remember him? You know he's your brother?"

Her spine grew stiff, and she began to tremble. "Brother?"

"Brother?" Snake asked at the same time.

Skeeter removed his hat and scratched his head, making his mop of blond curls stick out in all directions. "That's what he says."

"How can that be?" Snake asked.

"He wants to come in and talk to you. Is that all right?" Skeeter's eyes were on Summer.

She clutched onto Snake's arm, her tiny nails digging deep into the skin beneath his shirt sleeve.

"You don't have to talk to him," Snake assured.

"No, I want to." Her eyes met his. "Will you stay with me?"

He brushed his lips against her brow and held them there, wanting her to know how much he cared for her—about her.

"I'm not going anywhere." Snake glanced to Skeeter. "Send him in."

Skeeter replaced his hat as he stood. "Buffalo Killer's a good man, Summer. I'd be right proud to call him my brother."

She nodded.

Before Skeeter slipped out the flap, he turned back to them. "He can talk in full sentences. I told him to knock off the one syllable shit."

In his own way, even Skeeter was looking out for her. The knowledge was doubled-edged to Snake.

Summer squirmed out of his hold and stood beside the bed. He rose to stand beside her, keeping one hand on the small of her back, where he could still feel the trembles rippling her spine.

Chapter Seventeen

Summer didn't realize she was holding her breath until her lungs grew hot and hard. She parted her lips, letting the air flow out, and gulped in another breath as the flap opened again. The moccasins were the first thing she saw. The familiarity tickled her spine. His footsteps were silent in the hide that had turned black from wear. The ties holding the footwear in place were brown, as were the deerskin pants that hugged the man's thick thighs and waist. That was where any type of clothing stopped. Buffalo Killer's chest was broad and golden brown, not unlike her skin. His flesh was darker, exposed regularly to the sun.

His hair was uncontained. No hat, no headband, just long black tresses that hung past his shoulders. Summer, growing lightheaded from holding her breath for so long, let the air flow out of her mouth again.

Buffalo Killer walked toward the bed. His gaze moved to Snake, standing stiffly at her side. She felt rather than saw the nod of acknowledgement her husband offered. The Indian accepted the greeting with like actions and then settled his dark eyes on her.

"Summer Dove," he said, bowing his head slightly.

"It's just Summer," she answered, for no particular reason, other than it gave herself a sense of who she was.

"I'm sorry. I didn't mean to frighten you. I was just shocked to see you. We thought you were dead."

Buffalo Killer stopped directly in front of her. His eyes seemed to inspect her from head to toe.

"I'm very much alive. As you can see."

"And very much married," Snake added.

Buffalo Killer looked as if he tried to hide a smile. A small smirk lifted the corners of his mouth as he turned to Snake. "Your wife is my sister."

"Just so you remember she's my wife."

Buffalo Killer nodded.

"How can I be your sister?"

"Shall we sit?" Buffalo Killer pointed to the bed.

Summer didn't move. Part of her wanted to run from the tent. Not only was it warm, she was beginning to feel smothered. Did she want to know what Buffalo Killer had to say? How much did he know?

Snake eased her onto the mattress, giving her no choice but to sit beside him as Buffalo Killer took a seat on the chest Skeeter had sat upon earlier.

"Your mother, Silver Bird, was my father's second wife. She came to live with us when I was a boy. Her family had died on their way to the big waters. She was happy. We all were. There were many buffalo then. I remember her laugh. It was like a singing bird, happy and full of song. We had a great celebration when you were born." Buffalo Killer's eyes sparkled, and his voice carried a sense of happy memories. "We had good moons. Happy moons. The Great One kissed you."

For a moment the sound of her mother's laugh filled her ears. She remembered it, too, just as he described it. The rest of his words settled. "The great one?" she asked.

He nodded and gestured around the room. "The Great One."

A flood of warmth encompassed her. Summer stilled her thoughts, wondering if it was Jonas, The Great One, or Snake's arm which had settled on her shoulders. She glanced over and met the concerned gaze of her husband. A smile grew easily on her lips. He grinned back, and his hold tightened.

Turning to Buffalo Killer, she asked, "What happened?"

"The white man's army came and took you and Silver Bird. There was much bloodshed. Many of our people were captured and taken to the Ok-la-ho-ma land. The ones they couldn't catch, me and our father and several others, tried to find you, but the yellow haired Chief said you were dead. He said we could stay if we promised not to fight with the settlers. Our father agreed because he believed you were not dead. He said you'd come back some day, and he'd be there when you did."

"I-is he still alive?"

"Yes."

"What's his name?"

"Chief Red Elk."

In all her years of making up stories as to whom she was, she'd never once proclaimed to be a Chief's daughter. The knowledge made something she had to consider as pride—since it was an unusually new sensation—settle inside her chest. Questioning the feeling, and her hearing, she asked, "My father is a Chief?"

"Yes. Our father is the Chief."

She planted both hands on the mattress beside her hips, stabilizing herself as the room began to swirl. All the years of not knowing, of wondering, came like a spring flood. Summer closed her eyes to the rush of emotions. Doubt stuck its head up like a vicious serpent. Her eyes snapped open.

"Maybe you're wrong. Maybe I'm not your sister."

Buffalo Killer folded his arms across his mighty chest. "I not wrong."

"But it's been years. Perhaps—"

His interruption was stern. "I know my blood. You are my sister."

"There are others...like me. Half breeds."

His eyes grew narrow. The sight was fearsome. "I have no other sisters. No other brothers."

Half afraid of offending him further, yet needing to know, she continued, "But how can you know? I don't look like my mother, and I must have been a toddler the last time you saw me—for I don't remember any of it."

He let out an exasperated sigh, and his expression grew soft and caring. "You look like our Grandmother. That's how I know."

"I do?"

"Your eyes. They're just like Grandmother's. You see things others cannot. You know things others don't."

A chill raced up her spine. She dug her nails onto Snake's knee beside hers as the chill sent her heart tumbling inside her chest. It landed in the pit of her stomach. Buffalo Killer knew. He knew about Jonas.

****

Snake had spent most of the afternoon working on the house. It was coming along quickly, and by tomorrow they would be able to move the furniture in, but today, his heart wasn't in it. It was jumbled up in his throat, choking off his airway and leaving a rotten egg feeling deep in his gut.

The sun was lowering itself in the blue sky, sending ribbons of crimson and orange to float amongst the fluffy white clouds. Ma's old dinner bell had rang across the prairie a few minutes ago, and moments later the pounding, sawing, and overall racket of men working had faded as the others stopped for the day. He should pack up his tools, too, and climb down from where he sat. The shake shingles covering the peaked roofs of the dormer

206

windows on the back side of the house were all in place. Had been for the last half hour or so. The ladder leaned against the side of the house, patiently waiting for him to climb down, but he didn't. Instead he let his gaze wander, to find the meadowlark chirping it's melody in the tree limb nearby and then move on to watch the wind rustling the leaves and spindly branches of the weeping willow.

He'd left Summer in the capable hands of his sisters-in-law, after she'd recovered from the shock of learning her parentage, but later he'd seen she and Buffalo Killer sitting together beneath the shade of an elm in the front yard, deep in conversation. He'd wanted to join them, wanted to know what they discussed. Yet, he knew she needed time alone with her brother. His sour stomach erupted again, sending bile to the back of his throat.

She'd found her family, or her family had found her. Whichever way he looked at it, it disturbed him. He wanted to be happy for her, knowing her lack of history had been a disturbance to her, but there was another deep down, gut feeling, eating at him.

He removed his hat and swiped his brow with his shirt sleeve. The problem was he understood the feeling. It was fear he felt. Fear she'd want to return to the Badlands with Buffalo Killer. Did she feel more of a draw to her long lost family than to the one she'd recently acquired? He had no way of knowing. He loved her deeply, and unconditionally, but their love was new—could it withstand this?

They had a deep connection—of that he had no doubt. And she responded to his touch with ferocity, but he had a feeling it was all on the surface. There was something deep down inside her, a place he couldn't touch, nor get a glimpse of, that had never opened up to him, and that's what haunted him now.

The ladder jiggled, and he glanced down to see who climbed the rungs. Kid peered over the roof edge a moment later. "Hey, little brother, didn't you hear the dinner bell?"

"Yes, I heard it."

"Need some help finishing up?"

"No. I'm coming," he answered, but didn't move.

Kid climbed another rung and rested his elbows on the shingles covering the eve running the length of the first story. "Who would have thought it? Buffalo Killer and Summer. Pretty amazing."

"Yeah. Amazing."

Kid's brows crinkled. "You don't sound right. What's up?"

"Nothing."

His brother glanced around, staring for a moment at the leaves hanging on the spindly branches and dancing in the wind before he turned back and let out a half chuckle. "You know, there was a time when I thought I knew it all. I criticized Pa for the life he lived. I criticized you boys for being young and inquisitive. I doubted things, too—like Jessie's love. That is until she showed me how wrong I could be. And that I didn't know it all. In all actuality, what I did know didn't amount to a hill of beans."

Snake had an idea where Kid was going with his revelations, but he rested an elbow on his knee, and listened, figured there would be a moral in it somewhere. There always was with Kid.

"Until I met her, I thought I had it all. Cattle. A ranch. A fine house. Money in the bank." Kid's gaze grew serious. "In reality, I had nothing. Oh, I had the basic necessities, but a man can get those practically anywhere. In Jessie, I found my life. Without her I was a shell, walking around empty. I got along just fine, but only because I didn't know what I was missing. Now that I do, I have a different outlook on things. I wake up every morning excited to work, not because I want to succeed, want to have the largest ranch in Kansas, but because I want her and the children to have food, clothing, shelter, and most of all, happiness."

Snake understood; he, too, had a new outlook on life since Summer had arrived that hot, sunny day, still, he had to wonder if Kid was—in his own way—trying to say something more.

Kid cupped the rounded tops of the ladder legs, and stretched like he had a kink in his back. "If Jessie told me she wouldn't be happy unless we packed up and moved to New York City. I'd load the wagon up today."

Frowning, Snake asked, "New York City? That ain't likely to happen."

"No, it's not, but that's not the point."

"Then what is?"

"If my wife wanted to travel across the state to be reunited with the family she'd lost years ago, I'd say, let's go."

"You would?"

"Yes."

"What about all this?" Snake waved a hand, indicating the homestead.

"What about it? It'll still be here when you get back."

"What if she doesn't want to return?"

"Then Bug and Ma have a brand new house all to themselves."

"What about my wheat fields, my irrigation systems, my..." he let the words fade before anymore formed on his tongue. He already knew the answer.

"They don't matter as much as Summer does, do they?" Kid asked.

Snake shook his head. The rotten eggs in his stomach had faded away as gently as the new emotions had flooded in to take their place. The feelings that said he loved Summer, and would rather live with nothing, than without her. He glanced at his brother, ready to admit how he'd felt.

"I guess I just didn't like the idea of sharing her."

Kid nodded. "I worried about that when Jessie was pregnant. Wondered if she'd still have time for me once the baby was born. Want to know what she said to me when she figured out my worries?"

"Yeah," Snake admitted, nodding for Kid to go on.

"She said her love wasn't divided between the baby and me. It was multiplied. And you know what?"

"What?"

"She was right. The more people we have to love, the bigger our hearts become."

Snake had to blink a couple times to clear the film from his eyes. Kid, nor any of his brothers were sappy philosophers, yet, listening to what Kid said was like reading Revelations, and understanding it.

A chuckle coughed up his throat. He let it out and leaned down to grab the long handle of his wooden tool chest.

"You know," he said as he hoisted one leg over the dormer roof. "I never imagined there'd be a day when I was jealous of Buffalo Killer."

Kid laughed. "Don't feel so bad. I remember a day when I was jealous of Joe."

"Joe?" Snake was astounded. Kid's old ranch foreman had to be seventy if he was a day.

With a grimace Kid admitted, "Actually, it was more than a day."

Snake hooted then. The image of Kid jealous, was one thing—for everyone knew how protective he was of Jessie. Snake had almost met his demise once for losing her—but "Joe?" he repeated aloud.

Kid, laughing good naturedly, began to climb down the ladder. "Yes, Joe. I can laugh about it now, but at one time, I was mad enough to shoot the old coot."

They were still chuckling when they rounded the house to where the women had the tables set with enough food to feed half the state. Snake took a moment to consider his family as he set aside his tool box and moved to the water basin. Randi loved to cook, and she put great efforts into every meal she prepared. Hog, who loved to cook so much he opened a restaurant, had willingly stepped aside so his wife could prepare meals at their fine establishment. Skeeter, who'd never had a care in his life, had tossed aside every carefree manner in order to provide for his family. Matter of fact, he was probably the most serious one of the family anymore. And Kid, well, he knew exactly where Kid stood when it came to his oldest brother's family.

There wasn't one in the bunch who'd question his leaving if Summer wanted to go meet her family. Especially not Ma. Family meant more to her than the sun did to the earth.

He wiped the water from his hands and face, and tossed the towel over the hook on the side of the stump. Hell, he'd been worrying all day for nothing.

Turning around, he noted his wife walked toward him. As their eyes met, he grinned. The relief in her face grew into a wide smile. They met halfway to the table, and not caring who watched, he folded her into an embrace and while the sun filled the horizon with an evening glow and the wind fluttered by on its way to Missouri, he kissed the dickens out of her.

It was the hooting and giggles that finally made them break apart. For the first time since their marriage, she didn't seem to mind his public affections. She'd never shied from his private ones, but before now, he'd always sensed her nervousness when it came to kissing or touching in front of family. This time, when he settled his arm around her shoulders, she leaned against him, and stayed there as they walked to the table.

The meal proceeded leisurely, with mellow conversations and playful teasing amongst the brothers. Randi had outdone herself again with a savory chicken dish smothering fresh biscuits, and beets boiled with light seasonings that made him favor the vegetable he'd often avoided in the past.

After everyone finished off the large slices of spice cake, which August devoured, claiming it was as good as chocolate, the women started to clear the table. Skeeter rose and with a nod, he gestured Snake to follow. The rest of the brothers were already moseying toward the house, as if there was something that needed all of their attention. Snake glanced to where Summer stood, hands in the dishwater. He loved the curves of her slender frame, and smiled at the graceful way she swayed aside as September lowered another handful of dirty plates into the basin of water.

A weight landed on his shoulder. "Come on," Skeeter said. There was a touch of urgency in his tone.

Snake rose, after tossing a wink toward Summer when she turned his way, he followed his brother across the yard. The rest had gathered near the end of the porch, where everyone had stacked their tools and supplies for the night. Skeeter was not his normal happy self. He was quiet and thoughtful. And that alone was enough to make Snake wary. By the time they arrived on the porch, his nerves were skating beneath his skin.

"What's up?" he asked before climbing the final step.

Skeeter pointed to Buffalo Killer. "He knows who started the fire."

"Started the fire?" Snake stopped shy of asking what fire, realizing Skeeter meant the one that burnt the house. As far as he knew, Sheriff Turley hadn't identified the source.

"It was a grass fire. Lightning starts them all the time."

"Not this one," Buffalo Killer insisted.

"How do you know?" Snake stepped onto the porch and leaned back against the newly installed rail.

"I looked."

"That's it? You looked?" Snake questioned.

A rooster pheasant cackled in the distance, the sound was ominous as the men stood silent. Stone faced, his brothers, glanced between him and Buffalo Killer. Regret at snapping his thoughts, made Snake shake his head.

"Sorry. What do you mean, you looked? You found where the fire started?"

"Yes. And several others. But they died out before traveling far. This one was herded to your house like a stampede of buffalo."

Snake took in the solemn faces of his brothers before asking, "What are you saying? That someone burnt us out on purpose?"

Buffalo Killer gave a single head nod.

"Who?"

"Wainwright would be my guess," Bug said, straightening out the end of a shovel with the toe of his boot. "Seems like something the coward would do."

Snake's chest grew tight. With everything else going on, he'd forgotten the man was still out there. Or had been anyway. The fire had been weeks ago. By now the Mexican trader was probably on the other side of the Rio Grande, trading off some poor little girls he'd captured along the way.

"What do you want to do, Snake?" The sound of Kid's voice snapped his attention.

"Me? What do I want to do?" He scratched at the

back of his head. Kid was the oldest. The rest had always looked up to him for the answers, for the decisions as to what came next. They were all looking at him though, and Snake didn't have an answer for them.

Buffalo Killer crossed his arms. "He left a trail."

"He did?" Skeeter asked, pushing off the rail to stand stiff.

"It probably leads all the way to Mexico," Snake guessed.

"No," Buffalo Killer said.

"Where to then?" Bug voiced what they were all wondering.

"I didn't follow, but he's not far."

"Not far?" The sensation of being watched made Snake spin around. The rest of the brothers did the same. Without speaking, they stared across the plains searching for whoever was out there. It was Wainwright. The man had probably been watching them the entire time. How had he forgotten? Overnight his world had gone from taking care of little more than wheat fields and irrigation plans to a wife, two children—a family—an entire family— including a hat-wearing Maisy and floppy-eared Jerome.

Unprepared for the responsibility, he now accepted wholehearted, he let his thoughts smolder for a few moments, before he turned to Kid. "We need to gather some information. Know what we're dealing with."

Kid nodded. "I'll ride into town tomorrow and talk to Turley."

A few years ago, Kid wouldn't have sought out the Sheriff's help if his life depended on it. Actually, his life had depended on it. His brother had changed. It had been subtle and happened over time, therefore Snake hadn't noticed how drastic the change had been. Or maybe he had noticed and had been frightened by what he saw. At the time, he'd thought marriage was the last thing he wanted. But now, after all was said and done, he wouldn't change his life for all the wheat in Kansas.

He turned to face the group of men behind and beside him. His brothers, Kid, Skeeter, Hog, and Bug, and their friend, Buffalo Killer. They were a formidable bunch and a sense of thankfulness—that they were on his side—swelled in his chest.

"That's a good start, Kid. I appreciate it. Bug, you go with Buffalo Killer. Do a bit of scouting. Check out the fire lines he found and check out the trail."

Bug slapped Buffalo Killer on the back.

The Indian stared at the hand, frowning.

"We're on it," Bug said once a grin formed on Buffalo Killer's face.

"Yes." Buffalo Killer's agreement was simple, yet Snake knew it was deep and sincere.

Snake then turned to Hog and Skeeter. "We have to be extra diligent. Make sure the women and children are never alone." The past few weeks flashed before his eyes. Times when he'd been so busy on the house he hadn't known where Summer, or September and August had been. That would never happen again.

"The house is completed enough. Let's move everyone out of the tents tonight," Hog said, his barrel chest puffed.

"No," Skeeter, looking willowy next to Hog, said, "That might upset the women. There's no sense in upsetting them if we don't have to. They're ready to move in tomorrow. Nothing is going to happen tonight. We'll take turns guarding the place."

"We'll act tonight just as we have every night," Snake insisted. "You'll all head to Kid's, and the rest of us will stay in the tents. If someone is watching, we don't want them to know we're on to them."

Chapter Eighteen

The men remained on the porch long after she'd finished the dishes. The way they hovered made Summer wonder. Engrossed in what the men might be discussing, her gaze roamed from one to the other, trying to decipher their facial expressions. They gave nothing away. Her heart however, skipped around in her chest as her eyes naturally roamed back to Snake's broad shoulders. Just the sight of him, no matter how innocent, sent butterflies fluttering in her insides.

Buffalo Killer, her newly found brother, came into view beside her husband. Her insides flittered again. This time with apprehension. They'd sat for hours under the tree, talking about a time she didn't remember, but he talked as if she should. Faint memories had speckled her mind. Surely she'd been too young to remember, yet she had a sense that she did. Not really people or places, but feelings. Happiness and love.

July Austin had been with the riders who'd raided the camp. She told Buffalo Killer about July's death. It had been then that Buffalo Killer asked her a poignant question.

Grasping her cheeks, looking deep into her eyes, he'd asked why she let a dead man steal her joy. At first she hadn't understood, but then, after he walked away, shaking his head, she comprehended. Why did she still allow July to influence her life?

All of a sudden something hit the back of her knee. Stumbling to keep from falling, she grabbed for the makeshift counter. Jerome, wrapped in the yards of gingham between her ankles, twisted to be released.

The basin, thankfully empty, slid across the narrow shelf, and squealing as her feet went out from beneath her, Summer hit the ground. With a ringing clatter, the basin bounced off her head and then clanged on the ground. Yipping and tearing up the dirt beneath his claws, Jerome shot out from beneath her skirt like a bullet.

Before she had a chance to catch her breath, Snake was lifting her from the ground.

"What happened?" he asked. "Are you hurt?" His hands patted her arms and waist. When he knelt down, inching up her skirt to examine her legs, she batted his hands away.

"I'm fine. I'm not hurt."

"Are you sure? What happened?"

She wasn't certain what had happened and glanced around. August, clutching a squirming Jerome to his chest, had tears rolling out of his eyes. Wary, his watery eyes bounced between her and Snake. The fact of what the child expected hit her.

She stepped toward August, but Snake was already moving that way. Her throat locked up, remembering how July had punished the child more than once.

Hiccupping and trembling from head to toe, the child stared at Snake. "You gotta whip me, don't you, Snake?"

A crowd had gathered, and every person, man, woman, and child, went stone silent. August's statement seemed to echo off the wind.

Summer wanted to rush forward and put herself between Snake and August, but there wasn't room, Snake had already knelt down in front of her brother, and his hands were resting on August's small, shaking shoulders.

"What happened, August?" he asked.

The sound of his voice reminded Summer it was Snake, not July the child had to answer to. She slumped with relief. A hand settled on her shoulder as Lila came to stand beside her. The comfort was appreciated.

"I threw a stick for Jerome. It landed behind Summer." August paused to take in a shaky breath. "Jerome runs faster than me. He got there first and slid under her skirt." Squeezing the puppy, he shook his head. "He didn't mean to make her fall. Honest he didn't."

"I'm sure he didn't," Snake said, rubbing the pup's head. "But you know better than to throw sticks near people, don't you?"

August nodded. Tears continued to run down his face.

With the edge of a thumb, Snake wiped one of August's red cheeks. "A dog is a lot of responsibility. It's your job to teach him how to behave. What if he'd knocked over one of the little kids?"

Bowing his head, August answered, "They could have gotten hurt."

"That's right. And Jerome could have been hurt, too."

August lifted his head, meeting Snake's gaze. "I understand you gotta whip me, Snake. I won't hold it against you."

Lila gasped and her arm wrapped around Summer's shoulders. She glanced at her sister-in-law. Tears fell from Lila's eyes, too. Summer turned back to her little brother. Snake had pulled the boy and the dog into his big arms.

"I'm not going to whip you, August." He held the child tight for several seconds. When they separated, he kept the child's attention by looking him straight on. "I'm not saying some day you won't do something that I'll have to punish you for, but this, today, was an accident. I do need you to promise it won't happen again."

August's chin had fallen. His mouth gaped open. Blinking, he asked, "You ain't gonna whip me?"

Snake shook his head. "But you have to promise this won't happen again."

"It won't. I promise."

"Good enough, then," Snake said, patting August's cheek.

August set Jerome on the ground and wrapped both arms around Snake's neck. The child whispered, but the crowd was so quiet, everyone heard, "I sure do wish you were my Pa, Snake. I sure do wish it."

Snake held the child, rocking him back and forth, for some time before he gripped August's teary cheeks. "I'm not your Pa, August, we both know that."

The child nodded.

"But I'd be right proud if you pretended I was."

August reached up and laid his little hands on both sides of Snake's face. His steady gaze was deeply sincere. "You mean it? I could pretend you are my Pa?"

Snake nodded.

Beside her, Lila was sobbing now, softly, but Summer could hear it, even over her own crying. The tears trickling down her face increased when August asked, "September, too?"

Snake turned and held one hand out to September. The girl stepped forward, tears covering her cheeks as well. "September, too," Snake said, pulling September into a three-way embrace.

Lila pushed Summer forward. Questioning, Summer glanced at the other woman.

"Go hug your family," Lila whispered. "I know how strongly this family loves children who aren't of their blood. Trust me, there's no difference in their eyes."

Summer looked back to the kids holding on to Snake.

"It doesn't matter where you're from, or how you came to be, once you're a Quinter, you're always a Quinter," Lila said, pushing Summer harder.

Snake turned his neck, glancing up at Summer as September hugged his one side and August his other. His eyes said it all. Summer stepped forward, dropped to her knees, and wrapped her arms around all three of them. Life couldn't get any better.

Jerome, sitting between Snake's knees, decided he needed to be part of the affection taking place and started licking everyone's chin. His lapping, as well as the giggles and squirming his love ensued made everyone lose their balance. Soon they were all four on the ground. Summer's head was on one of Snake's shoulder, September the other, and August, still holding onto Snake's neck was plastered on his chest. Jerome, with great enthusiasm leaped about, lathering each one of them with his non-stop tongue.

Snake planted a kiss on September's crown, then August's, and then Summer's lips, before he grabbed the dog. His arms, still around her and September, tightened as he lifted the pup, and kissed Jerome's puppy head before he asked, "Will someone please take this little monster?"

Laughter boomed across the plains. Bug took the dog while others reached down to offer a hand up. The incident was over, yet the significance of it would last forever—for her, Snake, September, and August.

Buffalo Killer helped her rise, and when Summer reached down to brush the dirt from her skirts, he gathered both of her hands. "Hold the joy you're feeling right now, little sister. Don't let someone steal it from you again."

Her mind wasn't fast enough to respond before he let go and walked away. As Buffalo Killer paused to speak with Lila, Summer's head spun. She had more questions than answers. What had Lila meant about children that weren't theirs?

Snake's arms, wrapping around her waist from behind changed the route of her tumbling thoughts. She pivoted inside his hold, wrapping her arms around his neck as she spun.

"Thank you," she offered, kissing his lips.

His brows tugged down, but the playfulness of his eyes said his frown was made up. "You want to call me Pa, too?"

She giggled, accepting the light twist he put on the emotional episode. She knew how deeply he loved the children. He hadn't once tried to hide the fact.

"I don't know," she teased, "Are you going to call me Ma?"

His gaze shot around and landed on his mother for a moment. He swallowed, quite exaggeratedly, and shook his head soberly. She laughed and allowed his kiss to completely absorb her, take her to that wonderful place only she and he knew.

When they separated, the horses had been harnessed to the wagons, and the families were gathering their items to head to Kid's for the night.

Snake held her for a moment longer, not wanting to ever let go. All the days of his life, he'd never forget looking into August's little face and hearing the child tell him he wouldn't hold a whipping against him. The child had no way of knowing how deeply the event affected Snake. But Summer did. He could feel it in her chest. The way her heart beat in unison with his. Kid had been right. The more people you have to love, the larger your heart becomes.

The others were waiting; the way they glanced their way said so. "I guess we better mosey on over and say good-bye."

"I suspect you're right." She lifted her head to glance toward the barn.

Whispering near her ear, he asked, "Do you want to go skinny dipping later?"

"Skinny dipping?" Her brows furrowed.

"Skeeter says it's swimming without any clothes on," he explained, running a hand up her arm.

"There's no place to go swimming around here. Is there?" Her voice held a hint of excitement.

"The tub."

"Everyone will see us."

"Not if they're asleep."

She giggled.

He grabbed her hand and pulled her toward the barn, as if saying good-bye quickly would make the minutes until everyone else was snoring go by faster. It may have, because not long after the wagons rolled away, everyone, including Buffalo Killer who bedded down in the barn with Bug, August, and Jerome, were settled in for the night.

Snake helped Summer undress, an act he took great pleasure in, and looked forward to doing for years to come. Her reaction to his aid was to assist him in removing his clothes, a procedure he found just as enjoyable.

The skinny dipping opportunity didn't manifest, not because of lack of interest, but because the wind picked up as if there was a contest of which breeze could cross the nation first. Every gust blew faster and more furious than the one before. Heaving in and billowing out, the sides of the tent must have stretch a good two feet in every direction before the poles gave out and collapsed upon he and Summer with the force of a mighty oak tumbling to the ground.

Finding their clothing amongst the flapping and twisting canvas was not an easy task, but Summer, was as always, resourceful and tolerant. He loved her more for the way she took light of the situation, laughing as the wind tried to steal her dress before he managed to help her get it over her head. Ma and September had taken shelter in the barn before their tent went down, so they were already settled on a mound of hay when he and Summer blew into the barn.

Snake had recovered some blankets, and Summer quickly prepared a place to bed down. Snuggled together as the east to west race continued, he and Summer drifted off to sleep to the lullaby of snores and snorts besides the whistling wind.

The following morning, other than the downed tents, there was no damage to report, and while the women, including his sisters-in-law who arrived as bright and early as ever, packed up the campsite in the front yard, the men worked double time to make sure the family would be moved in before nightfall.

Shortly after noon, a freight wagon rolled into the yard. Ma's shouts brought the men scurrying out of the house and across the yard. The porcelain bathing tub they'd ordered before the fire had arrived.

For Snake, Ma's joy and enthusiasm, as well as that the other women expelled, was short lived. Kid followed the wagon into the yard, and as soon as the freight was unloaded, he pulled the men aside.

His face alone was enough to send Snake's nerves on end. "What did you learn?" he asked. "Did Wainwright set the fire?"

Kid shook his head sadly. "Appears so, but that's not the important thing right now."

"What is, Kid? Hell, the way you're acting gots my toes jittering," Skeeter said.

"Dora Zimmerman has gone missing," he said.

"What?" Bug asked.

"The hell you say?" Skeeter slapped his leg with

his hat.

"When?" Hog wanted to know.

"Who?" The last question came from Buffalo Killer.

"She's a family friend," Snake explained. Unable to totally comprehend what Kid had said, he continued, "Tell us all you know."

"I was in Turley's office, asking about Wainwright when Stewart Zimmerman came in. Dora wasn't in her bed this morning."

"Maybe she's at a friend's house," Bug offered.

"No, we checked. Furthermore, outside her bedroom window we found a piece of cloth. Rosalie swears it's a piece of the nightgown Dora was wearing last night." Kid removed his hat and played with the brim.

The entire group stood silent for a moment. The news hung heavy in the air.

"Did they hear anything?" Bug broke the silence by asking.

"Aw, hell," Skeeter thumped his hat on his thigh several more times. "The way that wind blew last night, a man wouldn't have heard a freight train until it crashed through the front door."

The others agreed with grunts and gestures. "Do they think she ran away?" Snake asked, almost wishing Kid would say yes. Dora was spoiled, but Snake doubted she'd set out on her own, yet it painted a far brighter picture than the alternative.

"No." Kid's straightforward answer held no reservations. "We checked for tracks, but the roads leading in and out of Scott are well traveled. Men volunteered to start searching in all directions. I stopped at my place and sent ranch hands out to cover my land and told Stewart we'd scour the area out here."

"We best go saddle up," Bug said.

"I go, too," Buffalo Killer said.

Snake glanced to the trail of women carrying armloads into the house. Household supplies had been ordered during the past weeks, and stored in the barn as they arrived. There was also a large supply of things that folks had donated, including the Zimmermans. He released the heavy air in his lungs.

"We can't all leave. I don't want the women and children alone."

"I feel the same way, Snake, but I gotta admit, Lila can out shoot me." Skeeter stepped up beside him. "And if it came to protecting this family, she'd shoot long before she asked questions."

Kid stood on his other side. "I agree. We may want to think they need our protection, but those women we married are of good stock. They're amazingly tough and can be downright intimidating when they want to be."

Hog nodded toward the house. "They'll be fine. The house is solid, and once we tell them what's happened, they'll keep the kids inside. There's nothing here to worry about."

"We can't tell them what's happened," Snake disagreed.

Everyone stared at him. "What?" Skeeter shook his head. "I can't ride out of here without telling Lila where I'm going. I already told you she's a better shot than me."

"Secrets have no place in a marriage, Snake." Kid laid a hand on Snake's shoulder. "We have to tell the women."

"Yes, we do." Skeeter said, clearly relieved by Kid's judgment.

Snake frowned at Skeeter. Surely his brother wasn't that afraid of his wife. As if Skeeter could read his mind, he said, "Remember, my wife blew up half of the badlands. Kid's wife has already shot two men. Hog's wife captured two outlaws, shooting one

225

of them in the arm pit." His gaze went to Hog. "That had to hurt."

Hog nodded. "I'm sure it did."

Bug stepped forward. "Summer's no softie, Snake. She's been raising those kids by herself for years. Have you forgotten that she saved your life?"

While Snake was contemplating Bug's statement, Hog offered two more cents, "And don't let any of us forget Ma."

All five brothers swallowed. Ma was definitely not afraid to shoot someone.

Buffalo Killer grunted. "Maybe we should send the women out to find Dora."

The brother's turned to stare at him. The Indian glanced at them, one at a time, and then shrugged his broad shoulders.

"All right," Snake agreed, convinced the women were far from helpless. "Let's go tell them and figure out a grid to ride."

Summer was in the kitchen, lining the cupboard shelves with flowered paper. A stack of unpacked dishes sat on the table in the center of the room. Snake paused in the doorway, enticed by the way her back stretched as she smoothed out the paper. Behind him, he heard Kid moving up the stairway to where Jessie made beds, and on the far side of the living room he could hear Hog speaking to Randi and Ma who were getting Ma's new stitching room settled. Skeeter had gone around to the back of the house. Lila had their children, Kendra and Charles, as well as Kid's two, Joel and Winifred, playing in the grass with August and Jerome.

Worry tugged at his brow. "Where's September?"

Summer spun about so quickly, she almost made a complete circle. "Oh, my, you startled me. I didn't know you were there."

He moved across the room. "Where's September?"

"She finished a new hat for Maisy. The other one is about to fall off. She went out to see if she could convince the mule to let her switch them. Did you get the freight unloaded?" Summer gaze grew serious. "What's wrong?"

Sidestepping around her, he went to the window. The edge of the barn and the corral came into view. There was no mule with a flowered hat.

"Is Maisy in the barn?"

Summer stretched on her toes, peering out the window. "She was in the corral when September went out. Maybe she led her into the barn."

His veins grew icier every moment. He pushed open the back door and seeing Bug leading a horse out of the front of the barn, he yelled, "Bug? Is September in the barn?"

Summer clutched his elbow. "What's going on? What's happened?"

He turned and fought with what he had to tell her. He wanted to keep her safe, make her happy. Not tell her sad or bad news. His name floated across the yard, and he turned, sticking his head back out the door.

Bug ran across the yard. "She's not in the barn. Is she supposed to be?"

Skeeter and Lila, each carrying two kids, climbed the back steps behind Bug. "Who's not in the barn?"

"September," Bug said.

Others gathered in the kitchen through the living room doorway.

"What's happened?" Kid asked, pushing his way to the front.

"That's what I want to know!" Summer planted herself in front of Snake. The air cracked with gloom and her nerves were eating at her skin. "Snake? What's happened? Tell me!"

He spun back to Bug. "You're sure?"

"Yes."

Snake pushed him aside and tore out the door, taking the back steps in one leap. The rest of the men followed, all yelling her sister's name.

"What's going on?" Summer screamed.

Ma took her arm. "Someone stole Dora Zimmerman out of her bedroom last night. The boys think it might have been Wainwright."

Summer's knees buckled. People caught her by the elbows and leaned her back against the cupboard. A second later Ma set a chair in front of her. Jessie holding one arm, and Randi, holding the other, lowered Summer onto it.

"No," she whispered, pressing a hand to the ache deep in her chest. A chill tickled her spine. "September?"

"Don't worry, the boys'll find her," Ma said.

"September ain't in the barn," August said from the doorway.

"Where is she?" Lila asked, standing beside the door, keeping the toddlers from exiting the room.

August shrugged. "I dunno." He set Jerome down on the floor. "She went to meet Dora awhile ago."

"What?" Every woman in the kitchen yelled at the same time.

August scooped up his puppy before anyone stepped on him. Summer wasn't sure who made it out the door first, all she knew is she was in the front of the crowd, running across the front yard and shouting for Snake.

He met her in front of the barn door, caught her when her feet, still in motion, couldn't stop.

"What?" he yelled above the screaming women behind them as they collided. His fingers dug into her arms. "What?"

Her throat had locked up. She tried, but when she opened her mouth, no words would come out.

Tears blurred her vision.

"August says September went to meet Dora," someone behind her said.

Questions and answers. Male voices and female. Summer couldn't decipher who was saying what. Her throat, heart, and mind were on fire. Snake pulled her across the yard, back toward the house.

Her senses, voice, and strength returned simultaneously. She twisted out of his hold and pushed at him with both hands.

"Wainwright is here, and you didn't tell me?" The fire filling her insides turned into fury. She slapped away his hands as he tried to catch on to her again. "Why didn't you tell me? Why?"

"Summer! Calm down. I have to go talk to August." His fingers caught a hold of her dress sleeve.

She tore it out of his grasp and ran for the house. The air in her chest burned as it flowed in and out. Part of her was running to August, to hear what he knew, but an inner part, screaming with pain and hurt, was running away from Snake. As far away from him as she could get.

When she landed in the kitchen, gasping for air, and with her insides twisted into knots tight enough to cut off every ounce of blood flow, August was sitting in the solitary chair, staring up at the men circling him. Summer brushed past them to kneel in front of her little brother. Before she had a chance to catch her breath and ask him where September was, Snake, already beside her, took both of August's hands and started talking.

"When did September leave?"

Summer wanted to shove him away, and ask August herself, but she knew the important thing right now was September. Not her anger. There would be time for her to deal with Snake later.

"I don't know, Snake. Is something wrong?"

August's voice shook.

"Yes, something is wrong. We have to know exactly what happened. Did you see Dora?"

August nodded.

"When? Where?"

"While you were unloading the freight wagon. Jerome and I were in the barn loft. Grandma told me to get my bedding from up there." His cheeks turned red, and he bowed his head. "Jerome made a pile while we were up there. I knew I had to clean it up and while I was throwing it out the loft door, I saw September and Maisy. I was gonna shout at her, tell her to not step in the hay I was throwing out, but she was too far away already. That's when I saw Dora. She was on the far end of the corral. Waving at September."

"Did you see anyone else?"

"Nope. Just September and Maisy, and Dora. Dora must've wanted to see Maisy's new hat 'cause she was waving really big."

Skeeter, at least Summer thought it was Skeeter, slapped Snake's back. "Come on, they couldn't have gotten far."

Snake didn't even look her way, as he stood and then barreled his way through the crowd and out the door.

The rest of the men followed, and in the silent moments that followed, Summer's heart landed on the floor.

It was a moment or more before she could stand, feeling hollow inside. September had to be all right, she just had to be. The air flowing in her lungs helped, and by the time she'd taken a couple steps toward the doorway, she was ready to join the search.

Ma caught her arm and the door slammed shut. "No. We gotta stay here."

"No, I don't. That's my sister. I'm going to find

her." She twisted against the hold.

Ma's grip grew as firm as a man's. "The men will find her. We'll stay here."

"No, I won't. Let go."

"I can't let you go," Ma declared.

Chapter Nineteen

Summer tugged harder and glanced up, looking for someone to aid her. Lila, with baby Charles on one hip, stood in front of the closed door. Her eyes were sad as she shook her head. Summer turned around, looking toward the doorway that led to the living room and ultimately to the front door. Jessie stood in that opening, holding Winifred. She, too, shook her head.

Randi wrapped an arm around Summer's other elbow. "I know it's hard. I know you want to go help. We all feel the same way."

A sob exploded in her chest. "I have to do something. I can't just stand here."

A rumbling not unlike thunder sounded outside, close enough to make the new windows rattle. Lila leaned over and glanced out the window beside the door. "It's just the men leaving."

"What direction are they headed?" Jessie asked.

"South," Lila answered.

"All of them?" Jessie walked across the room and handed Winifred to Randi.

"Yes."

"Then I'm going to ride to our place. Kid said he sent a group of cow hands out to search. I'll steer them this way." Jessie looked at Ma. "I'll need your shotgun."

"It's in my sewing room."

Lila moved away from the door. "Do you have another gun, Ma? Preferably a rifle?"

"Yes. Why?"

"I'm going to ride into town. Skeeter said the

sheriff sent men in all directions. I'll go tell them we need them out here. There's a lot of open country to cover." Lila handed Charles to Ma.

Ma pointed in the direction Jessie had gone. "There's a rifle and bullets in the long trunk in my room. Be careful, it hasn't been shot in years. It was Jay's."

Summer closed her eyes, willing Jonas to descend, or to hear her plea. *Go to September,* she begged. *Go to her and keep her safe.*

Something warm wrapped around her fingers. She opened her eyes.

August squeezed her hand. "What you want me to do, Summer?"

Randi knelt down beside August. "I need your help. Can you help me watch the babies? We don't want them to be scared."

His blue eyes, worried, glanced up to Summer. She swallowed the lump in her throat. "Randi is right. Can you and Jerome play with the babies?"

August looked around, a bit unsure.

Randi rested a hand on his little shoulder. "You told me Jerome is a good watch dog. Didn't you?"

He nodded.

"We need a good watch dog to watch over the children."

"All right," he said, still not sounding convinced.

"Come on," Randi encouraged, as she held one hand out to Kendra and Joel who were sitting on the floor petting Jerome. "Let's take the children in the other room. I bet we can find something for Jerome to fetch. The kids will like that."

"There's a rag ball in my stitching room." Ma glanced to Summer. "You ain't gonna sneak out if I take Charlie in there to play with the others, are you?"

"No, I won't sneak out," Summer promised. The feeling of helplessness had now settled on her

233

Lauri Robinson

shoulders. She'd always been the one to act, namely because there had only been her.

"I'll be right back."

Ma's words entered her ears, but Summer didn't respond. Instead, she sank into the chair. Wainwright was near. September was missing. Dora had been stolen out of her own home. Everyone had something they could do to help—Jessie, Lila, Randi, Ma, the men, even August—everyone except her. She was as useless as a knob on a tree. When had that happened?

"Holding down the home front can be more work than riding into the sun." Ma settled another chair near hers. "But this is where you're needed. September will need you to be here when she comes home. August needs you to be here."

The fear of not knowing what had happened to September held strong, but the anger she'd felt toward Snake had turned into sadness. "Why hadn't he told me Wainwright was here?"

"Men." Ma let out a long sigh. "They think women are soft and need protecting all the time. I suspect Snake didn't want to worry you. He's a lot like his Pa. He never wanted me to worry, either. Remember I told you he wouldn't go get Kid until he was sure Skeeter and I had everything we'd need?"

Summer nodded, recalling the conversation they'd had that morning weeks ago.

"I wanted to go with him, but I was carrying Snake, and Jay thought the trip would be too hard on me. He worked night and day, filling the cellar with meat and gathering enough wood to last us a year. I knew he was preparing to make the trip to Missouri, but he never said a word. Not until the night before he left." She tilted Summer's chin so they looked at each other eye for eye. "Because he didn't want me to worry."

Summer shook her head. "That's not the same."

234

"Maybe not to us, but to men, anything that might cause worry, is something they think they need to hold in, protect us from."

"The other men told their wives. Jessie, and Lila, and Randi, knew."

"Yes, they did."

"Why?"

"I don't know for sure, but the way I see it, they've been married long enough that they no longer have secrets from each other."

A chill made the hairs on Summer's arms go stiff. "Secrets?"

"Yes."

"Did you and Jo-Jay have secrets?"

"Not after he returned with Kid. Oh, we kept surprises from each other. Like my stitching machine. I had no idea he'd bought it for me until a freight wagon delivered it after his death. But we never had secrets about important things."

Summer's heart was on the floor again. Somehow she knew Ma was talking about her father's part in Jonas' death.

Ma's aged and wrinkled, but warm and friendly hands, wrapped around Summer's. "Trust is like love, honey. You have to give it to get it."

****

The red cloth petal looked as out of place lying on the brown summer grass as it did on the straw hat he'd watched September decorating for Maisy last week. The girl had been snatching up the bits and pieces left over from Ma's stitching. She'd proudly displayed her art work as she fit the scraps together and stitched them into flower shapes on the new hat. He'd cut the wide slots in the brim for Maisy's ears, since the straw was too stiff for September to manage. Snake plucked the flower from the ground. He'd known he was on the right trail. A very strong, yet invisible presence had told

Lauri Robinson

him so. The flower simply proved it.

He bit his lips together. Wainwright wouldn't want the slow moving mule with them, yet the tracks they'd found on the far side of the corral proved the animal traveled with two horses. Shod horses. He pinched his nostrils, stopping the sting that emitted when he sucked in air. The hoof prints had disappeared as their travels moved out of the tall grass and onto the stiff, course Buffalo grass that stretched out endlessly. Hell, he could see for miles, yet at the same time, between the patches of shoulder high grassland and the rougher terrain that hid small hills and valleys, he couldn't see a damn thing.

Far to the west, he could make out a hat but didn't know for sure which of his brothers it was. They'd split up, grid out the perimeter, and each took a section to search. They'd been looking for hours already, and this flower was the first sign they were on the right trail. It most likely was Kid, and closer in, where the grass swayed, would be Hog. To the east were Skeeter, then Bug, and Buffalo Killer. None could be seen, but he knew they were there.

Tucking the flower in his pocket, he climbed back in his saddle but kept his body low. Wainwright had a long range rifle. Snake had already been shot by it and didn't want a repeat.

The tracking was slow going, for they scoured every possible hiding spot. Wainwright couldn't be traveling much faster, not with two girls and a mule—who liked to stop for breaks. He should have told Summer about Wainwright. Told September as well. But he hadn't wanted to worry them. Figured they were safe at the homestead.

It was his job to keep them safe. Not let them fret or be bothered by things. His fingers clutched the saddle horn until they stung. A hell of a job he'd done. By not telling them, they hadn't had any

236

reason to be cautious.

The squawk of a crow, irritatingly loud and flying overhead, caught his attention for a second, but then it was the sun, angling down that held his consideration. It would be evening soon, and then night. His stomach plummeted.

The ground beneath him shook, and he spun about, recognizing the thunder of hooves behind him. Dust clouded around the group, and he tugged on his hat band, shielding the setting sun so he could make out the riders.

His brothers arrived at his sides before the posse did. Stewart and Rodney Zimmerman, as well as Sheriff Turley, led the charging troop. Their horses skidded to a stop, heaving and glistening with sweat, and stirring up a miniature tornado of soil and dried buffalo grass.

"Did you find their trail? Which way does it go?" Rodney asked, as his horse pranced about.

"South." Snake gestured with a head nod. "How'd—"

Stewart Zimmerman pointed at Skeeter. "His wife rode into town. Told the deputy to come find us and tell us to ride out here. She said Dora was spotted."

Snake used as few words and the least amount of time possible in filling the posse in on what August had saw and what they'd found so far. The group was dividing up, to start searching again, when a trio of horses rode in from the south.

Kid's ranch foreman, Joe, headed up that group. "Jessie rode out to the ranch, told us to come help with the search over here," he said as they rode in. "We found something along the way. Someone's held up in that old soddy on the far side of Dry Lake. I left a couple cowboys to watch 'em." He twisted his horse about. "Come on!"

The rumble of horses, at a full gallop, made

conversations, tough, but Snake had to know. "What did you see, Joe?"

"That gall darn mule of yours! She's braying up a storm and a man's trying to run her off."

"Wainwright?"

"Can't say. I ain't never seen the fella. But I don't think so. The man chasing the mule was as skinny as a bean pole."

Wainwright wouldn't work alone. He'd have convinced someone to help with his dirty work. And if Maisy was there, September had to be, too. Snake dug his heals into Buster's sides, making the horse surge into a faster gallop. The others kept up, there was probably close to twenty of them, if he took the time to count. Which of course he didn't. It didn't really matter. All that mattered was there was enough of them that Wainwright would go down.

The short buffalo grass and long prairie grass soon disappeared and nothing but parched dirt with cracks and crevices deep enough to trip a horse covered the gray-white ground. The animals were surefooted, and the men kept their speed up as they tore across Dry Lake. In the spring, when the snow melted and the rains fell, over three miles of land turned into a shallow lake, providing water for animals and humans, but by this time of the year, when the summer sun was at its peak and the wind blew Colorado into Missouri and Oklahoma into Nebraska, the lake disappeared.

The soddy Joe spoke of had been there for years. Probably some sodbuster who'd once thought the lake would provide for them year round. When the water had disappeared, the settler most likely had, too, since no one ever knew who'd built the crude home.

Snake had been out near the crumbling sod shanty more than once but had never gone inside. A churning in his guts reminded him why. The hissing and distinct rattle of the western diamondback had told him the place was infested with rattlers.

There was a slight slope where the lake ended, and on the down side of that knoll was where the soddy was built half in the earth. He held up his hand and as if he had the power to stop all twenty animals himself, the earth beneath him stilled.

Nobody spoke as the men dismounted and dropped their reins. The horses felt the urgency as strongly as the humans and silently shuffled away, cooling their heated shells with slow, quiet snorts.

The men gestured, indicating the way they'd go, pairing off in small groups and checking the rounds in their pistols and cocking their rifles. On his belly, with Sheriff Turley on one side and the Zimmermans on his other, Snake crawled to the peak of the knoll. A sagging roof, covered with grass still tinged green from the moisture the blocks of sod held, stared up the other side. The place looked as abandoned as ever, except for the mule sitting on her hind end about five hundred yards away from the shanty.

He would have smiled if he'd been able to gather the gumption. Maisy wasn't dumb. She sat just out of rifle range. How good of eyesight a mule had, he really didn't know, but Maisy's head pointed his way. Then she leaned her head back and brayed loud enough to be heard in Kansas City.

The sound made him shiver like a wet goose. Rodney Zimmerman started to move, and Snake grabbed his pant leg.

"Not yet, wait a second."

Maisy brayed again, and again. When no movement came from the house, Snake glanced to the men flanking him. "Let's go, but stay down. It's hard to say if they have a bead on us through the cracks in the sod."

As they worked their way down the hill, crawling through sticker patches and goat heads, the rest of the group, his brothers, the cowhands, and men from town, snuck toward the soddy from all directions. Maisy kept braying, and Snake kept waiting for Wainwright to exit the house to silence her. That didn't happen. And when he was only yards from the house, the noise he'd remembered, the hissing and rattling, grew so loud it vibrated his entire body.

Leaping to his feet, he ran around to the front of the shanty. The door, held precariously by one leather hinge, hung crossways over the open. A mass of hissing, slithering rattlers swarmed the opening. Amongst their bodies of muted browns, grays, and blacks, and decorated with the distinct yellow diamond shapes, was a red, swollen hand. It was a man's hand, not a girl's, but the sight made the sweat on his forehead pour into his eyes.

Blinking past the sting, he grabbed Rodney's hand as the man pointed his pistol at the mass of snakes.

"Don't shoot. We don't know where the girls are."

Maisy's braying still filled the air. He swore he heard a faint cry amongst the mule's squalls. He spun about.

"Maisy, shut up!"

A vast amount of clicks split the air, every man cocking the guns they had aimed at the house. Maisy quit screeching. The silence was ominous.

Snake leaped forward when September's voice barely sounded though the thick sod, "Snake, is that you?"

"Yes, honey, it's me." He jumped as a large rattler struck. Open mouth, its fangs bounced off his boot. Twisting his ankle before the critter fell back to the ground, he caught its underside with the toe of his boot and flipped it aside. The diamondback landed several feet away, in front of Buffalo Killer, who promptly stomped on its head. The long body, flipping and twisting, curled around the Indian's leg.

Buffalo Killer planted his foot harder and grabbed the withering body. With a solid jerk, he tore the snake in two. "Damn things."

"There's rattlers in here. Lots and lots of them," Dora Zimmerman yelled.

"Dora! Dora honey, are you all right?" Stewart Zimmerman shouted.

"Pa! Pa! The snakes killed the men. They're everywhere!" Dora answered. Screams came next. Loud and frightened.

Snake clenched his fists, feeling useless, and wondering how many snake bites it took to kill a man. If he was fast enough, maybe he'd only suffer half a dozen or so getting the girls out of there.

"Move out of the way!" Joe, carrying what looked like an old corral post, shouldered his way through the crowd. "Stand back!"

"Give me that!" Kid snatched the pole away and started flipping snakes aside. Men fired their guns as the diamondbacks landed too close for comfort.

"Quit shooting!" Snake yelled. "You'll irritate the ones inside to strike. Kid! Knock the door down so we can see where the girls are."

The worn plank door hit the ground with a thud and a renewed mass of slithering and hissing creatures covered it in a matter of seconds. Two men, Wainwright, even larger due to the swelling of his body, and a skinny man that Snake couldn't have recognized even if he knew him, were sprawled on the floor just inside the doorway. Deep puncture marks, red and oozing, covered their exposed skin, and blood stained their clothes from boots to collars.

The rattles and hisses were louder than a train of cattle rolling in at high noon. Picking a trail as Kid banished the rattlers with his pole, Snake eased toward the door. The one side of the shanty roof had caved in and the girls were sitting on a small ledge that had formed near the top of the back wall. They were tightly tucked into a small alcove beneath the roof. Diamondbacks of all lengths leaped from the ground, striking the crumbling sod. Some hit the wall just inches from where the girls cowered.

"Don't move. We're going to get you out. Just don't move," he instructed.

"What are we gonna do?" Stewart Zimmerman asked. "We gotta get rid of those snakes."

Racking his brain, trying to come up with a plan, Snake spun about. "Water. I need water. Rattlers hate water." The ability to find any was dismal. The lake they'd just ridden across was as dry as a sun bleached bone.

"There's water in this well!" Bug yelled, ripping weathered boards from the ground. Dirt and grass flew as others joined him in tearing the protective covering off the old hole. "I need a rope and a bucket."

"I got a rope, but it's back on my horse," a cowboy offered.

"Stay put!" Snake said to the girls. He turned, tugging on his suspenders. The buttons holding them to his britches fell to the ground as he ran toward Maisy. The mule, as if happy to see him, clambered to her feet and met him halfway across the yard.

She didn't protest as he untied the leather strap holding the hat beneath her long chin. Tying his suspenders to the strap he raced to the well. "Here, use this." He pulled his hat from his head. "Dump it in here." As Bug fell to the ground, dropping the suspenders holding Maisy's hat into the well, Snake spun back to the others. "The rest of you, come fill your hats."

The men looked at him oddly, but knowing their options were few and far between, they formed a line to get their hats filled. Snake ran back to the house. Water seeped out of the bottom of his hat, but when he dumped it, sloshing water towards the slithering mass on the door, the rattlers scrambled, detangling like a skein of yarn.

He grabbed the hats as men carried them over, handing them an empty one in return, and continued to splash the rattlers. Jumping left and right as they slithered out of the soddy and from under the broken door, Snake kept tossing the water. The rattlers hissed and shuddered. Irritated more by the water than by him, not one struck his way as they slithered away from the house. The hats kept coming, and he kept tossing the water at the slowly decreasing number of diamondbacks. Every rattler in Kansas must have decided to make the soddy their home.

"Stay there," he told the girls. "Don't move until I get them all out."

The last ones were still slithering over the broken door, when he and Rodney jumped over the prone bodies of Wainwright and his assistant. Snake snatched September from her perch. Hisses and rattles echoed off the sod. The sounds vibrated up his spine, but he didn't take the time to investigate where they came from as he leaped back out.

September clung to his neck, and he held her tighter. Hugging her with all the love he felt for his family. Rodney was right on his heels, and it wasn't until they were several yards away from the soddy before they stopped.

Setting September down, he lowered himself to the ground in front of her. "Are you bit anywhere?"

"No," she mouthed, crying too hard to speak.

"Are you sure?"

She nodded.

"We saw the rattlers as soon as the men shoved us in there. We got on the ledge before they struck us," Dora explained, crying. "That man made me trick September into coming with us."

"Shush, now, your daddy's here," Steward Zimmerman said, pulling his daughter into his arms.

Snake cupped September's cheeks. "You sure you didn't get bit?"

She nodded. Maisy stomped over, sniffing at September like a dog would. September patted the mule's head. "Maisy followed me and wouldn't leave no matter what those men did to her." Her gaze went to the sod shanty. "The rattlers struck the men as soon as they walked in."

Her little body trembled. He sat down and lifted her onto his lap. "Shh, don't think about it. It's all over."

Tears rolled down her face, onto his chest. "I knew you'd come for me," she hiccupped. "I knew it."

His heart swelled nine times its size. "Of course I'd come for you. I'm your Pa."

She stiffened in his arms. He wasn't sure how to react to it, and holding his breath, waited for her next move.

Her brilliant blue eyes lifted to gaze at him.

He had to take the chance, convince her. "I love you, September. I love you as much as if I really was your Pa."

"I love you, too, Pa." She melted against him. "I love you, too."

Chapter Twenty

The hoof beats were slow and steady, but thunderous nonetheless. Summer ran to the doorway even before August started to shout, "They're here! They're here!"

She was down the steps and in the middle of the front yard, outpacing August by a good ten feet. September, sitting in front of Snake on his big, gray horse, waved as the horse walked the final few steps to stop in front of her.

"Thank God," Summer whispered, head dizzy and knees weak.

Snake lowered himself from the gray and then reached up to lift September down. Summer folded her arms around her little sister, letting every ounce of her body absorb the reality September was safe and sound.

"Where were you, Sissy?" August asked. "Did you find Dora? Hey, Pa, why's your hat wet? Yours, too, Bug. Heck, even Maisy's hat is wet. Why's that?"

Summer let September go and watched as the girl was immediately encompassed in a smothering hug from Ma. Having put off the action long enough, she let her gaze lift to her husband.

"Wainwright?"

"We'll never have to worry about him again." His look went from somber to slightly smug. The corners of his mouth twitched as if he fought to hide a smile. The action, or maybe it was the wonderful sight of him, filled her with happiness. He spread his arms wide, giving her the option to step into them. She took the opportunity of course, for there wasn't a strong enough will on earth to deny how badly she wanted those arms to fold around her.

He held her, rocking slightly on his heels as she poured herself against him. No place on earth, or in heaven, could be a more wonderful, righteous place to be than in his arms. She lifted her face, and there, too, he didn't disillusion her. His lips landed on hers, hard, demanding, and oh, so pleasurable, for they were packed with passion, love, and devotion.

She welcomed him home with all she had. He provided her with so much, and the deep down reality was—he always would. The past was just that—the past. But the future was hers, and she was going to make it the most wonderful life anyone had ever known.

Their connection grew then, as if he read her mind and soul. Beyond the singing of her heart, sounds slipped into her ears, trickled her mind.

"Pa? Pa? What happened to everyone's hats?" August was asking again.

"Come on, August. Leave them alone. I'll tell you what happened to Pa's hat," September said.

Summer broke from the kiss, turning toward her sister. September, holding August's hand, led him toward the house. Ma had an arm around September's shoulders, and the Quinter brothers either had their arms around their wives or carried a child on their hip, walked toward the house as well.

"Supper's almost ready," Summer said, not attempting to slip out of Snake's hold.

"In a minute," he said. "We need to talk."

She met his gaze, eye for eye. Not feeling an ounce of remorse, she admitted, "Yes, we do." The devil himself would need help keeping her from fighting for the man and family she loved. She'd tell Snake about Jonas and face whatever the outcome might be.

He took her hand and started walking. The

horses were gone. The yard empty. For a split second, she wondered just how long they'd been kissing. Snake led her to the water tub and set her down on one of the benches beside it. Night had settled, covering the earth with a dark but comforting blanket. Reflecting the light of the stars, the tub of water shimmered behind Snake as he paced the ground in front of her for a few stilled moments.

She swallowed, wondering where to start. Blurting out that she held his father's head as Jonas took his last breath didn't seem like a conversation starter.

"I'm sorry I didn't tell you about Wainwright," Snake said, stopping in front of her. "But I didn't want you to worry or be afraid. I realize now that was wrong. If you'd known, you could have been more cautious. I should have told September, too, so she would have known."

"Yes, you should have." She sounded firmer than she felt and tried to soften her declaration. "It's easier to react to something we know than to something we don't."

He sat down beside her. "It won't happen again. I promise." His fingers found hers, threading hers with his. "I promise from this day forward, I'll never keep something from you again. And if you want to go to the badlands and see your father, we'll leave tomorrow."

That took her by surprise. She hadn't given much thought to meeting her father. Perhaps someday she would, but right now she had other concerns to deal with. "I would like to meet him, someday. When the time is right."

"You just say the word, and we'll go."

Closing her eyes, she bit her lips together. A soft and relaxing warmth settled on her shoulders. She wondered if it was his arm, but then knew it wasn't.

It might be Jonas, but then again, it might just be her. Years ago she'd learned to be resourceful, strong, and honest. It hadn't been until she found a life she was afraid of losing that she'd started to question her abilities. That would never happen again. She'd never allow doubt to shroud her thinking again. Never allow gloom to overshadow the love she'd found.

She met her husband's gaze. "I have something to tell you, too."

"First," he said, wrapping his other hand around their clutched ones. "Do you forgive me?"

"Yes, I forgive you."

He kissed her temple. "I am sorry. I know I caused you more pain by not telling you. I never meant to do that."

The need to tell him washed over her. "Do you remember when I told you we lived over by Cimarron?"

"Yes, why?"

"After the grasshopper plague, we had to leave. There was nothing left. We packed everything into a wagon, and started for Dodge. Our horse, too old and weak for the trip, died the first day. A few nights later a man came along." Tears bit at her eyes. "He shared his food with us. I don't remember what we'd eaten before then, but I do remember how good his beans and bacon were. He spent the night and told us about his family. His wife and kids. The next morning, while he was saddling his horse..." she had to stop to draw in a breath. "July shot him in the back."

Snake didn't say a word, and she didn't look his way. Staring at the water, watching the mirror image of the stars dancing overhead, she continued, "I ran to him and tried to stop the blood. But it poured out of his chest. It just kept coming and coming. I begged him to keep breathing, but he said he couldn't. He said his time had come and that if he had to die so I could live, so be it." The tears flowed freely now, and she let them fall, feeling everything she'd felt that morning so long ago. "I sat with his head on my lap. He smiled and said I was a good girl. No one had ever said that to me. And then he died. Right there on my lap, he stopped breathing."

The arm around her shoulders, tightened, and though she didn't remember when Snake had wrapped it around her, she leaned against him, needed the comfort. "His name was Jonas Quinter."

Snake didn't know what to say. The emotions swirling inside him were more entangled than the den of rattlers back at the soddy. Actually, he wasn't surprised. Something deep in him had known July had killed his father. Probably since the moment he saw the watch. But he'd never imagined Summer had witnessed it. The need to protect and comfort her lifted above all the rest.

"Shh," he murmured.

"I'm sorry," she cried softly. "I'm so sorry."

"It's not your fault."

She sat up and met his gaze. He saw the woman then. The proud, strong one, who'd stormed into his bedroom and proclaimed they were married, had reappeared.

"My father murdered your father."

Hearing the words, learning the truth of who killed his father, wasn't as hard to hear as he'd imagined. Perhaps the years had softened the news, or maybe it was because of who said them. He rested a palm against her cheek.

"Yes, he did." Never taking his eyes from hers, he asked, "But does it matter? Today, right now, does it really matter?"

"Of course it matters. I—"

"You what? You were just a child. There wasn't anything you could have done. And there isn't anything you can do about it now, either."

"But, your brothers. Ma..."

The heartache in her eyes ate at his chest. "Do you honestly think they'll hold something July Austin did against you?"

"He was my father."

"No, he wasn't. He was a man who stole you from your real family. He hurt you as badly as he did us."

"He was September and August's father."

"No, he wasn't a father to them. He was a burden to all of you. One you'll never have to worry about again." He tried to pull her close, but she refused.

"We—I have to tell your family."

"We have to tell our family. And we will. They may have questions, want to know how it happened. But there's no one who'll blame you, or be upset with you."

Her glance went to the house. The windows were lit and the back door open. Soft laughter filtered into the night air.

"Trust me, I know my family. They may appear to be rough on the edges, but they have hearts of gold. And they love you. You and September and August. And they always will."

When she turned, and once again met his gaze, a way to banish July Austin came to his mind. "There is one thing I want. I hope you'll agree and talk to the children with me."

She frowned slightly. "What is it?"

"From today forward, I would like September and August to start using Quinter as their last name."

Her eyes shone. He hoped it was happiness and not just from the tears she shed.

"They'd like that. I know they'd like that very much."

"And you? How do you feel about it?"

"I like it very, very much." She patted his cheek. "I have something else to tell you."

"All right," he assured, willing to listen to anything she had to say.

"It might sound unbelievable."

The transformation in her had been a wonderful thing to watch. The scared little girl he'd seen the past few weeks had disappeared, and he hoped she wouldn't ever need to return.

"I think I can handle it."

A smile touched her lips, and she glanced around, as if looking for someone. When her gaze settled on him, he felt more than saw a peace within her.

"Your father is my guardian angel. Since the day he died, he's visited me, especially at those times I really needed help. He..." she paused as if trying to think of a way to explain herself.

Snake pressed a finger to her lips. "I know."

"You know? How could you know?"

"Because he's visited me, too. He's the one who told me to marry you. He told me to nod. He was also the one that told me which direction September went."

"He did?"

"He did."

"He told me about the fire. Or showed it to me in a dream," she whispered

Snake nodded. "Sheriff Turley confirmed it had been started."

"Wainwright."

"We figure as much. But it really doesn't matter. Does it?" The time for talking was over. Snake pulled her close and kissed her until they were both swimming in a sea of passion.

Moments before he lost all control, he ended the embrace, knowing they couldn't act upon their obsession until later. After a few minutes, when they both were able to breathe, he pulled her to her feet.

"Come on, we best go eat before it's all gone."

She glanced to the house, squared her shoulders, and then with a smile, nodded.

Hand in hand, they crossed the yard and entered their home.

The transformation of the kitchen was remarkable. Full of furniture, family, and food, it barely resembled the shell he'd left a few hours ago.

His mother understood his shock. "Your wife has been very busy today."

"I see that," he said, tugging Summer closer to his side. "I can't believe it."

"The rest of the house is done, too. Curtains are up, furniture is set out, beds are made. I swear, if she'd had a few more hours, that fancy tub would have been installed as well," Lila said.

Summer's cheeks turned red.

He smiled. "You like it?"

"I love it," she admitted, and then stretched on her tiptoes to kiss him.

"Sit down and eat," Willamina said. "Eva has something to show you two as soon as supper is over."

"Hello, Willamina, I didn't know you were here," he said, leading Summer to a spot on the long table lined with two benches.

"Where'd you think I'd be? One of my family was missing. I had to be here when she came home." Willamina patted September's head. The girl beamed as bright as the noon day sun.

The meal continued, and the conversation lasted long after the chocolate cake was served. After August finished his second piece, the last dish was washed and put away. It was then that Willamina insisted everyone move to the living room.

The large fireplace, made out of the same stones

that had built the one in their old house, was in the center of the room. On its hearth was a sizeable canvas draped package. Having seen the paintings Eva created for his brothers, Snake knew what was beneath the canvas, and he was anxious to see how the young girl had depicted he and Summer.

Summer frowned at the canvas. It hadn't been there earlier. Yesterday, still allowing doubt to cloud her world, she may not have been aware of it, but today, once she decided for the first time in her life she had a life worth living, she would have noticed it. While the men were searching for September, and her sisters-in-law were riding the country, gathering more help, she'd decided to take action as well.

Setting the house in order, unpacking the crates of furniture and household goods, had not only given her something to do, it had renewed her spirit. This was her home. Her family. And she was proud of it. Of them. Never again would the actions of another claim her joy.

Snake held her hand. It was an undemanding and effortless action, but one that signified a connection that could never be broken. Her gaze was on his profile. He was so handsome. So strong and kind and caring. Best of all, he was hers. Forever.

The sound of the crowd around them sucking in air made her turn to the hearth. Eva, with the help of Bug, had uncovered a huge painting. Summer's heart jolted then stalled as her eyes settled on the scene.

The background was of the Kansas sky, a blue so brilliant, Summer couldn't believe the girl had found the right color paint to imitate it. The blue, softened now and again by white, summer clouds, eased down until it touched a field of wheat, golden brown with red tinted seed heads that danced so gracefully she could almost feel the breeze blowing through the tall stalks.

The images of people then caught her attention. It was her and Snake, standing proud and strong, hands entwined as they were that very moment. In front of them, laughing with the joy only children know, were September and August. Near the boy's feet, gazing up at his owner with adoration was Jerome, and a flower-topped Maisy stood beside September.

"It's him," September whispered. "It's him."

"Who?" August asked. "Me? That's Jerome. It looks just like him."

"No. Yes. That's you, but..." September moved forward and pointed to the sky above Summer's head. "That's him."

Summer had one hand on the heart that now raced in her chest. Her other hand squeezed Snake's so hard it throbbed. Painted faintly into the sky, to where you couldn't see him until you really looked, was the very image of Jonas Quinter.

"That's Pa," Skeeter shouted, excitedly. "Lila, that's my Pa."

September looked up at Snake. "That's the man that lifted Dora and I onto the ledge at the soddy. It was too high. We couldn't climb up there. Out of nowhere he appeared, lifted us both at the same time and set us up there. Away from the snakes. He told me my Pa was on his way and to stay put. I knew he meant you."

Snake hooked his hand around September's neck, pulling her to his other side.

Ma's voice cracked as she declared. "That would be my Jay. That's just what he'd do." She then wrapped her arms around September and pulled her to her breasts.

Summer's gaze went to Eva. The girl blushed. "His face just appeared. I didn't even realize I'd painted it until the picture was done."

"It's perfect." Snake reached out and rested his

hand on Eva's shoulder. "It's perfect. That's my wife's guardian angel. My Pa."

"Summer's got a guardian angel?" August asked. "Do you got one, too?"

"I don't need one. I have a guardian bride," Snake said. He turned then, drawing Summer's gaze to his. "Which means we'll all always be watched over. In times when we need help, and in times when we think we don't, there'll always be a greater power overseeing our welfare."

Summer closed her eyes, absorbing the warmth oozing into her body, mind, and soul. She welcomed Jonas, and thanked him.

"I want a guardian angel, too," August admitted.

"You got one, honey. That there's your grandpa," Ma said.

"It is?"

"Yes, August, it is," Kid said reverently.

A smile sprang to life on Summer's lips as August declared, "Whoopie. You hear that Jerome? We done got a Pa and a Grandpa! Whoopie!"

Laughter broke out, filling the room with glee. Summer opened her eyes and met the loving gaze of her husband. A hand settled on her shoulder. She turned.

Buffalo Killer's eyes glistened with moisture. "You're home, little sister. You're home."

She bowed her head in acknowledgment. "Yes, I am." Turning back to her husband, with her heart full and beating strong and steady, she added, "I am truly, finally home." Her gaze then went to the painting. "We all are."

Everyone else was too busy laughing and carrying on, but she saw Jonas wink. Snake squeezed her hand. He'd witnessed it, too.

A word about the author...

Lauri Robinson lives in rural Minnesota where she and her husband spend every spare moment with their three grown sons and four (soon to be five) grandchildren.

She works part time, volunteers for several organizations, and is a diehard Elvis and NASCAR fan. Her favorite getaway location is the woods of northern Minnesota on the land homesteaded by her great-grandfather.

Stop by and say hi to Lauri at
www.laurirobinson.blogspot.com

www.ingramcontent.com/pod-product-compliance
Lightning Source LLC
Chambersburg PA
CBHW070906180626
46817CB00003B/932